DEAD GORGEOUS

DEAD GORGEOUS

Elizabeth Flynn

LION FICTION

Published by Lion Fiction
an imprint of
Lion Hudson plc
Wilkinson House, Jordan Hill Road
Oxford OX2 8DR, England
www.lionhudson.com/fiction

ISBN 978 1 78264 131 5
e-ISBN 978 1 78264 132 2

First edition 2014

A catalogue record for this book is available from the British Library

Printed and bound in the UK, September 2014, LH26

Prologue

Early May

The *Passionista* magazine third anniversary reception had begun well. With the lights, the wall coverings, and the highly polished black floor, the stevedores who once worked in this converted docklands warehouse would have had trouble recognizing the place. Designers, columnists, editors, models, trendsetters, fashionistas, and a galaxy of stars mixed and mingled, making air kisses as they came together and small talk as they moved on. *Passionista* had laid on the champagne and hors d'oeuvres with a lavish hand, and every one of the "faces" obliged with a photograph in return, adding their smiling, designer-clad endorsement to the grand *Passionista* logo sparkling on the wall.

A fashion show added attraction to an already glamorous evening. The magazine had persuaded a couple of the big houses to let their junior designers loose to showcase their work. In a large salon just down the hall from the main party, a whole team of people had been working all evening to get ready for the event.

Amid the maelstrom in this other room, a young woman stood, tense with excitement. Behind her, chaos reigned. One of the fledgling designers, in meltdown, darted here, there and everywhere, not even trying to hide his panic. "Is *Vogue* in?" he asked, of nobody in particular. "Where's my coffee? That hem's dropped a bit. This is a disaster; everything's going wrong. What about *Style* and *Harpers*? That button's coming loose; we need a stitcher – over here – *now*! Has anyone seen if their seats are filled? Oh my! I really think that's got more tease than the law allows. Turn round, darling, I need to see if that back seam sits right." Somebody called in a stage whisper that they'd seen one or two well-known fashion bloggers taking their seats, and a fraction of the anxiety disappeared from his face. Nobody paid him a great deal of attention; they were all too busy trying to get his collection onto the catwalk. Only the models remained still and docile as make-up artists covered incipient zits and downplayed the shadows of too-deep cheekbones, hairdressers hoped and prayed the gel was up to the job, stitchers got on with last-minute alterations and dressers eased them carefully in and out of garments few of them could afford. And when they were ready, they were checked again, the hair, the make-up, the threaded eyebrows, the waxed and spray-tanned legs.

The woman had her back to them all. This booking meant so much to her; she was determined not to blow it. An event like this could get her noticed by Balenciaga, Gucci, Ivano King or someone like that. Her family back home in Russia, in a village near the Estonian border would easily recognize such a name. They'd all chipped in to help her get to England and she wanted to make them proud.

She was the first on and stood ready, even though most of the guests still hadn't come in from the reception. Someone shouted her name and she turned carefully so as not to dislodge her hair, and saw her new-found Polish friend, Asia, threading a way towards her through all the chaos.

"Klara!" said Asia, as she reached her. "Is so exciting; I speak with assistant to a designer who thinks her boss will like my work." Asia's eyes shone. "Even more, there is possibility of internship at her company. She will show him my designs and contact me."

"Brilliant!" Klara responded, keeping as still as she could. "I also have news. We have chance of rooms in a house."

"Oh *tak*! Wow! Is true?" Both young women longed to leave the hostel where they had met and really get started on their big adventure in the London fashion world.

"*Da, da,*" said Klara. "Is in nice place – Richmond – I get details later when I see Igor."

"OK, OK," said Asia, "is on tube line, I think." They were new to London but had quickly grasped how pivotal the underground transport system was to life in the capital. "I go now; cir… er… cir-cu-late some more." She beamed at her friend. "Many people now coming in from reception; fashion show will start soon."

Klara inclined her head carefully and turned back to face the direction in which she would move onto the catwalk. She knew the excitement she felt right now could not compare with the rush of adrenaline she would experience when her turn came.

The show began. Her music. Her signal. She raised her six feet of beautifully proportioned frame onto the runway, allowed herself a second to savour the moment and moved forward into the glare of the lights. She'd come a long way to make this short walk.

An hour later she could tell it had gone well. Klara's part finished with the first collection, and she was able to get changed and watch the second from the back of the room. She heard the buzz, sensed the excitement, watched the nodding heads and animated conversations and knew the evening had been a success. Two columnists passed her and she heard a snatch of conversation.

"I've always had a bit of a pash on *Passionista*."

"Oh, darling, that's excruciating, but I won't forgive you if you don't use it in the byline." They laughed and passed on to more champagne. Klara didn't get the joke. Her English wasn't up to it. She scanned the room looking for any sign of Asia, but couldn't see her. She presumed her friend must be networking until the last possible moment. By this time she had other concerns. She looked around for Igor and saw him on the other side of the room. He'd been helping set up the show earlier and would no doubt soon be busy with dismantling it all again. Right now, though, he was leaning against the wall, watching her, knowing she would have to seek him out eventually. He stood up as she approached, a small, malicious smile playing around his mouth.

"You have it?" she asked.

"*Da*." He reached into his pocket and brought out the tiny plastic pouch with its precious stash of white powder. He held it up as though to keep it out of her reach.

"Give!"

He shrugged and handed it to her. "Relax, Klara; I tease only."

She snatched the packet, turned away from him and moved across the room. Orderly, disciplined activity had replaced the earlier sense of chaos and panic as everything that had been used in the show was packed up and moved out. Klara, oblivious to it all, made her way to the ladies' toilets. She hoped she wouldn't have to wait too long for a cubicle.

Chapter One

A Monday morning, late June

Kirsty Manners drove her Ford Ka past the Lebanese food wholesalers which marked the beginning of the trading estate. She went along the uniformly constructed row of buildings, pulling up in front of the one at the far end just beneath the sign, Ivano King.

In the rear-view mirror she saw a silver Porsche convertible gliding by. It slid into a bay further along. The occupant emerged, unfolding his sinewy form as he stood up. He was Ian King, the man behind the label. As he came past her to enter the building, she made sure her bare, silky legs were just emerging from her car. He paused, letting his gaze travel all the way up from her perfectly turned ankles to her beautiful face. She stood up, smoothed down her very short skirt, ran a hand through her luxurious dark hair and treated him to one of her smiling pouts.

Ian hid a sense of irritation. They were having a fling, for goodness' sake, so why keep on preening and posing like she. was trying to impress him? Then he remembered. "Morning, Kirsty," he said in a non-committal tone. "I think Jenni's got quite a bit of paperwork for you to do today. I know it's still a way off, but things will become very busy in the run-up to London Fashion Week."

Kirsty's pout took on a mulish character. She wasn't about to be deflected. "Yes, but you're having a shoot here today and I don't see why – "

"Tall women only, Kirsty, and we've got shed-loads of them. Minimum of five-ten, for a magazine campaign, and it's nothing to do with us; they're just using our premises." Ian turned towards the front door and Kirsty fell into step beside him.

"But they're using your girls, though," she said, as they reached the building. Ian paused and looked questioningly at her. "From Massingham's," she explained.

He frowned. "Just because we use models from Massingham's agency a fair bit doesn't make them 'ours'. Other people use them as well." He held the door open for her to precede him into the building. Kirsty smiled to herself as she entered. If she couldn't be a part of the shoot she'd at least managed to ensure that her flatmate, Sandra, a model who did meet the height requirement, wasn't on it either. She'd known of the casting but hadn't given Sandra the details. She wasn't having her strutting about the flat going on about it.

From a first-floor window, Eleanor Chandler watched the arrival. In spite of herself, her heart softened for a moment, as it always did at the sight of Ian. Her lip curled, however, as she watched Kirsty's performance.

Seated at her desk on the other side of the room, busily sorting the post into separate piles, Jenni, who ran the office, paused in her work and glanced up. She watched Eleanor's face, saw its expression soften then harden again, and addressed the safest option. "Kirsty's arrived, has she?"

Eleanor turned towards her. "How can you tell from over there?" she asked.

Jenni grinned. "I don't need to look out of the window. I just know from the look on your face."

Eleanor pursed her mouth into an expression of disapproval and came over to Jenni's desk. "I do wish Ian wouldn't mix business and pleasure. She's in Gucci today. I bet it's a knock-off. I don't suppose for one moment she earns enough for the real thing. Not as a clerical worker and receptionist."

"And in-house model, don't forget," Jenni reminded her.

"Yes, and I get the impression that she thinks the next step is the catwalk at Fashion Week. As if."

"She doesn't even walk all that well, really, does she?" said Jenni.

"No. She doesn't stand a chance. She'd be advised to stick to photographic work because it's probably all she's going to get." Eleanor looked down at her jacket and checked the creases of her sleekly fitting trousers. As Ivano King's head stitcher, she knew more about clothes than most.

"That's a nice outfit, Ellie. Is it new?" Jenni asked. She knew it had been a mistake to mention Kirsty and leapt at the excuse to steer the conversation into another channel. Eleanor could be a bit of a stuck record on the subject of Ian's women.

"Thank you; Julien Macdonald, in case you didn't recognize it; I decided to splash out a bit."

"It's very elegant," said Jenni. 'I've got to hand it to you, Ellie, you've really come on since – " She stopped abruptly, blushed and cast a hurried glance up at her colleague.

Eleanor smiled. "Don't worry, Jenni, I know what you're thinking and you're right. I've spent years turning out the most gorgeous clothes for the industry but was never seen in them myself. It's true; until Mother died I looked a complete frump."

"Things weren't *that* bad," said Jenni, "but in any case, nobody could call you that any more."

"Thank you," replied Eleanor. "Sometimes I feel a bit guilty when I think of how I've moved on from her ways, but there you go; nothing's going to bring her back, is it?"

"No, you're right about that." Secretly Jenni often used to wonder how a woman in her forties could be so under her mother's thumb, but here stood the evidence right in front of her. She sniffed the air. "That's nice; you don't normally do perfume."

"I got it last Christmas; thought I might as well give it a whirl."

"It's lovely!"

Eleanor smiled. "Ta." She went to the sewing room, sat at her machine and gazed, without seeing, at the material-laden shelves, the stacks of cottons and the bindings. Several mannequins were festooned with a variety of fabrics. One had on a complete outfit while another, tucked into a corner, was draped with a piece of beaded, diaphanous stuff that would have done Salome proud. A few moments later the door opened. She caught the scent of a very familiar, very expensive aftershave as Ian entered the room and came across to her desk. Her heart did its usual little leap at his presence. She'd given up trying to kid herself she didn't care for this man years since, even though she knew she had no chance. At least he was straight. She'd known some undiscerning female colleagues over the years fall for gays with very embarrassing results.

"Morning, Ellie, good weekend?"

"Morning, yes thanks; how are things?"

"Busy; been fine-tuning the collection. I'm not at all sure about the hemline on those jackets now."

"That's only the third change of mind. What's the betting you end up back with the first choice," she joked.

He grinned. "It's because I'm more nervous than usual, I keep thinking I've left it rather late in the season to change direction. It's all a bit risky."

"Yes, but I think it's a gamble that's going to pay off, Ian. It's a younger, fresher look from you. I think you'll knock 'em dead come September." She became aware that his eyes were on her. He seemed to be studying her almost as if he had never seen her before. "Is everything all right, Ian?" she asked.

"What? Oh sorry, was I staring?"

Eleanor smiled. "Stare, stare, stare; drink me in," she wanted to say. "No problem," she answered.

"Hmm. I just hope you're right, about the gamble, I mean."

Eleanor said nothing. She could guess what was on his mind and knew he wouldn't thank her for pointing out that his last two collections had been given the thumbs down by the media. Besides which, Jenni had told her Harvey Nichols and Harrods had both dropped his stuff. They had no outlet left in London at the moment but their own shop in Chelsea. And a batch of dresses had been returned from New York last week.

"Right," he said. "I'd better get on." He grinned at her and left the room.

Eleanor sat at her desk watching his back as it disappeared into the corridor. *Unrequited love; it sucks,* she said to herself.

Two types of photographs lined the walls of Ian's bright, cheery office which overlooked the front of the building. They were either of celebrities wearing his creations on a variety of red carpets or they were of Ian with his arm around said celebrities at some reception or opening. Normally, just looking at them gave him a thrill, but this morning he sat at his crowded desk and stared moodily at the original jacket design. He felt his mobile phone vibrate in his inside pocket. He reached for it and checked the message. Kirsty had written *11 out of 10 for last nite u hunk.* He deleted it and put the phone back in his pocket. He could see this developing into a problem. He'd have to do something about it, but Kirsty was a slightly different kettle of fish from his previous women; he'd need to disentangle himself with some care. Meanwhile, he had more urgent matters to consider. He ought to touch base with his business partner at the shop in the King's Road.

He picked up the office phone and pressed the speed dial. A few seconds later he heard a clipped, no-nonsense voice. "Nigel Summers."

"Nige; Ian. Morning."

"How goes it in Wandsworth?"

"I still can't quite decide about those jackets."

"You'll sort it," said Nigel, with confidence. "Is everything set up for the shoot?"

"Yes." Ian stood up and looked out of his window. "I can see some of the models arriving. Oh – and the photographer's here now. It's Leon; he gets around, doesn't he?"

"Ah yes, much in demand, from what I hear," agreed Nigel.

"I must say, I wasn't at all sure about taking these premises at first, but that big space at the back has proved to be a nice little earner for us, hasn't it?"

"You see, you just stick to designing the clothes, *Ivano*, and leave the business side of things to me."

Ian grinned. "Yeah, your decisions have all come good so far. Want to sort out my love life while you're at it?"

"What; has Kirsty come to the end of her tenure, then?"

"I think so, but she sees me as her ticket to a supermodel existence or a rich and glamorous lifestyle, and I don't think she'll go quietly."

"Mmm. I found her quite tenacious, too. I had to be very firm in the end. And she's still stringing Darren along, isn't she?"

"Oh yes, she was his girlfriend even when she was seeing you. But you knew that. She's the sort who always has someone on the back-burner. Why did you dump her, by the way?"

"A couple of things, really. It dawned on me she thought we were a real couple, you know, like, long-term. And she showed far too much interest in things that are no business of hers."

"Oh, really?"

"Yes, well, I thought I'd give her a taste of how things go in this industry, took her to a bash in Wapping, you know, the one *Passionista* magazine threw. You remember? You couldn't go because you had the flu."

"Oh yes. Was that wise, taking Kirsty, given who provided the entertainment that night?"

"Oh, you'd have to be *really* in the know to suss that one out. Leon was there too, come to think of it, busily snapping away. Anyway, Kirsty was surprised by all these Ukrainian and Russian models being there. She asked me how they got to know about the 'in' parties when they could hardly even speak English. 'Well, darling,' I says, 'that's what it's like now. There are loads of them over here. The old Eastern Bloc has more tall model types than you can shake a stick at; and they learn English soon enough.' Then she got into conversation with one or two of them and I left them to it, although, I have to say, I didn't take her to the party to network on her own account. I expected her to stick with me because, you can't take it away from her, she looks good on your arm. And then there were the lines."

"Ah. Shocked was she? Had no idea it goes on?"

"Oh, I think she knew it went on, but to see it happening so blatantly pulled her up a bit. Then, if you please, she wanted to know who supplied the stuff."

"No way!"

"I kid you not. 'Kirsty,' I said to her, 'you're a big girl; be sensible.' It's there if you want to try it, but either snort up or shut up. There are some questions you just don't ask."

Just at that moment the door to Ian's office opened and Kirsty walked in with some letters in her hand.

"Ah, Kirsty," said Ian loudly, so that Nigel would hear. Into the phone he said, "I'll catch you later," and replaced the receiver. Kirsty, with the same smiling pout that had been on her face in the car park, walked over to his desk and perched herself on the edge of it.

"I'm loving the hemline like that," she said.

A sudden silence came over the room. "What do you know about this hemline?"

A look of alarm came and went in Kirsty's eyes. "Nothing, Ian, I'm just saying I like it."

"Hmm, of course; thanks for the post."

Kirsty relaxed and smiled. "Leon wants to know if you're up for a drink when the shoot breaks for lunch."

"I'll let him know," replied Ian. "Don't bother to go back to him with a message. I'll go down and see him in a minute. You just get back to Jenni."

Kirsty shook her head in a way that made her hair fall languidly back over her shoulders. She opened her eyes wide and let him take in the pose before she spoke. "OK; you'd be amazed at how much I'm learning about the business in this job. I could be a help to you."

Ian seriously doubted that. It would take more than a smattering of knowledge to turn this self-regarding princess into a useful colleague.

"Really?" he said in a voice heavy with sarcasm.

"I thought you were interested in taking on an intern. I could put you in touch with a good one."

"Don't bother. Nigel's already told me about one, a Polish woman. I interviewed her and thought she was suitable but she didn't turn up for work; so much for wanting to get on. Anyway, I've changed my mind about employing an intern now. I'll see you later," he said, by way of dismissal. He shook his head as the door closed behind her. She really didn't get it; that stride was never going to get her onto the catwalk. As he leaned over and switched his computer on, his eyes flicked to the calendar on his desk. Only a few weeks to go and he'd be celebrating his forty-fourth birthday. What a thought. He could still pull the young women, though. And the not-so-young ones, he thought, as a picture of Ellie came into his mind. He'd known for ages how she felt about him.

Suddenly he sat bolt upright. A thought had entered his head. Ellie… She could be the solution he needed. He definitely had to do something about Kirsty; now, Ellie… Would it work, hmm? There were distinct possibilities in the idea. He couldn't imagine it would be difficult. She had become a presentable woman these days, no problems there. A bit older than him, but that didn't matter. She'd blossomed a lot recently. He sat there for a while before getting on with his morning's work. A plan began to form in his mind.

Standing by the window of his office, Nigel Summers put the receiver down after Ian's call. It rang again and he turned away from the window, giving himself a mental shake. A framed photograph of him with his mother at a gala dinner stood by the phone and he smiled at it. "Good morning, Mother; I'll call you later," he said to the picture. He picked up the phone once more and gave his customary salutation: "Nigel Summers."

In a cluttered room at the back of the unit. Darren Carpenter walked along racks of garments methodically checking the items against his inventory and pushing everything back to make more room. Very soon now a small army of leggy females, all part of the magazine shoot, would descend on this place. Although, in theory, only the room next door had been hired models, make-up artists and dressers always overspilled into his section as the day wore on. He could neither see nor hear Kirsty's car from here, but he knew she had arrived nonetheless. She'd go past his bike in the rack, of course. He thought proudly about the new white mudguards and reflector tape he'd stuck onto them. He left it on the end stand especially so that she would see it. Darren and Kirsty were an item, a situation about which he wished he didn't feel so insecure.

He heard his mobile phone ring from the desk in the corner and went across to answer it. He recognized the voice of Kirsty's flatmate. "Hi, Sandra, thought I might see you here today."

"Oh, really, why?"

"We've got a shoot on. From the look of the girls, I reckon you're the same type."

Sandra let out a wail that was half-anguish and half-anger. "My agent never mentioned anything, but I bet Kirsty could have given me the details so I could have tried out for it. I bet you. The cow!"

Darren let a moment pass without saying anything. The uneasy relationship between Kirsty and Sandra bewildered him. "I know what you're going to tell me," he said.

"You do?"

"Yeah, I seen her, didn't I? She was with him."

A brief pause ensued. It briefly crossed Sandra's mind to wonder about this "sighting" but she didn't want to go down that route. All she could do was to add a rider. "She came in around midnight and left at the usual time this morning."

Darren's jaw hardened and the pulse in his temple throbbed. "So much for the girls' night in with you, then," he said.

"Is that what she told you she would be doing?"

"Yeah."

Sandra could see at once that Kirsty hadn't even bothered to think up a plausible lie, but she didn't say so to Darren. She didn't want to upset him too much. Sandra had her own hopes for Darren, and getting him to look upon her as something other than a listening ear into which he could pour his woes about Kirsty was proving to be a delicate business.

"Don't worry, I'm here for you Daz," she said.

"Thanks, Sandy, you're a star. I'd better go; talk to you later." He put the phone down and stared into space. He clenched his fists and flexed his muscles, making the huge biceps bulge at the tops of his arms. If things went on like this, he knew he would soon be teaching her a lesson. Kirsty was his girl. She had to get that through her head.

Kirsty sat at the desk opposite Jenni's and got started on

her day's duties. She looked at the pile of filing she'd been given with dismay. Office work hadn't been part of her career plan, but almost the first thing she'd learned in this industry is that you didn't spend your time dashing from one exciting modelling job to another. In fact, some weeks you considered yourself fortunate to even get sent to a casting. Still, she had an ace up her sleeve. Things had gone well with Ian the previous evening; a top designer like him must surely be able to use his influence to get her jobs. She had high hopes for her future.

Raj Wickramasinghe, the pattern cutter, breezed into the room. "Morning each," he said. "Hope we all had a good weekend."

Kirsty smiled uncertainly at the newcomer. Raj seemed impervious to her looks and charms so she didn't really know how to relate to him. Jenni did, however. She took in the rolling-eye signal he threw at her with an infinitesimal nod. "Kirsty," she asked, "would you mind popping down to the café and getting me a latte, please? You know how I like it."

"Ooh, be a doll and get one for me please, Kirsty," added Raj.

"Sure," responded Kirsty, jumping up from her seat, glad for an excuse to put off the filing for a bit longer.

Left alone, Raj smiled and raised an eyebrow at Jenni.

"Come on, out with it," teased Jenni. "I know that look on your face, you've got some *goss*."

Raj grinned and came over to her desk. He leaned forward, speaking in an unnecessarily low voice. "Our lot, the family, went out for a drink last night."

"Oh, really, still trying to persuade you to marry and produce grandchildren?"

Raj clicked his tongue. "Ha! Yes my mum is anyway – in her dreams! Still, she means well, bless her heart."

Jenni gave a guffaw of laughter. "I don't see it somehow," she said.

"Yeah, tell me about it," said Raj. "Anyway, we went to this nice little pub in Hampton Hill."

"Oh yes?" Jenni knew that Raj liked his listeners to pick up on the nuances of his gossip, so she added, "Quite a way out."

"Yes indeed, but however far you go, you can never count on being safe from prying eyes, can you?" Jenni shook her head, smiling in expectation. "Well, who should I see?" Raj leaned in closer to her. "*She* was there," he said, pointing his thumb in the direction of the door through which Kirsty had just disappeared, "with Ian."

"That's hardly juicy gossip, Raj. Have you made me send Kirsty out for a coffee I don't really want just for that?"

"No, no, no, listen. We all know about Ian and Kirsty."

"And her plans to get her feet under his table," said Jenni.

"Yeah, silly tart; like *that's* ever going to happen." replied Raj. "No, the thing is, Darren was there as well, hiding in a corner. He was watching them."

"Oh wow!" Jenni shivered. "Are you sure it was him?"

"It was him all right."

"I must admit I've always found him a bit intense, but that's more like borderline stalking."

"Creepy," agreed Raj.

The door opened and Eleanor came into the room. Raj straightened up and Jenni spoke. "So your mum hasn't given up hope, then?"

"No, but I've learned to live with it. Morning, Ellie."

"Morning, Raj," replied Eleanor. "I left some swatches down here." Just at that moment, Ian walked past in the corridor. Eleanor quickly grabbed the swatches and hurried to take the opportunity to walk along with him. "I'll catch you later at coffee," she said to Jenni, as she headed through the door.

When Ian and Eleanor reached Ian's office, he had to cut across her to enter. Suddenly he paused in the doorway. "Ellie," he said quizzically, his nose twitching. "You're doing perfume today; that smells nice."

Eleanor could hardly believe what she was hearing at first. *Keep it cool, Eleanor,* she said to herself. *He's got a good nose, remember, that's all it might be.* "Yup," she said. "I don't normally, but I thought I'd give it a go."

"Hmm," he smiled and, Eleanor could have sworn, nearly winked. "Well, it's very sexy; I approve."

Sexy; he said sexy. He did, didn't he? Yes he did. Eleanor went slowly back up to the stitching room. Well, this was a turn-up. What was *that* about?

Kirsty's mobile phone vibrated in her pocket as she made her way back to the office laden with coffees. She'd received a text from Darren. *U on 4 lunch?* She stifled a sigh as she balanced the cardboard tray of coffees in one hand and texted back with the other. *Yeh, c u @ 1.* She had been getting weary of him even before she started seeing Ian. She found Darren intense and possessive. She felt certain he'd been lingering outside the house where she shared a flat with Sandra, more than once. He hadn't been loitering outside last week, though. She'd come back from the gym to find him in the living room talking to Sandra while he waited for her. Kirsty paused in her thinking. She'd better watch that. She had a suspicion Sandra liked Darren and she wouldn't stand for that. Darren was her boyfriend and she hadn't finished with him yet, Ian or no Ian.

Still, it would all stop when she and Ian could finally take their relationship to the next level. Kirsty gave a smile. Oh yes, that would raise eyebrows. Kirsty Manners would be somebody then.

Chapter Two

A Sunday afternoon, one month later

Detective Inspector Angela Costello and her husband, Patrick, slotted a desk neatly under the window in the second largest bedroom of their house, and stood back in the doorway to survey the results of a morning's hard work.

The room, until early that day, had had the appearance of the dumping ground it had become for the past couple of years. It now looked fresh, inviting and cosy. They could finally see the bed, they had cleared the floor of boxes and bags, the windows sparkled, and the stale, dusty smell had disappeared. Later, they would welcome Patrick's daughter back to the house in which she had grown up, and until as late as yesterday Angela had feared they might have to park Madeleine in the cramped quarters of the smallest bedroom unless they managed to get their act together.

"Looks just as it did when she was ten," remarked Patrick contentedly. "All that's missing is a ballet poster and her teddy bear."

Angela laughed, her gaze travelling over the walls, the duvet cover and the lampshade, all in a similar shade of pink. "Very girly," she nodded.

"Interesting psychological insight there," said Patrick. "As a teenager Madeleine was a rebellious Goth, really into black – hair, clothes, make-up – very grim. But she didn't once try to change the decor in here."

"She remained pink at heart. I hope she stays for a while, so I can get to know her."

Patrick picked up on the nervousness in Angela's voice and pulled her to him. "It's going to be just fine, darling. You two will get on like a house on fire."

Angela felt grateful that with her face buried in Patrick's shoulder he couldn't see the sudden tears springing into her eyes. She'd become increasingly apprehensive as the big day of Madeleine's arrival approached, and surprised at how vulnerable she felt. Something of the depth of her feelings must have communicated itself to Patrick, though, because he sat on the bed and drew her down beside him. "OK, enough of the hearty platitudes; I've been jollying you along for a while now, but it's got through even to my dull wits that it hasn't worked." He fixed her with a penetrating stare. "Tell me."

Angela picked at the duvet cover. "I'm just being very silly."

He grinned. "Quite probably, but tell me anyway."

"Well, I know that Maddie and I have got on fine every time we've met, but we haven't ever lived under the same roof and this is the house she grew up in. I can't rid myself of the feeling that once she's here she's going to resent me… resent me…"

"Yeah?"

"You know."

"Say it, sweetheart."

Angel took a breath. "Taking her mum's place." The words came out in a rush. "There, I've said it. I know you'll think I'm stupid and you might be right but, anyway, that's what's been worrying me. This was her home first, you loved her first and – "

There was a pause.

"Come on, you might as well get it all out."

Angela shrugged diffidently. "You loved Louise first."

Patrick gave a gentle laugh and hugged Angela tight. "You soppy old thing," he said. "Actually, I didn't love Louise first. I'd been in love at least twice before I met her."

"Yeah, but you didn't marry those others."

"True." He thought for a moment. "OK, Angie, here's the deal. I loved Louise, very deeply. When she died I thought the world had ended. I cried, I raged, I got seriously drunk and I shook my fist at God. And you know what?"

"What?"

"The crying made me hoarse, the raging exhausted me, the drink caused me to throw up, and I discovered that God doesn't get uptight when you shake your fist at him."

"What's your point?"

"I did grieve for Louise, for a long time. But that was sixteen years ago. I've moved on and so has Maddie." Angela looked doubtfully at Patrick. "Honestly, when we were courting and I told her of our plans to marry, she was thrilled to bits."

"You're joking?"

Angela's face presented such a picture of puzzlement that he laughed out loud. Finally he said. "Don't you realize, you set her free?"

"What!"

"Yes, you numpty, she was quite concerned about her poor old dad."

"Old?"

"She was only seventeen when we met, remember. She could see me getting old, doddery and more and more lonely. She felt responsible. In spite of her Goth phase, the teenage moods, the tantrums about staying out late and all that, you know, she's a good kid at heart. She worried about leaving me to go off and live her own life. And then you came along."

"Oh." Angela felt her spirits lift. "I hadn't thought about it like that; a bit like a knight-ess in shining armour."

"Exactly."

Angela was silent for some moments. "Thanks, Paddy."

"Are you still nervous?"

"Yes, but in a different way now."

"What am I married to?"

"You're married to a numpty," she said, embracing him.

Kirsty Manners smiled with satisfaction as she looked at her computer screen. What she had produced looked businesslike. It would create just the impression she wanted. She glanced at her mobile phone. The text she'd just sent was still visible. *Go on, ring,* she thought. She wanted to see her plan working.

It rang. Ian's face appeared on the screen.

Kirsty snatched up the phone. "Ian?" Her voice sounded tremulous, near to tears.

"Kirsty, this is outside of working hours. You know what we agreed."

Kirsty made a quick assessment of the depth of irritation in his voice and decided there was only a low-level risk of annoying him further. "Yes, I know, Ian," she said, with a realistically weepy sniff, "but I'm having a particularly hard time today. You know how it is. Some days are worse than others."

"Yes, I do, but I had no choice. I have to be free – I told you that – otherwise I can't work, I can't create. Anyway, it's only a trial separation so that we can assess what we both want."

Kirsty homed in on, to her, the most salient point. "You're hardly free now you're having a thing with Ellie."

"That's different; Ellie's an older woman and... It's just different."

"It's OK, Ian. I know why you're going out with Ellie."

"Oh, really? And why is that?"

"Pur-leese; you're trying to make me jealous, that's all. You think I haven't done that myself? It's all right. I understand. You want to be calling the shots when we get back together."

"You seem very certain we'll get back together."

"Ian, we're good together; you know we are."

"What about Darren? Aren't you still stringing him along?"

"I finished with him just before you broke up with me, remember? I wanted you to be sure you're the only one for me. He's going out with my flatmate now." A smirk stretched itself across Kirsty's face as she thought about that. Darren had been to the flat a few times with Sandra – all very civilized and polite. They had behaved like grown-ups. But Kirsty hadn't failed to notice Darren's eyes constantly straying in her direction. She knew she would only have to click her fingers and he'd come running.

"Oh I see, well…" said Ian, clearly at a loss.

Kirsty, wondering if she'd sounded a little overconfident, thought a tearful note would restore the balance. "Anyway, you've spoilt me for other men. It's just you I want. I really miss you, Ian," she sniffed. "I can't bear the thought of you and Ellie together."

"Hmm, perhaps it's as well we're having this little talk. Kirsty, you're being very naughty, you know."

"But Ian, I really can't bear it. We're meant for each other. I know we are."

"The fact remains that Eleanor and I have a relationship and you really mustn't goad her about it. It doesn't make you look good, Kirsty."

A malicious grin danced around Kirsty's lips as she listened to him. She had let slip no opportunity to make snide comments in Eleanor's hearing, whether about her age or that she wouldn't be able to hold on to Ian. She took pride in her ability to get under the other woman's skin.

"OK, Ian," she replied meekly. "You're right. I'll behave better in future," she lied.

"Good girl."

"It was great just talking to you, Ian."

"It wasn't bad, was it? And who knows what the future holds?"

"Yes, I'll be waiting when you're ready, Ian." Kirsty finished the call and threw the phone onto her bed. It had gone well. She'd broken the office hours only rule and managed to engage him in conversation. And she could tell he wasn't honestly outraged at the way she behaved in front of Eleanor. She gazed with satisfaction at some photographs stuck around her dressing table mirror. Few women could match her looks, which hadn't ever let her down in the past. Oh yes, she'd get him back again, no doubt about that. Kirsty had never had any trouble getting the man she wanted. Ian offered a bit more of a challenge, that was all. *And once we're back together again,* she thought, *I'll make sure he cuts out that "good girl" rubbish.*

Just as she turned back to her computer, the front door bell made her jump. She hastily saved the file she'd been working on and closed the computer, aware that one couldn't be too careful. Then she went down to answer the summons.

Eleanor Chandler hurried into her kitchen and sat down at the breakfast bar breathing heavily and feeling the heat of her flushed cheeks, a complete contrast from her cool composure when she left the house earlier. She deeply regretted having set out in the first place. After a few moments she felt steadier, and she got up and took the kettle to the sink. A hot drink right now would restore her completely to herself.

As the water ran into the kettle, her mind wandered back over the past year and a half.

She wouldn't ever have believed her life could change so radically. Eighteen months ago she'd been a dowdy woman dominated by an overbearing and autocratic mother. The only place she'd shone had been at work. She knew her stuff there. For that one thing she felt grateful to the late Mrs Chandler; her mother had taught her to sew from a very young age. Eleanor turned slightly and cast her eyes upwards in the direction of the old woman's bedroom. For more years than she cared to remember, she'd fetched and carried for the cantankerous invalid. Eleanor shuddered at the memory of the humiliations she'd taken, the sniping comments, the put-downs.

She'd known she had finally cast off the maternal shadow when she and Ian first made love. Could it really have only been three weeks ago? It had happened in the very bed from which her mother had refused to rise for the last ten years of her life.

Just at that moment the front door bell rang and a smile lit up Eleanor's face. She wasn't expecting anybody, and only one person ever visited her spontaneously. She put the kettle down and hurried along the passage, her heart pumping now for a completely different reason.

She threw the door open and smiled into Ian's face. "Hi, Ian. I didn't expect to see you today."

Ian returned her smile; the arm held behind his back now came round to reveal the bottle of champagne in his hand. "Neither did I; I've still got an appointment this evening, but my afternoon became free when my golfing buddy cancelled at the last minute, so I thought, is this an opportunity or is this an opportunity?"

Eleanor beamed delightedly but still hesitated on the doorstep, unsure of herself. In spite of her many years in and around the fashion industry, she had little experience with men. And she'd wanted this one for so long she felt uncertain how to handle the situation now she'd got him. She liked to think of herself as a quick learner, though, and as Ian stepped across the threshold she found a riposte she thought worthy of the occasion.

"Did you bring any oysters to go with that champagne?" she asked, injecting a suggestive note into the question.

Ian smiled as he shut the door behind him and glanced up the stairs before fixing his eyes on her face. "I don't think we need any oysters, do we?"

She gave a small laugh, knowing she sounded like a sophisticated woman now, not a gawky schoolgirl any more. "You're right! However, we do need glasses. You go up and get to work on the cork. There are some champagne flutes in the dining room but I'll have to dig them out."

Ian bent his tall frame over her and kissed her gently on the lips. "Don't be long," he said.

She felt the warm flush of anticipation rising up through the whole of her body. "I'll be right there," she replied. She knew just where to find her champagne flutes, having recently transferred the box of glasses from the old sideboard to her new wall unit, along with a pile of other things. A cousin had given her the champagne glasses in a rush of uncharacteristic generosity one Christmas, and she had never taken them out of their wrapping. Eleanor's mother had considered both the giver and the gift frivolous – ridiculous. She found the package and pulled it open, setting out four of the flutes behind the glass-fronted shelf higher up and hastening upstairs back to her lover with the other two.

Sandra Hodges fed another coin into the pinball machine in the Tone-Up Gym's coffee bar, and pulled on the handle to start the game. Her heart wasn't really in it. Much as she liked sports and keeping fit, even she felt a little surprised at Darren's capacity to work out. If she'd wanted any confirmation that she really loved him, hanging about here a good hour after finishing her session, just because he was on the premises, would have provided it. Disconsolately, she left the game and ambled over to a table near a small bar where a muscular man with close-cropped hair stood spooning coffee into a percolator. He looked up and winked at her as she sat down. Darren and Sandra had been coming to his gym for a couple of years, long before they were an item. He'd got to know them very well, and on occasions even trusted one or the other of them to guard the reception for him if he had to be elsewhere. He had a pretty good idea what was on Sandra's mind.

"Want a cup, Sandra? On the house."

"That's nice of you, Tone. Yes please."

The eponymous Tone, owner and manager of Tone-Up, brought the drink over to her table, straddling the chair next to her and turning a sympathetic gaze on her face. Not for the first time he wished Sandra didn't regard him as merely a good friend. He sighed and put the thought out of his mind. "It'll come good, Sandy," he said, after a few moments.

Sandra gave a rueful grin. "Yeah, I'm sure; it's just a bit difficult right now."

"The path of true love and all that."

"Yeah, I know. It's just that when you first start going out with someone, that's when you expect it to be very intense, all hearts and flowers. I mean, it seems to me we got on better when we were just friends. I knew he was paying attention to me then; really listening, like, you know? It was great."

Tony said nothing. He knew, and felt sure Sandra did too, the reason she and Darren got on so well as just-good-friends was because Sandra provided the perfect listening ear into which Darren could pour all his sorrows about Kirsty. Only a month had passed since Kirsty had finished with Darren, and in Tony's opinion he'd jumped into this relationship with Sandra too quickly. He had his own ideas about why that had happened, as well.

"I'm sure it'll be great again, Sandy," he said, to comfort her. "You just need to give it a bit of time; let the dust settle."

Sandra smiled at him. "Thanks, Tone. You're right. I'm expecting too much too soon, really." She looked gratefully at him.

"There you go," said Tony. "It was a real blow to his pride, getting dumped by Kirsty. He thinks the body beautiful is all any woman could want in a man and, you've got to admit it, his is honed to perfection."

Sandra gave a small laugh. "You're not kidding. I've never known a man who could hit the weights like he can. It's either that or the cycle racing. He's like a man possessed, sometimes." She looked at Tony and her expression became conspiratorial. "But let's face it, Tone, that's not what motivates Kirsty, is it?"

"Oh, no way! I saw that early on when she first turned up here. I tried to hint as much to him, but I don't think he got it. You could be an old crock but if you've money, power, prestige – especially money – Kirsty's going to be interested in you. She and Darren were never going to go the distance."

Sandra laughed. "No. He'll realize that in the end. He's much better off with me." She pulled her shoulders back and smiled, feeling more optimistic. She'd had a few little talks like this with Tony recently and he always managed to make her feel better.

Tony discerned the change of mood and moved on to a different subject. "How's the work going? Earning enough to pay the rent?"

"Nearly. I'm doing less and less temping to fill in. Got a shoot tomorrow, as it happens, for a catalogue; sportswear."

"Sportswear? That's right up your street," said Tony, as he began to fish for something in his pocket.

"Off into the back room to indulge your vice, Tone?"

He stood up and grinned ruefully. "Had one already, just don't want to squash the packet." Tony limited himself to two cigarettes a week, which he smoked in a little room behind his counter. Now and again he was joined by Kirsty, who liked the occasional smoke but hadn't wanted Darren to know.

"OK," said Sandra, standing up. Something she could see through a glass-panelled door at the other side of the room suddenly caught her attention. "Oh, there's Darren's bike!"

Tony followed her gaze through the glass to the covered passageway alongside the building, shielded from sight of the road – he allowed some of his more regular, trusted clients to store their bicycles there. "Yeah?" Tony looked puzzled. The door opened and a customer came in, so he began to move towards the newcomer as he spoke. "Where else would it be?" he said.

"Well, there, of course – but it wasn't there earlier; not that far along, that is."

"It must have been," said Tony.

"I didn't see it earlier."

"Well, nobody else would have moved it, except me, and I didn't, so maybe you just didn't notice it."

"Yeah, maybe." She didn't want to seem obsessive, so she let the matter drop; but it focused her mind. Her real problems were nothing to do with Darren being such a keep fit fanatic and keen cyclist, those things she could deal with. He hadn't really got Kirsty out of his system. That was the crux of the matter. She'd seen the way his eyes strayed to Kirsty when he came to the flat and she was home.

Sandra suddenly felt a frisson of fear. Darren was a brooder, and once or twice Sandra had definitely sensed that he could become violent. She sighed. It would all be all right if only Kirsty wasn't around.

Chapter Three

By the end of the afternoon, Madeleine had been installed, or rather, reinstalled. The only reminder of the rebellious teenager who had set off for university three years earlier was that her teddy bear, perched on the corner of her pillow, wore a little black trousers and T-shirt outfit.

"I see Ted's still going through a Goth phase," remarked Patrick, hoisting the last few books onto the top shelf of the bookcase.

"He'll get over it," replied Madeleine, flopping onto the bed and stretching herself the length of it. Angela appeared in the doorway bearing a tray of tea and biscuits. Patrick looked up at her, correctly interpreted her hesitancy, grinned and beckoned her in. Angela came into the room, put the tray on a small table, then sat down.

Madeleine sat up. "Thanks, Ange, that's ace," she said, leaning forward to take a cup. Over her head Patrick winked encouragingly at Angela.

Madeleine slipped her shoes off, drew her legs up under her on the bed and munched contentedly on a biscuit. "That hits the spot," she said.

"Have you kept up with your old school friends?" asked Angela.

"One or two, but the closest ones have moved away. I'll check out the parish on Sunday, see who's around. How's it doing these days?"

Patrick and Angela exchanged surprised looks. "The local parish? The church?" he asked.

Madeleine grinned. "Yeah, you know, where I was baptized and went to Mass for all those years."

33

"Yes, but I thought you'd become an avowed atheist," said Patrick.

"I tried to be, but it didn't take."

"Now there's a thought to conjure with," said Patrick. "Let's see, it's quite lively. I'm sure you'll find something you can get involved with."

"The parish priest these days is a young bloke called Martin Buchanan," said Angela. "He's a friendly chap. He should be coming here for dinner within the next week or so; we really must nail down a date, Paddy – oh – excuse me," she added, as she heard her phone ringing from her handbag in the other bedroom.

"That's your work mobile," said Patrick, inclining his head towards the sound. "You're not on call, are you?"

"I'm just covering Ronnie Bailey for this afternoon as he's got a family 'do'," called Angela, hurrying into the room at the other end of the landing. She leaned across the bed and grabbed her handbag, trying to keep any trace of either relief or hope out of her voice. In spite of Patrick's reassurance earlier, she knew that she was going to have to get used to Madeleine's presence in stages.

She could see from the screen on her mobile that it was Detective Constable Gary Houseman calling. Even while she was telling herself not to be silly, she knew she wouldn't be sorry to be called in to work just at this moment. "Hi, Gaz," she said, more loudly than necessary, knowing Patrick would hear and come to the obvious conclusion.

"Sorry, Angie; I know you've got something on at home, but DI Bailey said – "

"Not a problem," said Angela, firmly. "What have we got?"

"Unexplained death in Roehampton," replied Gary. "A young woman; sounds dodgy from what I can gather, but the person who found the body is in hysterics. The neighbours who came to help had the sense not to touch anything – well, apart from one of them trying to find a pulse. The doc's on his way. Rick and Jim are with me in the car. Shall we swing by your place?"

"Yes, Gary, thanks; see you when you get here." Angela finished the call, went back to the other room and stood in the doorway.

Patrick threw her a penetrating glance and raised an eyebrow. "You didn't say you were on call." The conflicting emotions of irritation and understanding battled with each other in his expression.

"Sorry, it's just for a few hours; once we got embroiled in all the clearing out in here I forgot."

"It reminds me of when I was little and Dad was still in the police," said Madeleine. She knew nothing of the tensions exercising Angela earlier, aware only that she had come back to her old home and a warm welcome from her father and stepmother.

Understanding won, and Patrick clicked his tongue good-naturedly. "I'll do the dinner," he said. "I hope you're back in time for it."

"I hope so too," she replied, gratefully accepting his olive branch. "I'll keep you informed."

"What is it anyway?" asked Madeleine. "Are you allowed to say?"

"A young woman in Roehampton; unexplained death," said Angela. "I don't really know any more than that at the moment." She saw Patrick's hand reach out automatically in a protective gesture to Madeleine and suddenly realized, just as she had her own reasons for wanting to be out of the house for a few hours, it would do father and daughter no harm to be alone together for a while.

The Homicide Assessment Team car barely pulled into the kerb before Angela was pushing open the front gate and heading towards it.

"OK, have you got any more information yet?" she asked Gary Houseman as she slid into the front passenger seat and clicked her belt into place. The newest and youngest member of the team, Gary's arrival had coincided with Angela's promotion to detective inspector recently. Two other members of the unit, detective sergeants Rick Driver and Jim Wainwright sat in the back.

"Not much, Angie. The dead woman's name is Kirsty Manners. Her flatmate, Sandra, found her about an hour ago. Apparently she – Sandra, that is – came home to find Kirsty lying face down across her bed. She called her name but didn't get a response, so she went close enough to see Kirsty's eyes wide open and staring; which is when she went screaming to the couple in the downstairs flat."

"Who did what?"

"Came back up with her and saw Kirsty. He tried for a pulse and she rang for an ambulance and the police. A couple of uniforms are in attendance."

"We can take them if you like, Angie," said Rick.

"Who, Mr and Mrs Downstairs?"

"Yeah," added, Jim. "We'll want to know if they were in all afternoon. If they heard or saw anything."

As a box-ticking exercise, what Jim said was accurate, but Angela preferred to take in the scene before making any procedural decisions. "Thanks for the offer, you two. Let's check it out first. For all we know, the woman died of natural causes and we're on a wild goose chase."

"She might not even be dead," added Gary. "Who's to say she wasn't playing a trick on her flatmate and they're having an argument about it at this very moment."

But Gary's optimism proved to be unfounded. Kirsty Manners was unmistakably dead.

Angela always waited for expert assessment, but just taking

in the scene at first glance it looked very much as though the young woman had been strangled.

She lay face down across her bed, the ends of a filmy pink scarf trailing out across her back. Her mid-length, dark brown hair had fallen across her shoulders, obscuring part of her face; so it was difficult to be exact, but it looked as though the scarf went all the way round her neck. She wore jeans, and a shirt that spread out at her sides.

Angela and her three colleagues said nothing for a moment, each taking in the scene in their own way.

Rick spoke first. "At least she had her own bedroom," he said. "That'll make it easier to seal the scene."

"Assuming this is her room," said Jim. "Oh yeah, look," he added. "There are photos of her stuck on the dressing table mirror." They all looked across at a selection of photographs showing the young woman in a variety of poses: in peach, as a bridesmaid, standing next to what was obviously a bride in the topmost view; in a bikini, relaxing on a beach; at a party; on the arm of a man out of shot.

"That looks a bit odd," said Angela.

"What does?" asked Rick.

"Oh, I know why," replied Angela moving round the bed towards the dressing table. "These photographs have been stuck on with Blu-tack, and look – there's just a blob of the stuff on the frame under the last picture, like there was another photo there and it either fell or has been taken away." All four officers looked down at the surface of the dressing table and on the floor all around the area.

"If there was another photo there it hasn't just fallen down," said Jim, finally.

"Hmm, I wonder if it'll matter to us," remarked Angela.

"It might turn up," said Gary, "the SOCOs will find it, if it's here anywhere."

"Or maybe the flatmate will know what was in it."

"You're right," said Angela giving the photographs another glance. She would look more thoroughly at them all later. They would go through the dressing table contents and the wardrobe. They would scrutinize her diary and address book, her mobile phone and her computer. They would turn over every detail of Kirsty Manners's life to find out who had ended it.

She continued to gaze silently down at the body stretched out on the bed. *She must be close in age to Madeleine,* she thought. She sighed, remembering Patrick's hand reaching out to Maddie as soon as he heard about the death of a young woman, and realized this murder enquiry would have a different resonance for her.

"*Everything makes a difference,*" she whispered to herself.

"Angie?" asked Gary.

Angela blinked and looked at him. "Sorry, just thinking aloud."

They heard a noise in the hallway. Jim slipped out, returning almost immediately. "The doctor and scene of crime officers are here."

"Yeah," replied Angela, stepping back from the bed. "We'd better get out of here and let them get on with their stuff." They filed out of the room, standing aside in the hallway to let the SOCO team and police doctor enter. They headed for a door at the end of the hall and found themselves in the flat's sitting room.

"Did you take a close look at those photographs?" asked Jim. "A hot girl like that must've had a boyfriend. We'll need to round him up."

I bet you had no problem with geometry at school did you, Jim? thought Angela. *You have a complete grasp on the fact that the shortest distance between any two points is a straight line.* "We'll

38

round up everybody we need to," she replied, putting a slight emphasis on the word "everybody". "OK," she continued, "I presume the flat downstairs has more or less the same number of rooms as this, so I'll take up your suggestion, Jim. You and Rick, ask if you can talk to Mr and Mrs Downstairs in one room while Gary and I see the flatmate in another. Did you say her name was Sandra, Gaz?"

"Yeah, Sandra Hodges," answered Gary, consulting his notebook.

"OK. Rick, you and Jim know what questions to ask. We'll meet back up here after we finish the interviews, and take it from there."

All four officers made their way down to the apartment below, whose occupants showed Angela and Gary into their bright, cheerful living room before withdrawing with Rick and Jim to sit round their kitchen table. Within a short space of time, a WPC led a pale-faced, shocked-looking young woman through the door. In the way with which Angela had now become familiar, Gary found a chair where he could sit unobtrusively, his notebook open and ready.

Angela assessed Sandra's build and colouring as very different from Kirsty's. Tall, she must have easily made about five feet ten or eleven, Angela guessed. Her slim body looked taut and muscular. She wore her blonde hair pulled back into a ponytail, and was dressed in trainers, jogging bottoms, and a T-shirt. Her eyes were red-rimmed and swollen and her face blotchy from crying. She stumbled a little as she walked across the room holding on to the policewoman's arm, and allowed herself to be settled like an invalid into the armchair.

Angela took out her own notebook as the door closed softly behind the WPC. "I know you've had an awful shock," she began, gently, "but you do appreciate that we need to ask you some questions, don't you?"

Sandra nodded. Her eyes filled with fresh tears. "I can't get that image out of my head… I just can't… They've been great, Mel and Jon, who live down here, you know. I don't know what I'd have done without them. They're going to let me stay with them tonight cos I don't think I can go back up… you know."

"I understand," said Angela. "Thank God for good neighbours, eh?"

"Yeah." Sandra managed a weak smile.

"Right," continued Angela, after a short pause. She found official spiel a useful tool for getting to the nitty-gritty, so launched herself into it. "I'm Detective Inspector Angela Costello and my colleague over there is Detective Constable Gary Houseman. There will have to be a post-mortem examination to find out exactly how Kirsty died, and until we know for sure we have to treat it as a suspicious death, hence the questions." She stopped. Through the clear signs of shock and distress, Sandra had turned a pair of very alert, very focused blue eyes upon her.

"Silly cow," she said. Across the room Gary glanced up and raised his eyebrows before bending his head back to his notebook and recording her words.

"Er…?" began Angela. She gave the other woman an interrogative look and waited.

Sandra shook her head in an exasperated gesture. "Oh, the way she was, with blokes and stuff. She was just so up herself and didn't see how she could upset…" She blinked and gazed directly into Angela's eyes. "If it turns out to be murder, you won't find any shortage of candidates, you know."

Chapter Four

Angela looked at Sandra Hodges for a moment and recognized what she had seen many times before in people caught up in murder. The shock was beginning to wear off. Very soon now, Sandra would realize the time had come for her fifteen minutes of fame and she would make the most of it. From this Angela deduced that she hadn't been overly close to her flatmate. *Hmm,* she thought. *I can see you can't wait to point the finger, Sandra. This could be interesting; but I'll set the pace of this interview, thank you very much.*

"That's an intriguing statement and I'll come back to it," she said. "But I'll need to get a few preliminaries out of the way first."

A hint of disappointment flared and died in Sandra's eyes. "Yeah," she nodded.

"Where were you this afternoon?"

"I... I was with my boyfriend, at the gym."

Angela noted the curious hesitancy in the way she said these words. "May I have your boyfriend's name?"

"Darren. Darren Carpenter."

"And where is the gym?"

"It's the Tone-Up Gym in the High Street."

So, less than two minutes away, thought Angela. "What time did you come home?"

"Four o'clock."

"Was Darren with you?"

Again she detected the curious hesitancy in Sandra's voice. "No," she said.

Angela made another note and looked up at Sandra. "Did Darren drop you off outside the house or did you leave him at the gym?"

"I left him at the gym." The hesitant note had completely disappeared. *Hmm, no problem answering that question,* thought Angela as she made another note.

"Will you describe to me exactly what you saw?"

Tears welled up in Sandra's eyes again and Angela had no doubt they were genuine. "I found her just like you saw when you went in," she replied. "I didn't touch anything."

"That's very helpful for us, thank you. Could you go through what happened from the time you came home?"

Sandra wiped her eyes. "Just as I was putting my key in the lock, Mel and Jon came through the gate. We said 'hello' and that, and they went into their flat."

Angela nodded. The house comprising the two flats had been built in the thirties as a family home. In the conversion process, the original front door giving on to a wide hall had been taken away. Two front doors, each opening on to a narrower passage, one containing the staircase, had taken its place. "So, then what?" she prompted.

"I came up to our flat. Kirsty had her door shut. The whole place was very quiet."

"Is that normal?"

Sandra thought for a moment. "It depends. One of us might have the telly on, or the radio. Sometimes we like to play computer games, which can be a bit noisy."

Angela nodded. *I wonder if Maddie's going to make a noise about the place,* she thought. "But you were struck by the quietness," she said.

"Well, you never know with... never knew with Kirsty. She could've had a guest in her room with her. She sometimes brought people home."

"So the fact that it was quiet made you wonder if she wasn't alone?"

"Not necessarily, but it was possible. Normally, even when

someone's in there, if you wait a minute you catch a sound – a laugh or a bit of conversation."

"Yeah, of course; so what made you think differently about this quietness today?"

"Well, I had this weird feeling that I was alone in the flat but, kind of, not alone."

"So what happened then?"

"I went closer to her room and then I saw the door wasn't shut, just pulled to; so I called out her name, just in case."

"Yes?"

"She didn't answer, so after a minute – well, it might not have been as long as that – I pushed the door open and looked into the room and that's when I saw… saw… you know." Sandra gave a shudder at the memory and the tears started to flow again.

"It's OK, Sandra, you're doing fine. You're quite sure you didn't touch anything at all?"

Sandra shook her head. "It's the one thing I was clear about. I just thought, Mel and Jon, I must get down to Mel and Jon. They'll tell me I'm being stupid or they'll say it's a joke and they're in on it. I was already thinking about what I would say if it turned out to be just a joke after all. I was going to go right ballistic, I can tell you."

"Yes, some jokes are just not funny. Do you know who Kirsty's next of kin is?"

"Yeah, that'll be her mum and dad. Their number is in our telephone book, by the phone in the hallway. We've got each other's parents' numbers and GP and all that, there."

"Very sensible. We'll take the details in a minute." Angela caught Gary's eye and he nodded. Angela turned back to Sandra. "There seems to be a photograph missing from around Kirsty's mirror. Would you know anything about that?"

Sandra shrugged. "No, I mean, I know she had pictures there but I don't know what they were of – well, Kirsty would have been in them all, of course." Sandra rolled her eyes a little. "But we weren't in and out of each others' rooms. We're not – weren't – that type of flatmates."

Angela nodded. "I think that's all we can reasonably get out of this line of enquiry at the moment, but you do realize that we'll probably need to see you again, don't you?"

"Yeah."

OK, thought Angela, *I'll let you out to play now.* "So," she said, "tell me what you meant earlier when you said there would be no shortage of candidates."

Sandra made herself a little more comfortable. "The thing is," she said, "Kirsty liked being the centre of attention. With her looks she never had any trouble getting boyfriends, and she didn't always bother to finish with one before she started with another."

"We'll need to know the names of Kirsty's boyfriend or boyfriends."

"Yeah, well, I can't help you there, I'm afraid. Kirsty was very cagey about them. She'd become very secretive lately… and excited."

"Excited?"

"Yeah, she's always been ambitious, ever since I've known her. She's a model – when she gets the work, which isn't as often as she likes – but lately I think she'd broadened her ambitions. She talked about going places."

"What did she mean by that?"

A look of frustration passed across Sandra's features. "I don't know. I got the feeling she'd managed to land some important boyfriend, and it was giving her ideas."

"But you don't know who he is?"

"No, someone she'd met through her office, I suppose."

"In the office? You said she's a model."

"Yeah, well, it's not that regular and she has to pay her share of the rent, so she has – had – a regular job. But that's in the fashion industry as well. She reckoned working there would give her inside knowledge of any jobs going. Lately, though, she'd started saying she wasn't going to be a clothes horse for much longer; she would be moving on to better things. I'm a model too; that's why someone introduced us, at the gym, thinking we'd have something in common. But recently she seemed to look down her nose at me a bit, even though I get a lot more work than she does. And she boasted about the posh *showbizzy* parties she got to go to."

"But her boasting didn't include giving you any names?"

"No." Sandra cast a knowing look at Angela. "You can make things seem better than they are if you keep a bit of mystery about them, can't you? And whoever she was seeing, she wasn't bringing him – or them – back to the flat."

OK, thought Angela, *you've thrown in enough key words now. I'll take the bait. I've got to know anyway.* "Where did Kirsty work?" she asked.

The satisfied look of a teacher, pleased with a promising pupil, passed across Sandra's face. "She worked for Ivano King."

Angela raised her eyebrows. Gucci, Jean Paul Gaultier, Balenciaga; and Ian King, the man behind the Ivano King label. He was right up there with them.

"You can see why Kirsty had such big ideas," Sandra said as she saw Angela's recognition of the name.

Angela nodded "And you don't know who she was seeing?"

Sandra shook her head. "No. She was always throwing famous names about when she wanted to impress me, but she could be very cagey when it suited her. She took a lot of calls she said were to do with work, when she wasn't actually in work."

"Oh, really?"

"Well, that's what she said, but it could have been a cover if she was seeing someone from the office."

"Or more than one person, as you suggested," replied Angela, pleasantly.

"Yes, of course."

Angela made a couple of notes. *You've definitely tried to point me in the direction of Kirsty's workplace, Sandra,* she thought. *And I have to ask myself why.* She smiled at Sandra, on whose face the pleased teacher's expression was still in evidence.

"So, you met Kirsty at the gym?"

"Yes."

Angela nodded, taking in again the honed physique and sports clothes.

"How long ago?"

There was a pause as Sandra pulled back a stray hair. "About a year," she said. The pleased teacher had disappeared and Sandra had stopped meeting her eyes.

"Was Kirsty very keen on fitness?"

The expression on Sandra's face now became almost a sneer; but, Angela reflected, she did look as though she took fitness very seriously. "I don't think so," she said. "Not really. She did enough to make it worth her while paying the fees, but that was about it. She knew she looked good in a leotard. You've seen her. Well, you can't take it away from her, not now. She was beautiful. And she knew it. You get a lot of blokes coming through a gym and they all liked to look at her. She enjoyed that."

Out of the corner of her eye Angela saw Gary shift in his seat. It was his way of asking permission to speak.

"Go on, Gary," she said.

"Was there any rivalry among the men, over Kirsty?"

Angela nodded her approval of the question.

"I don't think so... not seriously," said Sandra. "They all knew she was... spoken for." Angela looked sharply into Sandra's face but the other woman was gazing down at her fingernails.

Oh, you're definitely not comfortable parting with that snippet of information, thought Angela.

"Spoken for? Was she engaged?" asked Gary.

"No... nothing like that," Sandra looked up at him. "Kirsty was the sort of girl who was always spoken for. As I say, if you want to find out about the current man I suggest you talk to the people where she worked."

Oh, steer us away from the gym, why don't you? We'll leave things on that ambiguous note for now, thought Angela. *You'll keep, Sandra.*

"Thank you," she said. "I think that's all for the moment. I'll get back upstairs. Just give Detective Houseman your contact details – and Darren's, please, because we'll need to chat to him, too." Angela watched Sandra closely as she said this, but the prospect of bringing Darren into the investigation didn't seem to produce any further tension in her. "Is there a key to Kirsty's room?"

"Yeah, it should be in the lock on the inside of the door."

"OK. We'll lock the room for now, but obviously you'll need to come and go in the rest of the flat. I'll just check with our crime scene people and ask them to let you know when they've seen all they need to."

"I'll have to get my clothes and stuff, for tomorrow."

"Yes, of course. We won't keep you waiting any longer than we can help."

Angela emerged from the downstairs flat. She rang the bell to be let in upstairs, and as she waited she discovered that word of "something going on" had reached the neighbours. A couple of people were leaning on the front gate of the house across the road, ostensibly chatting to each other, though their eyes were fixed on the door to Kirsty and Sandra's flat. A dog walker hovered nearby. Casting her glance a little wider, Angela saw a couple of curtains twitch. A few more people walked past looking pointedly at the house, quickly averting their eyes when they saw Angela looking at them. By the time Jim opened the door, Gary had joined Angela and they all made their way up to the living room.

"OK, what have you got?" she asked.

"Jonathan and Melanie Bingham," replied Rick, flicking through his notebook. "Moved in about six months ago. Said Kirsty and Sandra already lived here then; nice pair, all got on OK, had a drink and a meal together now and again – nothing too heavy, but they were friendly. They thought there'd been a bit of tension between Kirsty and Sandra recently. They don't know details, but they think it might have been over a bloke."

"Hmm," said Angela. "I wouldn't be surprised if they're right. I'm sure the flatmate's got more to tell us."

"And the scene of crime team need to get in here as well, Angie," said Rick.

"Yes, of course they do. Just before we clear out of their way, what do we know about the scene?"

"No sign of forced entry," came three voices very nearly in unison.

Angela laughed. "Wow, we have a chorus; a couple of tenors and a bass if I'm not mistaken. OK, there's not much more we can do here at the moment, so let's get back to the incident room and feed what we've got into the computer." *I might even get to sit down to dinner with Patrick and Maddie,* she thought, realizing with a pleasant surprise that she looked forward to the prospect. From outside came the sound of a vehicle pulling into the kerb. Angela stepped over to the window. An undertaker's van had just drawn to a stop in the street. The few neighbours in evidence earlier had now swelled to a small crowd and abandoned all pretence of being anything other than intensely curious about whatever was going on. This reminded Angela of something she hadn't set up yet. "Rick and Jim, will you get house-to-house enquiries underway?" she asked. She turned back to a study of the people outside, but couldn't see anybody who looked like a journalist.

Her three colleagues joined her at the window. "No sign of the press as yet," said Rick.

"Just what I was thinking," answered Angela. Below them, two men were pushing a wheeled stretcher through the garden gate. "I think we'd better go while the going's good," she added.

They waited until the undertaker's men had gone into Kirsty's room before slipping out to the car. Within ten minutes they were settling down to open the case in the privacy of their own incident room.

A couple of hours later the car, now containing just Gary and Angela, drew up in front of Angela's home. "Thanks, Gary," said Angela, gathering up her handbag.

"Could I just use your loo, please?" asked Gary.

"Sure, no problem," she replied. "Come on in." She pointed him in the direction of the bathroom and went into the living room. Patrick looked up at her with a smile. He knew she didn't like to launch straight into shop talk, the minute she got in. Madeleine, not knowing this, had no inhibition about expressing her natural curiosity.

"How was it?" she asked, springing up from the sofa on which she'd been lounging.

Angela grimaced. "Not as bad as some I've seen. It looks like it might have been quick and clean but we'll know more after the post-mortem."

"Will you have to go and watch?"

"Yes, probably, unless D.C.I. Stanway chooses to go."

"What exactly do they do at a post-mortem?"

"Mads, darling," began Patrick with a note of caution in his voice. Just at that moment the attention of all three was arrested by the appearance of Gary in the doorway.

He blushed slightly at the sight of three pairs of eyes turned towards him. "Thanks, Angie," he said.

Angela went over to him. "Gary, I don't believe you've met my family, have you? This is my husband, Patrick, and my stepdaughter, Madeleine."

Patrick came over and shook Gary's hand. "Hello. I think you're fairly new to the CID, aren't you?" he asked.

"Yeah, still wet behind the ears," grinned Gary.

"Were you involved in that murder at Wimbledon?" asked Madeleine.

"Yes, that was my first case."

"Were you at that press conference – the one Angie had to make a statement at? That was really cool! I saw it on the telly in the uni bar with a load of my friends and I was telling everybody, 'That's my step-ma! That's my step-ma!' They were all dead impressed; so was I, to be honest."

Angela turned to Patrick and mouthed the words, "Step-ma? Impressed?" with a look of wonder on her face.

Patrick grinned and winked at her. "Numpty!" he said quietly.

"I was there," said Gary, "but not at the press conference. The new boys don't get to do that sort of thing. Where were you at uni?"

"Brighton."

"Oh, that was one of my choices! But I ended up in Nottingham." He looked around at them all. "Well, thanks for the use of the bathroom, Angie. I expect you're wanting to chill out and have some supper now, so I'll see you tomorrow." His glance took in Patrick and Madeleine, lingering infinitesimally longer on Madeleine. "Nice to meet you," he said.

Angela showed him out and came back into the living room.

"I didn't know police officers were allowed to be so cute," said Madeleine.

Chapter Five

DEAD GORGEOUS

Angel should . . . . the living room
I didn't know police officers were allowed to be so . . . .
said Madeline.

Eleanor gazed down on Ian's face as he dozed. She'd done a lot of gazing on this face in the past few weeks. She could still hardly believe the way things had changed between them. She'd loved without hope for so long, she hardly dared imagine really being in a relationship with him; yet here they were. She didn't lose her grip on reality, though. She, of all people, knew Ian's history with women. She would just enjoy the moment; that was a strict rule she had set herself.

Ian opened his eyes and she could see he wasn't immediately aware of his surroundings. She watched as he orientated himself, became aware of her gaze and smiled up at her. "I must have dropped off," he said.

She ran her hand gently across his forehead. "I like to watch you sleeping."

He leaned up on one elbow and kissed her lips.

"Who are you meeting later?"

"Oh, just Nigel; we're getting together for a drink. I know it's still a way off, but we need to make sure we've got our act together for Fashion Week."

"Oh, am I *not* looking forward to that," said Eleanor.

Ian grinned across at her. "I am; I'm getting a real buzz from this latest collection."

"Yes, but the working round the clock, the last-minute panics – all that."

"It'll be worth it, Ellie, you'll see. I expect to be the talk of the entire industry."

"You've certainly been adventurous. I've got to hand it to you. Getting away from shop talk, have you heard any more from your little pal?"

"I had a text this morning. Much the same, I'm afraid. Still in love with me and wants me back. Who knows how long this pining will last?"

"I think you've got her all wrong, Ian. I don't think she's pining at all. That is one very hard-nosed young woman, and it's my guess that all this 'pining', as you call it, is part of an act. She likes the idea of going out with a rich and famous boyfriend. She wants that lifestyle."

Ian smiled. "No flies on you, are there, Ellie? OK, the truth. I know she's a pushy, ambitious little cow and I know what she's after. The thing is, I'm keeping her sweet until I can be sure she hasn't got hold of any of my designs and might leak them."

Eleanor's opened her eyes wide. "Wow! Are you sure?"

"Well, that's just it, I'm not. I know she got at my laptop a couple of times, visiting my pad. She said she was just catching up on Facebook and Twitter but... I don't know. And I need to be sure."

"Of course you do. Do you think she *would* leak them?"

"Not while she thinks she can get me back. She called me this morning and I pretended I was a bit annoyed about her calling me at home, which isn't part of our agreement. But I'll let her think I'm changing my mind about breaking up with her and engineer a visit to her flat. Then I can make sure that, somehow, I get a good look at her laptop and wherever else she might have kept anything like that."

"That's more cunning than I would have given her credit for. She's been no end of a nuisance to me at work. I wish she'd just settle for Darren."

"I'm not sure what's happening there. That's what some of her texts have been about, actually. She did drop him but, apparently, he's now going out with her flatmate, which I suppose means he's still coming round to her place. To be honest I got the impression she was a bit frightened of him."

"I wouldn't be surprised, the size of him. He's a brooder, is Darren – the type to suddenly explode. Mind you, a bit of fear might be good for her; she's so cocksure of herself."

Ian grinned as he picked up his trousers from the chair where he'd draped them. "No prizes for guessing she's got up your nose!" He pulled his mobile phone out of his pocket and punched some of the buttons. "Just checking with Nigel; he wasn't sure what time he could meet me." He put the phone on speaker and laid it on the bed while he stood up and put on the robe that Eleanor had provided for his use. His call was answered on the fourth ring.

"Nigel Summers."

"Oh, hi, Nigel," replied Ian. He switched off the speaker and picked up the phone. "Yes... yes, you weren't sure... seven-thirty? No problem, Nigel, I'll see you there." He finished the call and smiled at her. "Look, Ellie, I'd better take a quick shower and dash, I'm afraid."

"No probs." Eleanor's eyes devoured Ian as he moved gracefully along the passage and disappeared into the bathroom. She still couldn't entirely get over this – as though she'd wake up and find it had all just been a beautiful dream. She was having an affair with Ian. Who would have thought it?

Well, she knew who wouldn't.

Mother; that was who.

In the neat and tidy living room of a small flat in Wandsworth, Darren Carpenter and Sandra Hodges sat close together on a sofa, conferring over mugs of coffee. Darren was having trouble coming to terms with the facts.

"It... seems really weird." He stared into the middle distance. "To think that she won't be in work tomorrow, that she won't come to the gym again. She won't do anything again. I know we were having problems in our..." He glanced quickly at Sandra. "I know we were splitting up." He tightened his grip on his mug as if to warm his hands.

Sandra stifled a sense of impatience. "You'd already split up, remember, Daz. I mean – you know – how we've been together the last few weeks, and all that. I told that policewoman you're my boyfriend."

Darren's eyes flicked towards her again and he looked at her as if seeing her for the first time.

"What?" she asked.

"What did she ask you?"

"Just about what I saw when I came home, how I found the... you know... Kirsty." Sandra thought it best to subject her conversation with Angela to a heavy edit.

"Still can't take it in, really," he said. "I..." He stopped. Just for a second she thought she saw a secretive look behind his eyes.

"What?" she asked.

"Nothing, I'm still coming to terms with the news... bastard!"

"Daz?" Sandra looked at him, puzzled, then her eyes widened. "Do you know something?"

He glanced briefly at her and away. "Nah, course not. What would I know? I'd just like to get my hands on the bastard, that's all. To think that while I was working out someone was – doing that."

Sandra repressed another impulse to give way to impatience. When *wasn't* he working out? "Yeah, I do know that, Daz. I mean, they're going to find out you were her boyfriend until recently, and they're naturally going to ask questions about how you got on. They'll be looking for someone with a motive. They might think, you know, as you'd split up..."

Darren roused himself then; he put his mug on the small table in front of them and sat up straighter. "I'll soon put them right," he said, with more energy than he'd shown since she'd arrived. "They won't be able to pin anything on me!"

Now it was a sigh that Sandra stifled. All she really wanted was for Darren to take her in his arms and tell her everything would be all right, they would get through this together. Inwardly she admonished herself. There were all sorts of different reactions to grief and shock; it was only fair that Darren be allowed to deal with the situation in his own way.

Not until nine had Sandra risked escaping in search of Darren; she had to be the one to tell him. Mel and Jon were concerned about her going out on her own so soon after such a nasty event, and for a moment, it looked as though Jon would insist on coming with her. She managed to reassure them she would be OK, though, and she'd be back soon.

Sandra put aside her personal frustration at Darren's response. Right now they had practical matters to deal with. "You're going to hear about all this tomorrow," she said. "And when you do, act surprised."

Darren looked at her and furrowed his brow. "Why?"

"Because it probably won't look good if you're seen to know already. If it comes out that I've been round here discussing the case with you, it might seem like we're... you know..."

"No. What?"

She fought against exasperation. "It might seem as though we've met up to, well, to get our stories straight."

Darren set his mouth in the stubborn way that Sandra didn't like. "I ain't got no story," he said, thrusting out his chin. "I was at the gym all afternoon and that's all there is to it. And you came round here to break the news to me. That's only natural, it's no secret."

"OK, you're right," said Sandra in her most encouraging voice. "I wasn't thinking straight. That's all you've got to say. I really wasn't thinking, it must be the shock."

"Yeah, well that's understandable, really." He gave her a smile, which was probably meant to show understanding, but he made no accompanying attempt to put his arms around her and comfort her.

As she made her way back to Mel and Jon's, Sandra found herself going over the events of the day. That little secretive look he'd given continued to puzzle her, because it was unlike him. What you saw was what you generally got, with Darren. And then there was the business of the bike. She didn't want to contemplate this, really, but Sandra hadn't ever been one to duck difficulties. Somebody had definitely moved that bike.

Ian King put one whisky and soda and one gin and tonic on the table, and sat down beside Nigel Summers. Both men sat in silence for a few moments, gazing out from the Richmond pub garden across the paved area separated only by a low wall from the riverside embankment thronged with people, all out enjoying a drink in the evening sunshine. "Nice place," remarked Ian, as he contemplated the scene.

"Isn't it, though?" replied Nigel. "I often come here of an evening, especially at this time of the year." He cast a sidelong glance at his companion. "I meant to ask; I haven't heard you mention her for about a month, so I presume you've sorted out your love life."

Ian smiled across the top of his glass. "That's a very discreet way of putting things."

Nigel grinned. "OK, I heard you had a thing going with Ellie, so I stepped back in amazement, gasped and said, 'What? Are you sure? Oh. OK, then.'"

Ian laughed. "Ellie's all right, she doesn't make any demands, she has no agenda and she's got a darn sight more conversation than Kirsty will ever have. But…"

"Oh? What's the 'but'?"

"I'm not quite free of Kirsty. She's always on the phone or texting me. She thinks she can win me back. And she's being really horrible to Ellie."

"You're not putting up with that, surely?"

"Only until I'm sure she's no threat to the new collection."

"*What?*" Nigel's eyes opened wide.

"Mmm. I think she managed to get into my programme and transfer some of the original sketches to her own laptop. She hasn't come right out and said so, but she's made one or two comments about the new designs, betraying suspiciously more knowledge than she should have. I'm going to soften her up and take a look. Then it'll be goodbye, Kirsty."

"I told you she showed too much interest in things that are no concern of hers, didn't I? Once you're satisfied about the safety of the collection, you want to get that girl completely off the payroll!"

"How nice to be in agreement with one's business partner," said Ian.

The two men chinked their glasses.

Chapter Six

The following morning, in the general office at Ivano King, Eleanor remembered that Raj had been planning to gatecrash a showbusiness event during the weekend. "OK, so did you get into the after-show party?" she asked him, as they poured their first coffees of the day.

"Oh, my dear, yes, all the humble pie I ate to get there was worth every morsel. I was *this* close to Lady Gaga." Eleanor widened her eyes, suitably impressed, as Raj brought his palms to within inches of each other. "I say, sweetie, are you OK?" said Raj, breaking off his narrative and staring at her. "You winced just then."

"Toothache," replied Eleanor. "It's been with me on and off since last week but I've got a dentist's appointment this afternoon."

"Oh, poor you. So there I was rubbing shoulders with the great and the good, when guess what?"

"What?"

"My contact, the one who got me in, had been rumbled and was being removed from the building."

"Oh dear, so – "

"Yes, it was only a matter of time before I met the same fate. This heavy bore down on me and thrust his face in mine in a most unfriendly manner. I don't know why he bothered, it's not like I wasn't going to go quietly."

"Sounds most unpleasant."

"Yes, I went from a study of Lady Gaga's perfect *maquillage* to making a close acquaintance with the bouncer's ugly open pores. Well, to be honest, they were more like slightly ajar; you know how I hate to bitch."

Eleanor was full of sympathy. "Oh, what a shame for the evening to end so badly."

Raj widened his large, brown eyes in astonishment. "Badly? What are you talking about? It was a fabulous evening. Imagine, being thrown out by Lady Gaga's bodyguards. It beats the time I was thrown out of the Brits by One Direction's driver."

Eleanor laughed. "You're amazing, Raj, you really are."

The sound of footsteps pounding along the corridor outside startled them both. As they looked up, the door flung open and Jenni burst in, evidently very upset. Her breath caught in a sob, and she sank down onto a desk chair, gasping. Her colleagues exchanged alarmed glances and advanced towards her.

"Jenni? Are you all right?" asked Eleanor. "What's happened?"

Tears welled up in Jenni's eyes as she stared up at Eleanor. "I've had the most dreadful shock," she said. "She rang here. Well, I'm the office manager, she would ring me, of course," she gabbled.

"Who rang you and what was the message?" asked Eleanor, speaking quietly and calmly. This worked. Jenni took a deep breath and gathered herself together.

"Kirsty's flatmate rang me to say that Kirsty wouldn't be in to work. I was just getting the sickness book out, thinking, 'Oh she's picked up a chill, or something – when she said that she... she's... *dead!*"

"Dead!" exclaimed Eleanor. She and Raj turned stunned eyes to each other before giving their attention back to Jenni.

"Jenni, that can't be right," said Raj.

Completely calm now, Jenni was ahead of her two workmates. She gazed at them with a solemn expression.

"She's not only dead. She's been murdered."

The viewing room of the public mortuary was devoid of any adornment whatsoever. The walls, the ceiling and the sheet covering Kirsty were all uncompromisingly white. Angela and

Patrick were silent as they stood respectfully by the body as it lay on the steel mortuary tray. "Well, at least it was quick," said Angela. The forensic post-mortem confirmed death by strangulation, identifying the scarf Angela had seen, trailing out from under Kirsty's hair, as the murder weapon; the time of death very close to three o'clock the previous afternoon. There had been no signs of a struggle. As far as the pathologist could ascertain, the girl had been caught unawares, from behind. It would all have been over in a matter of moments.

"I don't suppose that will be much comfort to her parents right now," observed Patrick, grimly. His duties that morning necessitated him being at the mortuary. Angela had to attend the post-mortem, and this gave them a rare opportunity to travel to work together.

"No, of course not," she agreed. They were silent for a few moments before Angela spoke again. "Jim's the only one who mentioned it yesterday, but I can see what he means about her looks now," she said, taking in the neat, regular features surrounded by an abundance of luxuriant brown hair. Kirsty had been about five feet five inches tall, with not an ounce of spare flesh on her slender body. "That's something her parents asked me about. Having been told she was strangled, they thought her face would be bloated."

"Ha! Readers of detective fiction," remarked Patrick. "But it doesn't always follow in real life, does it? Have they been in yet?"

"Yes, I was here when they formally identified her." Angela clutched Patrick's hand and let it drop again. "Rather harrowing."

"I can imagine. Where are they now?"

"I've left them with the Family Liaison Officer. I've got to talk to them, but I thought I'd give them a bit of time to move on from the initial shock."

"Of course."

Kirsty's parents were huddled together in the interview room when Angela joined them a few moments later. Tears fell unchecked over haggard cheeks. One of Mrs Manners's tissues was in shreds on the table and another was going the same way. Mr Manners had an arm round his wife and his head on her shoulder. Angela nodded at the FLO, took out her notebook and sat down near the grieving couple.

"Mr and Mrs Manners," she began in a gentle voice. "I can't begin to imagine how you must be feeling at the moment, but we have to set our investigation in motion as soon as we can. We want to catch the person who did this dreadful thing."

Both parents nodded and Mr Manners spoke. "We understand. We know you've got to ask us some questions."

"First of all, do you have any idea who might have done this?"

The couple shook their heads. "We've got no idea," said Mrs Manners. "It's hard to believe anybody would want to... to... She was such a lovely girl, Inspector."

"Beautiful," added her husband. "My beautiful little princess." He dissolved into weeping.

"She hadn't mentioned that she was worried about anybody?"

"Worried?" Mrs Manners's brow furrowed.

"Yes, in the sense of, perhaps a friendship that had gone sour and the other person had taken it badly, or somebody with a grudge for some reason."

Angela had been trying to keep things general, but Mrs Manners homed straight into one type of relationship. "She always had lots of boys after her," she said. In spite of her grief, her voice held a note of pride.

"Oh yes, no worries there. Well, she was so stunning, wasn't she, Babs?" said Mr Manners, rallying.

His wife nodded. "Right from when she started senior school; they were like bees round a honeypot, weren't they, Ray?"

"Yes." Ray turned to Angela. "With her looks, we told her she should be choosy."

"Choosy?" asked Angela.

"Yes, you know. Go for someone with a bit of class – well, class and money; someone who could keep her well. We told her she should be ambitious – that she could *be* someone. With her looks she could have been a supermodel."

There was something tragically naive about this notion, and Angela's heart went out to them. She thought back over what Sandra had said about Kirsty, and the suspicion that she was in a relationship with some kind of high-flyer. It seemed that Kirsty had taken her parents' advice on board.

"So, did she have a boyfriend?" she asked.

The look on both their faces gave Angela part of the answer. "He was a nice enough lad," said Barbara, damning with faint praise, speaking more to her husband than to Angela; evidently she had reiterated this opinion frequently.

"Bit too Neanderthal for my liking," said Ray, addressing Angela.

"Who are we talking about?" asked Angela.

"She met him at the gym," replied Barbara, "but they work at the same place too, now. He got her the job, in fact. She'd finished with him, actually, but he was still hanging around."

"No, they don't want to get the message, do they?" added Ray.

Ah! This looks promising, thought Angela, remembering her conversation with Sandra. "I've been told Kirsty worked for Ivano King," she said.

"Yes, she's the in-house model! Top designer's place, it is."

"She'd hardly begun there when she started turning heads – isn't that right, Babs?" said Ray, his voice full of pride.

"So – going back to the boyfriend," Angela persisted. "What can you tell me about him?"

In the small hiatus following this question, Angela realized that the last thing either of them wanted to do was talk about the boyfriend, ex or not.

"I think he's a hard-worker," began Barbara, in much the same tone she'd used to describe him as a nice enough lad.

"She could have done better for herself though," said Ray.

"What was his role at Ivano King?" asked Angela, intrigued.

There was another silence. Ray and Barbara cast quick glances at each other. It dawned on Angela that they were slightly embarrassed.

Ray shrugged and bowed to the inevitable. "I think he worked in the despatch department or the storeroom, or something," he said.

Barbara gave a small laugh. "OK, 'nuff said."

Angela was on the verge of asking them what was wrong with that when she realized that the "top designer" would be more what Ray and Barbara had in mind for their daughter. She decided to steer into safer waters. "What's his name?" she asked.

"Darren. Well, she called him Daz, of course."

Oh my, my. Are you the same Daz Sandra was talking about yesterday or are you a different one? Whatever, thought Angela. *I shall be having a little chat with you before either of us is very much older.* "Oh yes," she said in a carefully neutral voice. "I spoke to Kirsty's flatmate, Sandra, yesterday, and she mentioned a Darren."

Barbara and Ray exchanged looks before Barbara spoke, more to Ray than Angela. "The coast'll be clear for her now, won't it!"

"Did Sandra have her eyes on Kirsty's boyfriend?" asked Angela. She couched her question specifically to fall in line with their perception of their daughter. Ray's response proved that her strategy had been the correct one.

"Somebody's always got their eyes on Kirsty's boyfriends," he said. "That's the way it's always been. The boys all want Kirsty and the girls are always jealous. Not surprising, with somebody who looks like she does… did." Reality hit him again and his eyes filled afresh with tears.

I think that might be my question answered, thought Angela. "How did Kirsty feel about that – about Sandra's interest in Darren?" she asked.

Barbara gave a smug little smile. "She could handle it. It was no problem."

"Let's face it, she had enough experience," Ray added.

Angela didn't feel she could gain any more in pursuing Kirsty's attraction for men. It was time to change tack. "How did she and Sandra get on?" she asked. "Were they very good friends?"

Ray and Barbara looked at each other as they considered this question. "Well… they got on all right… I suppose," said Ray, eventually. "I don't think they were especially close, though. It just worked out for them, being flatmates."

"Yes, they met about a year ago at the gym Kirsty went to. It turned out Sandra needed a new flatmate and Kirsty wanted to move at the time. Like Ray says, it suited them. I doubt they'd have been best pals, though; they weren't the same type of person at all."

"Oh, really?" Angela's tone was inviting.

"Well, Sandra's a model too – I think that's why they were introduced. She does a lot of catalogue work, from what I can gather. But she's sporty – I mean, *really* into it," said Barbara. "Did you notice her muscles? She works on them all the time. I don't think that's very feminine, personally. Our Kirsty had a nice little figure and she just went to the gym to keep in trim. That's all you need to do, if you ask me."

"He was no different, was he?" added Ray.

"No different…?"

"Darren... always working out, lifting weights. And he rode that bike everywhere. Still, better than being a couch potato, I suppose. But the gun worried me."

"The gun!" Angela's eyes opened wide.

"Yeah, he does a lot of cycle races and once, when he was laid up with a pulled muscle or something, he was asked to do the starting pistol business. That got him into guns, and he got a real one in the end." Ray glanced at Angela and misinterpreted the interest in her eyes. "He's got a licence and a proper secure place for it. He's law-abiding, he's not a bad lad; but what I say is, why would anybody want a gun?"

Why indeed? thought Angela.

Angela decided she had gathered as much information as she could use. She thanked them for their assistance, mentioned that she might have to speak to them again, offered fresh condolences, and left as soon as she decently could without seeming hurried.

She popped her head round the door of Patrick's office on her way out. He looked up at her from his computer screen. "How was it?" he asked.

"Not as bad as I'd feared. I've got my first possible signpost on the way."

"Oh, really?"

"Yes, there's confusion over whether a chap called Darren was Kirsty's boyfriend or her flatmate Sandra's."

"Ah, the old three-sided love tussle! It's never very far away, is it? With any luck it'll turn out to be a jealousy killing – you'll charge either one or the both of them and be home in good time for dinner."

"If life were only that simple!" said Angela. "I'll see you later – " she blew him a kiss.

"*Ciao,* sweetheart," said Patrick, returning the gesture.

Half an hour later, Angela hurried into the incident room to find her boss, Detective Chief Inspector Stanway standing in front of Kirsty's case board taking in the information they had so far pinned or written there. Jim, Rick, Gary, and two other detective constables, Leanne and Derek were grouped around on chairs or the edges of desks. It pleased Angela to see them all together. This team had worked with her on the murder at the Wimbledon tournament, her first case after her promotion to D.I. and she couldn't help but feel a bond with them. She slid onto a vacant chair, just as Stanway turned round to face the room.

"Ah, good morning, Angie! No, you can come here – I'm putting you in the driving seat. I went to the scene last night, but I just missed you."

"Oh, I'm sorry, sir," said, Angela, annoyed with herself for blushing at the delicately implied criticism. "We spoke to the immediate neighbours and the flatmate, and set up the house-to-house, but I didn't think there was anything else we could reasonably do. If we'd hung around we'd just have been in the way of the scene of crime team."

"Absolutely, no problem," soothed Stanway. "I just wanted to touch base with you all, right at the beginning. You can see I've assigned you the same bunch of miscreants you had on the Wimbledon case." A burst of laughter met his quip. He turned back to the board. "It looks like you've got off to a flying start. I know it's early days, but have any angles emerged yet?"

"Just a couple, so far, sir. Kirsty's parents told me her boyfriend is a chap called Darren, but yesterday the flatmate – "

"Sandra Hodges."

"Yes – said she was at the gym during the relevant time with 'her' boyfriend, Darren."

"We're talking about the same Darren, I presume?"

"I think we are, but that's something we'll be checking out, of course. It also seems, according to Sandra, that Kirsty didn't limit herself to one boyfriend anyway."

"Hmm… this could get mucky."

"Possibly, sir."

"What's the other angle?"

"Well, Sandra didn't lose any time pointing me in the direction of Kirsty's workplace, and suggested we would find no shortage of candidates there."

Stanway's eyebrows rose up to his receding hairline. "Oh, did she, indeed?" He turned back to the board to refresh his memory. "Ivano King. Are we talking about the dress designer?"

"Yes, sir."

"Hmm, wasn't one of these people shot some years ago?"

"That was Gianni Versace; in Florida."

"Ah, American gun laws, not so easy over here, but... hmm, maybe some of them live a bit close to the edge. Is there something about the fashion industry that makes it more likely for somebody to be murdered?"

"I don't think so. It seems to me that Sandra may be pursuing some agenda of her own."

"Ah well, I'll leave you to it, Angie." Stanway rose and ambled to the door. "You know how to proceed. Let's hope it's a simple case of the old eternal triangle and you can soon wrap it up," he said, echoing something of Patrick's remarks earlier.

Angela took his place, facing the team. "I don't think we'll be getting off so lightly," she said. "If what the flatmate says is anything to go by, we're talking about an eternal polygon."

"Put it about, did she?" asked Jim.

"That's the impression I've been given so far," Angela replied. "But that could turn out to be wrong, of course."

"Hope so," said Gary. "A complicated love life won't make our job any easier, will it?"

"Quite," said Angela. "OK, then, let's get on with it. Where's her laptop and mobile?"

"With the lab," said Leanne. "Well, the laptop is. No mobile was found."

"Really? That sounds very odd."

"Yes, guv, the scene of crime team searched everywhere."

"Must be something incriminating to the perp on it," said Rick.

"You'd think so, wouldn't you? Right, you keep a close eye on that, Leanne. You know what we want off them."

"Yeah," Leanne grinned. "Everything that's on them."

"Absolutely; and you and Derek stay on top of the house-to-house. The minute you find a neighbour who noticed so much as a pigeon landing on the roof of Kirsty's flat yesterday, I want to know about it."

"What's the timeframe, Angie?"

"Quite wide, really. It could be several hours before the event. Even the previous evening, at a pinch. With no forced entry, she let someone in, or else they had a key. Kirsty's bedroom is at the other end of the landing from Sandra's. It would have been tricky, but not impossible, for someone to be there overnight without Sandra knowing."

"There were plenty of neighbours out in the street watching what was going on yesterday," said Gary.

"Weren't they, just!" acknowledged Angela. "They weren't bothering to hide their curiosity by that point, and I'm sure that among them there must be one or two who could curtain-twitch for England."

"Specially if she had a rapid turnover of blokes," said Jim. "The comings and goings might have been more interesting than watching the soaps, to someone."

"That's very perspicacious of you," said Angela.

Jim formed his mouth into the shape necessary for saying "What?" – paused and said: "I'll look it up."

Angela laughed. *You've worked with me before,* she thought. She looked around at the rest of her team. "OK, then, we'd better get ourselves over to Ivano King. Kirsty's colleagues have managed to rouse her flatmate's suspicions. Let's see if they'll have the same effect on us. In any case, that's probably where we're going to find this Darren, and he's got to be the first one we speak to."

Chapter Seven

Father Martin Buchanan sat patiently in the Immaculate Conception parish confessional. A good-sized room for its purpose, it had originally been used as an office at the back of the church. A screen at right angles to the door hid Martin from anyone coming in, allowing penitents the option of remaining anonymous behind a covered mesh opening in the screen, or moving beyond it to sit face to face with him. Confession was available after every Mass, but he didn't really expect to get many takers this early on a Monday morning. He had come to value the quietness, just sitting here. A light glowed above the door, announcing his presence. He picked up his breviary to take this opportunity of saying the next part of the Divine Office. He'd no sooner opened the book when he heard the front door slam. Almost immediately a shape appeared at the frosted glass panel in the confessional door and it was pushed open. A young woman, who obviously didn't care for anonymity, moved past the screen into the body of the little room.

In a previous life, before his ordination, Martin would have opened his eyes very wide at the sight in front of him and said, *"Wow!"* However, he'd changed a lot in his journey to the priesthood. He had learned to look behind a pretty face, for one thing, and he could sense a great deal of tension in this woman – even fear. Her eyes kept darting towards the door and she held her head at an angle, as if listening for a sound from outside. He smiled pleasantly at her and put his breviary down on the ledge at his side. "Good morning," he said, adjusting the purple stole round his neck.

She saw the gesture. "Please," she said, "not confession." Her accent wasn't English; some sort of Eastern European, he thought.

Puzzled, Martin lifted the stole from around his neck, brought it briefly to his lips and put it to one side. "Are you a Catholic?" he asked.

"*Tak* – yes." She perched on the edge of the chair, her whole body trembling, rigid, poised to fly.

"Then why...?" Martin stopped. It wasn't his place to ask. "No matter," he said. "How may I help you?"

But she volunteered an explanation. "If I confess, you not be able to tell peoples."

Martin's stomach turned over. "What's the problem?" He struggled to keep his voice steady.

"I come here for fashion industry, meet peoples, many fashion designers here and I choose one with same name like me." Martin's brow furrowed at this and he wondered what she meant but he didn't want to interrupt the flow. "He say he help but I no see him any more. Now, I am prisoner. They want me do bad things, with mans – men, at parties. The other girls, they accept but I no want do this – " She broke off, apparently unnerved by the sound of keys being jangled in the aisle beyond the door.

Martin kept his voice to a whisper. "Young lady, I can help you. Stay here and I will help you." His mouth felt dry. The room suddenly darkened and the young woman jumped. Martin peered round the screen and caught sight of a huge shadow passing by the frosted glass panel in the door. He got a fleeting impression of close-cropped hair and a dark bomber jacket – and bulk; the size of the man...

"Is Igor," she whispered. "He not look for moment and I run from house. I run round corner, along this street, that street. I think I escape, but then I see him. I see church, I run in."

Martin's stomach churned again. The idea of being watched by that giant was not a pleasant one. "Please let me help you," he said.

She looked at him. "Is no good; I have to go." She put her hands up to her cheeks; tears started in her eyes. "I frightened, I think they steal my looks. I need my looks." Gazing into her pretty face, Martin's heart went out to her. The shadow appeared again at the glass panel. "Hide so he not see you!" she said on a note of rising panic. Martin let himself be persuaded by the fear in the woman's voice. He moved further back behind the screen and crouched down. The door opened and he heard an angry grunt that sounded like "asher". The woman answered him. "Is quiet, empty; nice to pray here." Martin could hear the fear in her voice. Another grunt, this time more peremptory in tone, sounded from the doorway and the woman got up and left the confessional. After a moment, Martin rose and went into the main body of the church. He was just in time to see the front door swing shut.

Jenni saw the police car arrive. All morning she'd been drawn time and time again to the window, from her desk where she'd hardly done a stroke of work. She couldn't have said exactly what she was looking out for, but when she saw an unfamiliar car draw to a stop just by Ian's Porsche she knew it was the police and felt, strangely, as though a burden had been lifted from her. She didn't have to be anxious about the murder any more; the police were here to take over.

She watched three men and a woman emerge from the car, before getting up and heading along the corridor towards the stairs leading down to the pleasant, airy reception area.

Jim was just about to ring the bell when the door opened and the detectives found themselves staring into Jenni's mild, thirty-something eyes.

"Good morning, I'm Detective Inspector Angela Costello – "

"Are you here about Kirsty?"

"Yes."

Jenni stood aside to let them pass into the building. "So it's not a horrible mistake, or some sort of joke in very bad taste, then?"

"I'm afraid not," said Angela.

"I'm Jenni, the office manager. You'd better come into the general office, where I'm based," said Jenni, leading them up the stairs. As they went along she gabbled on about what a terrible shock it had been to receive the news. Angela made sympathetic noises as she walked, taking in her surroundings, walls arrayed with large photographic poses of models in elegant and stylish clothes. These were interspersed with a different type of picture – receptions, launches, gala occasions, celebrities, people in beautifully cut suits with smiling faces and champagne glasses. Here and there she could see the type of plaque that could only be an industry award of some sort.

Once in the general office, Jenni offered them seats. Angela introduced her colleagues.

"How was she killed?" asked Jenni, once they'd all turned down the offer of tea or coffee.

"It wouldn't be right to talk about the way in which Kirsty died, not at the moment, anyway," said Angela. "But there's no question of it being anything other than murder, which means we're going to have to talk to all the people who worked here with her."

Jenni nodded. "This is awful," she said. "It's like something from the telly or the films. Everybody's very shocked. I don't suppose much work is being done out there." She cocked her head in the direction of the corridor.

"I can imagine," replied Angela. "Would you have a list of the personnel here?"

74

"Hmm, we're not big on personnel as such," answered Jenni. "Most of the people working here are on a contract. We employ a lot of casuals, in the stitching room for example, and there's Raj, the pattern cutter and Ellie, the head stitcher. They always work here even though they're on contract. Mind you, Ellie's not here at the moment. She had a dentist's appointment today."

"The thing is," said Angela, "we'll need to speak to everybody here, whatever the terms of their employment. Are you a permanent member of staff?"

"Yes."

"OK, thank you for your help, Jenni. We don't want to disrupt your work any more than we can help. We're looking, first of all, for someone called Darren Carpenter."

Angela saw speculation flare behind the other woman's eyes and could immediately imagine the conversation at lunch with Jenni's confidantes: *She hadn't been in the place five minutes before she was asking to see Darren. You take my word for it; they've got him in their sights already.*

"He's downstairs at the back. Despatch is his official job, though he does some maintenance and a few bits and pieces, as well."

"OK, D.S. Wainwright and D.S. Driver will start with the stitching room, while we're talking to Mr Carpenter, if that's all right."

"No problem," replied Jenni. "If you go down the stairs we've just come up and along the little passage leading to the back, you'll find Darren." She nodded at Rick and Jim. "I'll take you up to the stitching room."

Downstairs, Angela and Gary found themselves walking through a cluttered room lined with wheeled clothing racks, packed with garments shrouded in plastic bags and sheets.

A man strode towards them through wide double doors set into the back wall of the unit.

Angela took in the bulging biceps, the top pulled tight across a muscular chest and the powerful-looking legs straining against a pair of combat trousers as he moved.

She raised her eyebrows. "Cor, thunder thighs," she murmured.

"Looks like a bruiser doesn't he?" agreed Gary. "You wouldn't want to get on the wrong side of him."

"Oh, you never know, he might be a gentle giant."

"Yeah… right."

Angela was still chuckling at Gary's cynicism as the man reached them.

"Yes?" he asked.

"Good morning. I'm Detective Inspector Angela Costello, and this is Detective Constable Gary Houseman. We're looking for a Mr Darren Carpenter."

"That's me." He stood back to let them pass, indicating a smaller room to one side. The two detectives entered to find themselves in a tiny office; clearly Darren's personal domain. A couple of speed bike posters decorated the walls, and snaps of riders lined up to start a race. Darren could be clearly seen in two of them, looking very solemn. One showed him as a competitor and in the other he held aloft the starting pistol. The office had only two chairs and very little room; Gary, glancing back into the despatch room, spotted a low stool which he commandeered, seating himself more or less in the doorway. He took out his notebook.

Angela sat down on one of the chairs Darren sat on the only other one. He picked up a cable tie, used throughout industry to close plastic refuse bags, and fiddled with it. Angela decided to use his obvious hobby as a starting point. "I see you're a keen cyclist, Darren. Do you mind if I call you Darren?"

"Nah, s'all right; yeah."

"Yes?"

"Yeah, I'm into cycling." Silence reigned in the little room, Darren clearly waiting for their next question.

Angela reminded herself that this man had just lost someone close to him and she couldn't know how he was dealing with it. She looked at the photographs of Darren with the starting pistol, and gave it another try. "I see you've got an official position in some races," she said.

Darren glanced briefly up at the photographs. "Yeah, I'd pulled a tendon; couldn't race for a while."

Another silence. A movement from Gary indicated that he wished to ask a question. Angela cast a glance at him and nodded her permission.

"Is there much difference between a starting pistol and a real gun?" he asked.

"Yeah."

"Is it easy to tell them apart?"

"If you're an expert." All Darren's utterances came out of his mouth and dropped like dead weights into the ether. Gamely, Gary battled on. He smiled; his tone keen and interested.

"Ah, you're an expert, then?"

Darren nodded and looked quickly at Angela. "Got a licence," he said.

Angela nodded and gave up on easing gently into the interview. Darren obviously didn't do conversation. "We're here about Kirsty Manners," she began.

Tears welled up in Darren's eyes and overflowed down his cheeks. "Yeah," he sobbed. "I knew you'd..." He was unable to continue. Angela waited, letting him regain his composure. "I knew you'd turn up," he said eventually, in a shaky voice.

"You've obviously heard what's happened."

"Yeah." More tears poured down across his face. "I was told last night."

"Who told you?"

"Sandra, my... her... Sandra."

"Sandra Hodges?"

"Yeah."

"I see. I'm sorry to distress you, but I'm sure you realize I have to ask you some questions."

Darren nodded. "Yeah, s'all right; I know."

"I believe you'd been in a relationship with Kirsty."

"Yeah, we'd... split up."

Hmm, I bet this wasn't a clean break, thought Angela. Her speculation was immediately answered by Darren's next words. "Well, she'd split with me, but I... well, I had, too, sort of. I was going with her flatmate, Sandra... er... " He stumbled to a halt.

Hello, hello, thought Angela. *I bet you'd taken up with Sandra in an attempt to make Kirsty jealous and get her back.* "When did you split up with Kirsty?"

"'Bout four weeks ago."

"And had you seen her at all in that time?"

"Yeah, well, at the gym – we use the same gym – and when I came round to the flat to see Sandra."

"You didn't find that awkward?"

Darren shrugged. "Nah, it happens, you just get on with it." He paused. "I don't think it was working out for her."

"What wasn't working out for her?"

"Her relationship, the one she'd split up with me for."

"Oh, really? She was seeing someone else?"

"Yeah, well, that's why she split with me; but something had gone wrong – according to Sandra, anyway."

"You've no idea what?"

"Think she was being dumped. Sandra heard her in her room on the phone. She said it sounded like she was arguing and pleading. And she thought Kirsty had been crying a couple of times but tried to hide it. It looks like it happened straight after she told me she didn't want to see me any more." He gave a small satisfied smile. "Serves her right, she should've stuck with me." He broke off and cast a swift calculating glance at Angela. He secured the ends of the cable tie so it couldn't come undone and pulled on the resulting circle of plastic with both hands. "I was thinking, maybe…" He shrugged and ground to a halt.

"Were you thinking that if her new relationship wasn't working out, maybe you and she could get back together again?"

There was a very long pause.

"Yeah."

"Tell me about Kirsty," said Angela, gently.

A large sigh escaped him, causing him to shudder. "She's lovely, a real looker; couldn't believe it when she said she'd go out with me. When the job came up here, I put in a word for her. She always said she wanted to be a model. She sent pictures to agencies and had done a bit of photographic, but she wanted to do the catwalk. So I thought this job would give her a taste of it, like. She was so keen." Tears coursed down his face again. Angela and Gary exchanged glances.

"Oh, really?" asked Angela.

"I didn't know she had big ideas. It wasn't just about modelling. She wanted to live the high life. She thought she could be somebody and get someone, way up there." He waved his hand towards the ceiling.

"Up there?"

"Yeah, you know; like, up the social ladder."

"And who did she want?"

"Someone rich and high class. Her parents had told her she could get anybody she wanted; but she didn't realize." Darren was overtaken by another bout of weeping.

"What didn't she realize?" asked Angela after he'd calmed down a little.

"Well, it's not just about looks, is it? You need other things. You have to have a bit more about you. You have to know how to – you've got to be able to walk the walk as well as talk the talk, ain't you? Kirsty was gorgeous all right, but apart from that she was just an ordinary girl. You know what I'm saying?"

Angela nodded. "I think so. Looks alone aren't enough. To mix in certain circles, the ones Kirsty was drawn to, you need education and culture."

"That's it," nodded Darren.

You need class. And it's looking like Kirsty didn't have any, thought Angela.

"Who was the man she left you for?"

"Ian."

"Ian King?"

Darren nodded. Angela made a note. "I see what you mean about her being a high-flyer."

"Yeah. Well, it was him that she split up with me for, but I think there was someone else before that. I don't know who the other person was, but that's when I first got suspicious, like."

"What made you suspicious?"

"She had texts here and there that she was cagey about. I'd go to the bar to get our drinks and when I came back, I'd catch her reading a text. When I asked who it was from, she'd just say it was her mum, or one of her friends, but I dunno, I just got a feeling. Then I reckon that finished 'cause she was, like, full-on with me for a while. Then it started up again."

"You mean that relationship, the first one?"

"No, I mean the cageyness, things that made me suspicious."

"And this time you think it was Ian King?"

"It was him. A couple of times she came to meet me and I caught a whiff of his aftershave. He always wears the same one. It's not cheap stuff. Kirsty used to like to give herself a spray of a bloke's aftershave here and there. She did it with me when we first started going out. And I saw them together."

"Where did you see them?"

Darren was silent for longer than consideration of the question required. "In a pub in Barnes," he said at last.

Angela made a business of writing the information down. "Anywhere else?" she asked, without looking up from her notebook.

The pause wasn't so long this time. "They went for a meal in Mortlake once or twice and they were in Hampton Hill a few times."

You've been following her, haven't you, Daz, thought Angela. She wasn't surprised. There was something brooding about him, obsessive even. "And you've no idea who the first man was?"

"Nah."

"Did it not bother you that she was seeing other men while she was supposed to be your girlfriend?"

Darren put his hand through the cable tie and pulled it up his arm in bracelet fashion. "Thought she'd soon learn, and then it would be all right, didn't I?"

"Learn what, Darren?"

"What I said; looks ain't enough; specially with him."

"Him?"

"Ian. He never sticks with 'em for long."

"Oh right; OK. Darren, I need to know where you were on Sunday afternoon."

Tears welled up in Darren's eyes again but he remained composed. "At the gym."

"From what time?"

"I got there after lunch; 'bout two-ish."

"And how long did you stay?"

"Till about five."

"That's a long time to be working out, isn't it?"

Darren shrugged. "I wasn't working out all the time. I

stopped, went to the loo; I helped out on the reception a bit. The bloke who runs the place is a good mate of mine so I hang out there quite a lot."

"Do you remember what time you stopped for the loo and to help out at reception?"

There was a pause. "Three – or around then." Angela looked up from her notebook to find herself being scrutinized by Darren. She bent her head to her notebook again. *Hmm*, she thought. *There was something going on in the back of your mind just then. I wonder what it was.*

"So there are plenty of people who could verify that you were there?"

Darren was completely relaxed. "Oh yeah, no problem."

Angela shut her notebook and stood up. She thanked Darren for his time and gave him the usual warning that she might need to speak to him again.

Once the door had closed behind them, Darren opened the bottom drawer of the desk. He took out a felt bag, extracted from it a gun and stared at it for a long while, running his hand lovingly over the gleaming metal.

Angela and Gary went out to the front of the building and called Rick and Jim to come and join them. "How did it go with the stitchers?" she asked, once they'd arrived.

"There were three of them there," answered Jim. "We've got their details. None of them could tell us much. They knew who Kirsty was, of course, had seen her in the office here, but hadn't really talked to her."

"What about the is-he-or-isn't-he boyfriend?" asked Jim.

"Well, that situation's a bit clearer," said Angela. "Darren who works in despatch is the ex who wanted her back. In the time he was with her, he suspected she'd been seeing someone else; and more recently, he knew for definite that she had gone out with the boss here – Ian King."

"Who's this Ivano King, then, Angie?" asked Jim, looking up at the sign above the unit.

"The same person; Ivano King is the label on the clothes, that's all. I suppose he thought it sounded more interesting alongside names like Prada and Armani. As it happens, I've quite liked some of his stuff in the past, but I haven't heard much about him for a while. I read somewhere that he's had a couple of bad years." She looked towards the building. "They seem to be in full production, though, so perhaps he's hoping for better reviews for the next collection."

"Really? Well, I'm strictly a Marks & Spencer man," said Jim. "I expect the girlfriend will have heard of him, though."

Angela didn't bother to point out the Marks & Spencer stake in the fashion market to Jim; she didn't think he would get it. "No matter," she said. "Gaz and I will take him on. And then we can talk to this person," she said, tapping the next name on a her list, "although I think she's not here this afternoon."

Jim cast a look down at the page. "OK, so do you want us to take the woman who let us in – Jenni – and this Paki bloke?"

There was a brief silence. "The what bloke?" asked Angela eventually.

Jim had the grace to look embarrassed. "The Asian gentleman, Angie."

"Yes, Asian gentleman," said Angela. "Raj Wickramasinghe; you'll probably find he hasn't ever been to Pakistan in his life and has little knowledge of either the customs or language of that country." She paused.

"Yes, Angie." Jim didn't meet her eyes.

"There's no place for racists on this team, Jim."

"Yes, sorry."

"OK, let's get to it then, chaps."

Chapter Eight

Angela realized what Darren had meant about Ian's aftershave the minute she entered his office. And he was right; it wasn't cheap.

Angela looked around, avidly drinking in the atmosphere. This was probably the only chance she'd ever get to be in a top fashion designer's office and she wanted to make the most of it. The whole place breathed creativity. She noted all the photographs of the glossy lifestyle but her eyes were really drawn to the sketches on the worktable, the swatches of clothes; silks and wools, linens and cottons, thrown here and there. She wanted to run her hands over them, to feel the textures. In her teens and early twenties she'd made many of her own clothes and had only stopped in her determination to rise through the police ranks. In clearing out the room at the weekend for Maddie's return, they had come across her machine. She was just thinking about how easy it would be to set it up in the smallest bedroom when she became aware of Gary looking at her with a puzzled expression on his face. Reluctantly she turned her attention to the other man in the room and tuned back into reality.

"I'm totally shattered by this," Ian sighed. "And not just me; everybody's very shocked."

"Yes, I'm sure," said Angela. "How did you all find out?"

"Jenni told us – well, she told Raj and Eleanor because they were in the general office."

"Oh yes." Angela consulted the hastily put-together list in her notebook. "Eleanor… Chandler? The head stitcher?"

There was a brief pause before he replied. "Yes."

Angela looked up at him and gave a small, puzzled, smile. "You don't sound too sure about that," she said.

Ian put a hand up to his forehead and took a breath. "Sorry," he said. "Not quite with it this morning. I keep thinking, 'Goodness… Kirsty… but there's work to be done…' and then I find it's some time later and I haven't done any work. I suppose I can't get my head round it."

"Yes, I can understand that. There's no gentle way to lead into this, so I'll just get on with it. Would you mind telling me where you were yesterday afternoon?"

A flash of annoyance appeared in Ian's eyes. "Well, to be honest I think I would, Inspector. Are you saying that I'm a suspect?"

"Not at all, sir, it's just routine."

The expression on his face lifted. "Yes, of course. Sorry, I'm overreacting. I think we're all a bit tense today." He paused for a moment as though thinking what to say next, running his fingers through immaculately cut hair; even the ensuing disarray looked fashionable. "This is why I hesitated just now. In the past few weeks, Eleanor and I have become rather more than just boss and employee and as it happens I was with her all yesterday afternoon."

"From?"

"Ooh, I got there just after two o'clock and I think I left around six."

"I see." Angela made of point of keeping her face expressionless. *So how long was the interval between dumping Kirsty and taking up with Eleanor,* she wondered. She jotted something down and underlined it.

"The thing is," Ian hurried on, seeing her making notes, "my relationship with Eleanor; it's not generally known and I'd be grateful if it didn't get out."

"We won't be telling anybody," said Angela.

He nodded; a man of the world.

Angela decided to squeeze a little. "Unless it becomes part of the evidence in the trial," she said.

Ian paled before managing a smile. "Oh, there's no chance of that. Our situation, Eleanor and mine, that is, has no bearing on what's happened to young Kirsty." He leaned back in his chair, completely at ease again.

Young Kirsty? queried Angela to herself. *Are you distancing yourself from her now or did you always call her that?* "How much do you know about what happened?" she asked.

"Only what Jenni could tell us this morning," he replied. "Apparently Kirsty's flatmate phoned in to say Kirsty wouldn't be in. Jenni was just about to enquire what was wrong with her, when the flatmate said Kirsty was dead – she'd been murdered. We're all still having trouble believing it, really."

"I'm sure." Angela smiled pleasantly at him. *Now, is my next question going to annoy you or is it not?* She made a play of flicking through her notebook before finding the correct page. "I believe you were recently in a relationship with Kirsty," she said.

Ian clicked his tongue. "I don't suppose it was much of a secret around here."

"So it's true?"

"Yes, we had a thing going for a while, but I had to put a stop to it. Jenni fielded a couple of enquiries from the tabloids recently, and said they seemed keen to move from my next collection to my love life. I don't mind my own people knowing, but I didn't want it getting into the press. I've got a bit of a reputation and I don't know that Kirsty would have done it any good."

"Really? Why not? She was trying to make it as a model, wasn't she? Isn't that the sort of person you'd be expected to consort with?"

"Oh please, Inspector! This industry is crawling with women who are trying to make it as models. The bottom line is, if I ran into, say, Mick, at a bash would I have introduced them?"

"Mick?"

"Jagger."

"Oh, right."

"I've got a feeling Kirsty was telling her friends about us as though we were a couple. I suppose I shouldn't be surprised; I think she was quite naive – a little gauche, perhaps. Not very sophisticated."

"Surely that's the type of thing gossip columnists look for anyway? Can you really be sure Kirsty was indiscreet?"

Ian spread his hands. "It was only a matter of time. A couple of occasions when her mobile battery was low she used my laptop – later I had to clear her Facebook and Twitter pages from my browsing history; you know how girls like to gossip."

Angela also knew how girls like to keep secrets when it suits them. She wondered for a moment how far the lab had got with trawling through Kirsty's computer. She decided not to let him get away with blaming Kirsty now she couldn't speak up for herself. "I find it's often impossible to trace gossip to its source," she said.

"You might be right. The poor kid's dead so there's no point in dissing her anyway, is there?"

"No. So, how long were you in a relationship with Kirsty?"

"Oh, I wouldn't go so far as to call it a relationship," said Ian. He smoothed one expertly threaded eyebrow. "I don't know, what's the modern term for a… er… dalliance?"

I could tell you but modesty forbids, thought Angela. She was beginning to feel defensive on "young" Kirsty's behalf. "Well, whatever you call it," she said, being careful to keep her voice neutral, "you were obviously seeing her for a while. Would you mind telling me when it started?"

Ian thought for a moment. "Where are we now…? Nearly into August, so probably middle to late May."

"And when did it finish?"

"I told her it was over about a month ago."

"Why did you decide to end the relationship?"

Ian sat forward in his seat, fully cooperative now. "Bottom line, Inspector; Kirsty looked good – knockout, in fact. But she didn't cut it, as one got to know her better. Her conversation was quite limited. There's only so much interest I can feign about which of her friends had said what about another one, or the goings-on in soap operas I've barely heard of. I'm afraid I tuned out a great deal of the time, or my head would have been filled with a significant amount of unwanted information. It's as I said before, would I introduce her to Mick – or Hugh?"

Yeah, Hugh Grant, I get it, thought Angela. "So you thought it best to finish it."

"Yes; I also think she was hoping her association with me would be a kind leg-up into modelling, but the fact is she had zero chance of setting foot on any catwalk of mine – or, I strongly suspect, of anyone else's."

"Why wouldn't she have made the grade as a model?"

"Too short for one thing; plain fact of life, I'm afraid. Also, Kirsty didn't walk well, and she liked to loom large in the picture. At the end of the day, we employ models to show off the clothes, we don't make clothes to show off the models."

"So how did she take it when you finished with her?"

"Ah. Not good, I'm afraid."

"Can you be more specific?"

"Oh, you know; tears and protests. I tried to let her down gently. I used the difference in our ages, tried to point out that she'd be a lot happier with someone nearer her own age. But she was very upset, said that she loved me and wanted me."

"That sounds as though it was difficult."

"It was. So I took the avuncular route. Well, that's what I was trying to do in my mind. Whether she took that on board or not, I don't know. I said we'd still be friends and that she could still come to me with any problem she might have."

Angela thought for a moment. She took in his high-end polo shirt, the pique detail as good as the Ralph Lauren label that was no doubt sewn into the back of the neck. He liked hobnobbing with celebrities and dropping their names into the conversation. He was very aware of his own image, and that image was youthful. She wondered if he was capable of being avuncular to his actual nieces and nephews, let alone his ex-girlfriend. "And did she?"

"What, come to me with her problems? Well, unfortunately yes, and they all seemed to centre on me. It was clear she was experiencing a great deal of difficulty getting over me, poor child."

Oh, get me a bucket, someone, I want to puke, thought Angela. She wondered what Gary was making of all this. "Were you still in contact with each other until yesterday?"

"The last text I had from her was yesterday morning."

"Do you still have any of these texts?"

"I'm sorry, I tended to delete them as soon as they came."

"Can you tell me the nature of yesterday's message?"

"Oh, the same as all the others; she wanted us to get back together again. She said she realized she'd been a bit shallow, but she was changing, learning lots of things, and she knew we could make a much better go of it this time round." He paused. "I'm a high-end dress designer, Inspector. I've dressed rock stars and Oscar-winning actresses. That's the world I move in. She wasn't easily going to come up to scratch, if at all."

"What about when you saw her here, at work? Did she try to speak to you alone?"

"Oh yes, she would come in and chat to me, mostly a tale of lovesick woe, I have to say. I was trying to help her through it."

I bet that was totally counterproductive, apart from feeding your ego, thought Angela. "Right, well, I think that's all for the moment, but I'm sure you understand we may need to see you again as the investigation progresses," she said.

"Oh yes, absolutely no problem," replied Ian. He was a picture of reasonable helpfulness, but didn't try to disguise his relief at the ending of the interview.

"Of course I'll need to speak to Ms Chandler, to verify your account of yesterday afternoon. I gather she's not here this afternoon."

"That's right. Would you like her address?"

Angela noted down the address, and a few minutes later she and Gary joined the others in Kirsty's office.

"Your eternal polygon theory is holding up," said Rick, looking through his notes.

"Oh yes?"

"Yeah, Raj Wickramasinghe was filling us in on the office gossip," Jim cut in. "He seems to have quite a sense of humour."

"Oh, really?" remarked Angela, noting the conciliation in Jim's words. "Let us in on the joke, then."

"He was with his family in some pub when he saw Ian King and Kirsty Manners come in; but he says Darren Carpenter was there as well, watching them and making sure he wasn't seen." Jim broke off and looked at Angela. "That might be important, eh, Angie?"

"Oh yes, noted," said Angela, doing so. "That confirms the impression I got from him."

"Anyway, Raj says she was making up to him like nobody's business," said Jim, adopting what they assumed to be Raj's voice. "She was going all out to impress him; bending over backwards, probably literally as well as figuratively, if you take my meaning. Silly tart, she didn't even have the sense to wonder why her date was happening in a suburban backwater.

A more savvy woman would have at least expected a Mayfair restaurant."

The chunky, darts-playing, macho Jim's efforts to reproduce Raj's crisply camp utterances and arch manner of expressing himself made them all laugh.

"Ah, bless!" said Angela. "Well, Ian King was very open about the situation with Kirsty. Mind you, he didn't go so far as to dignify it with the term 'relationship'; he called it a 'dalliance'."

"Not what I'd call it," said Jim.

Angela laughed. "Right, you two – get off to the incident room and start feeding what you've got into the computer. Gazza and I are going to talk to the head stitcher – the new lady in Ian's life, apparently, and his alibi for the events of yesterday."

The door of Eleanor's house in Putney opened to reveal a brunette in her forties, of average height and build. Her face, neither pretty nor plain, benefited from very well applied make-up. She looked enquiringly at them.

"Ms Eleanor Chandler?" asked Angela.

"Yes?"

"We're sorry to disturb you, I'm Detective Inspector Angela Costello and this is Detective Constable Gary Houseman."

Eleanor stood back a little. "Ah yes; I was told to expect you. Come in." She showed them into a comfortable front living room decorated in shades of peach and cream. Every single item in the room looked new, and Angela thought she could detect the faint smell of fresh paint.

"Have you been decorating?" she began, sitting down in the armchair indicated. Gary went over to an upright seat in a corner, and took out his notebook.

"Major interior overhaul, more like," replied Eleanor. "My mother died a year or so ago. Her taste got stuck in *her* mother's era – and she hated change. She'd been an invalid since my teens, bedridden for the last ten years of her life."

"That must have been difficult for you – juggling work responsibilities with caring for your mum."

Eleanor shrugged. "I managed. I tried to be the dutiful daughter. A home help came in each morning, and – well, we got into a routine." She straightened a little in her chair. "Still – you haven't come here to talk about my mother, have you?"

"No, you're right." Angela opened her notebook and looked down at it. "We've been speaking to Ian King." She looked up to see a softening of Eleanor's eyes mixed, intriguingly, with a hint of sadness.

"Yes, he sent me a text to let me know he thought you'd be here this afternoon."

Angela nodded. "Obviously we need to check on the movements of everybody who knew Kirsty, especially those who had been – er – closer to her." *I wonder if Eleanor knew about Ian and Kirsty,* thought Angela, but she saw a tightening of the other woman's mouth and guessed she knew the answer.

"I presume we're talking about yesterday afternoon?"

"Yes."

"Ian was here with me all yesterday afternoon, Inspector." She thrust her head up and opened her eyes wide.

Hmm, Angela thought, *you enjoyed telling me that, didn't you? Dutiful daughter, invalid mother since your teens; I bet there haven't been many boyfriends on the scene, if any.*

"What time did he arrive?"

"Around two-ish; I was downstairs when he got here and there aren't any clocks down here. It's taking a while, dragging the décor of this house out of the 1930s, and these rooms and the hall were only completed last week. I haven't found any clocks to my taste yet, and I tend not to wear a watch in the house."

"So you can't give me an exact time."

"Oh yes, the clock in Mother's bedroom keeps excellent time; that's where... It's the only room with a double bed."

"I see. So how long after Ian King arrived did you go up to the bedroom?"

Eleanor hesitated. "Very soon; Ian went up first and I followed a few moments later." A soft blush appeared on her face

You're not used to this, are you? thought Angela. "Did you notice the time when you got to the bedroom?"

"Yes, it was ten past two."

"And what time did he leave?"

"About six-ish. He slept for a little while and had a shower. He would have stayed, of course, but he had a business meeting."

"Oh, really?" replied Angela, making a note of these details. "Odd time for a business meeting, I would have thought."

"London Fashion Week's coming up and things are more manic than usual." Eleanor couldn't avoid a smile of satisfaction as she spoke. "I should think a great many meetings will take place outside normal working hours."

"I see. OK, Ms Chandler, that's very helpful, thank you."

Eleanor visibly relaxed. "That's no problem, Inspector. I'm glad to help, but the very idea of Ian being a suspect is quite strange. The fact is, I had much more cause than he to want Kirsty dead."

Chapter Nine

Angela opened her eyes wide and stared at the other woman.

"Sorry, I don't mean to be flippant. It's just that it's been quite a month, and Kirsty was involved."

"Involved?"

"That's probably the wrong word. How shall I put this? Her loss was my gain."

"I'm aware that Ian King had been having a relationship with Kirsty until recently."

"Ah, he's told you. Well, he had no reason to hide it, really. I know one isn't supposed to speak ill of the dead, but in spite of her looks she really was very ordinary; and since Ian finished with her she'd been quite a nuisance to me."

"Oh, really, how?"

"She wanted him back and she let me know in no uncertain terms that she was going all out to get him. She... you could say she mounted a campaign. I've never come across such blatancy. Every day I had an email from her talking about the things she and Ian had done together, or making it clear that she would get him back in the end. I tried to rise above it, but I found it wearing. Then we had an actual confrontation, which left me reeling, I can tell you."

"What happened?"

"She... she actually came into the sewing room one morning – when I was on my own, thankfully – to have it out with me. I could hardly believe what was happening."

"What did she say, exactly?"

Eleanor's cheeks turned crimson while the colour seemed to drain from the rest of her face. "What she said, 'exactly', was that the very idea of me sleeping with Ian disgusted her, as I'm way too old for any such thing. She said he would very quickly tire of me. 'He'll soon get fed up with an old wrinkly like you,' were her precise words; I remember them clearly. She said they had plans together, and I was kidding myself if I thought I could hold on to him. I've never been involved in such an unpleasant scene, but at least it showed me just what type of person she was – what my mother would have called a very common little piece."

"What did you say to her?"

"I made it clear that I was not prepared to get embroiled in a slanging match, especially with a child. That shaft went home, I can tell you. I said her behaviour lacked all dignity, and if that was how she normally carried on then it was no surprise Ian had dumped her."

"And how did she react to that?"

"Like the guttersnipe she really was: 'Ian and me 'ave a good thing going, Ellie, and I'm going to get him back.'" Eleanor mimicked Kirsty's Estuary accent. "Really, Inspector, the whole scene was ludicrous. And it's not as if she didn't already have a boyfriend."

"You're talking about…?"

"Darren Carpenter. His knuckles don't quite scrape the floor when he walks and he's OK if you like the sporty type. Perhaps that's the problem. Kirsty didn't strike me as being particularly sporty."

"Ah yes; we've spoken to Darren."

"Yes, I'm sure you have." A considering look appeared on her face. "I don't know if it's relevant, Inspector, but Ian mentioned that he thought Kirsty might be afraid of Darren."

Angela made a note. "Yes, it is relevant; thank you. When did he say this?"

"On Sunday – just after… shortly before he left for his meeting."

"OK, we'll look into it. And this scene between you and Kirsty; this was the only actual confrontation?"

"Yes, apart from the sniping and the emails. I was surprised how much it upset me. I've been in this business a long time, and I thought I'd come across every possible situation. She must have caught me on an off day. Ian had told me about her texts and calls to him. He was very laid back about them, but personally I don't think he was wise to let the situation drag on."

Angela smiled politely. She thought she'd learned all she could for the moment. She rose, nodded at Gary and they took their leave.

Leanne and Derek were the only two people in the incident room. From the way they both stood up and looked at her as soon as she entered, Angela guessed they had news to impart. *Either that or they've been having a crafty snog,* she thought. Derek and Leanne had been thrown together on the investigation at the Wimbledon tennis tournament, and after a short time of coy prevarication they'd gone public with their relationship a few days earlier.

She looked expectantly at them. "What have you got?"

"Three things," said Derek.

"A secret file," said Leanne.

"A woman and…" Derek paused for effect.

"… somebody on a bike!" finished Leanne.

Angela smiled. *They'll be wearing matching jumpers next,* she thought. "OK, let's start with the secret file."

"Ah," said Derek. "We can't actually tell you anything about that at the moment, except that it exists."

"The lab people have been back to us with most of what they found on Kirsty's computer. These are the printouts," added Leanne, indicating a pile of papers on the desk at which she stood. "It seems pretty innocuous stuff, but they also found some password-protected files; they'll get back to us once they've cracked it."

"That's intriguing," said Angela. "I wonder what Kirsty was keen to keep to herself."

"I don't suppose it'll take the lab long to find out," said Derek.

"No, I'm sure. Right, so tell me about this woman and the person on a bike."

Leanne and Derek exchanged smiles, apparently certain they were about to pass on an important piece of information. "Information from the house-to-house, guv," said Leanne. "One of the neighbours saw a woman near the house a bit before two o'clock."

"Description?"

"Smartly dressed was all we could get. The witness thought she wore a dark suit, but couldn't be sure about the exact colour."

"OK. And the bike rider?"

Derek took over. "Somebody came to the house on a sports bike at just before three o'clock on Sunday afternoon."

"Oh, wow. Tell me more."

His face fell slightly. "Um… there is bit more, but I don't know how helpful it will be." He read from his notebook. "This is from a lady who lives directly opposite the house where Kirsty lived. She says she just glanced out of the window and saw this person riding up to the gate. She's very clear about the time because she was timing some sponge cakes in the oven and had to keep her eyes on the clock. She went into the kitchen to swap over the oven shelves, then came back to check the clock and noticed the bike had been left in the front garden. She didn't think anything of it, but the next time she looked out of the window, which she thinks must have been ten minutes later because her cakes were almost ready, the bike was gone."

"Did she give a description of the rider?"

"Wearing an anorak was the only thing she was clear about. She 'thinks' he or she might have been wearing jogging bottoms."

"You're being very careful about saying 'a person' and 'he or she'," remarked Angela.

Derek grimaced. "Yeah, sorry, guv; she thinks the person was tall-ish so she was thinking it might be a man, but she wasn't certain and didn't want to commit herself as to gender. She also says they were wearing a baseball cap with the peak turned round the back, and sunglasses. She's used to seeing a bloke on a bike come to the house so she didn't take a lot of notice."

"Never mind; what about the bike?"

"She reckons it was just like the one she's seen before, a rust colour, apparently, and whoever owns it has fixed reflector tape on the mudguard so it's quite noticeable."

"That's what she's used to seeing?"

"Yes, guv."

"OK, get Darren's bike checked out before you do anything else."

"Will do," chorused Derek and Leanne.

Angela looked at Gary. "OK, so we've got a smart woman in a dark suit and *a* person on *a* sports bike," she said.

"As regards the bike, I know he said he was at the gym all Sunday afternoon but Darren Carpenter's got to be our first guess," said Gary.

"No question of it," she agreed. "We get the pleasure of thunder thighs again, but not today; it's getting late and I want to go through the stuff from Kirsty's computer, see if I can get an angle on her."

An hour later Angela got up, stretched and yawned. "That's enough," she said. "I'm calling it a day." She looked across to where Gary was sitting, gazing intently at a computer screen, and saw he was playing Patience. "There's a black nine in that top right-hand corner that can come down on that red ten in the middle," she said.

Gary jumped and turned round, a deep crimson blush suffusing his face. "Oops, sorry, Angie." Angela laughed. He closed down the game, stood up and came over to her desk. "Did her laptop throw up anything of interest?"

"Hmmm... the jury's out..."

"Oh yes?"

"I'm somewhat intrigued. There's a great deal of what you'd expect; emails between Kirsty and her friends, between Kirsty and her mum and dad, and all the usual jokey ones that go round. She didn't do a great deal of surfing – mostly to dress shops, fashion houses, Facebook and Twitter. In the last few weeks, though, she'd trawled loads of modelling agencies, and gone to Companies House a few times, and two or three other sites which give advice about setting up a business."

"That's a bit odd for an aspiring model – maybe related to these big ideas she's supposed to have had?"

"Yes, that's what I wonder. We should be able to shed more light on that once the lab has broken open these password-protected files. It's a blooming nuisance about her mobile phone."

"Its absence has got to be significant, hasn't it?"

"It certainly looks that way – unless she lost it somewhere, which I think is unlikely." Angela wandered over to the whiteboard to scrutinize the pictures taken from Kirsty's dressing table mirror. "These might have been taken on a mobile phone. Ah!" She raised her eyebrows and looked pointedly at him.

"Ian King! He said he'd had a text from her yesterday."

"Well done, that detective constable," smiled Angela. They both reached for their notebooks. Angela found the relevant page first. "Yesterday morning, which would be... oh, it's still

Monday, so it's still yesterday morning. '*The last text I had from her was yesterday morning*,'" she quoted.

"So we know she had her phone on the morning of her death."

"The perp must have taken it. Something on it is very incriminating."

"That makes sense," agreed Gary. "They didn't just delete whatever it was, they took the phone."

"Time must have been of the essence."

"Which would tie in with the bike being there and gone again in about ten minutes."

"Yes, indeedy. I suppose it could be anything – a text, a contact detail." Angela frowned at the whiteboard again. "But a photograph had been pulled away from the dressing table mirror. Suppose the missing picture was also stored in her phone?"

"We've got no way of finding out for certain," said Gary.

Angela grinned at him. "Oh, I'm not so sure. Who knows what will come to light as we go along? OK, just before I switch off for the night, let's set down a marker. We're definitely talking about premeditated murder, most likely perpetrated by someone well known to the victim."

"That's about the size of it, Angie."

Angela stretched again. "Right now I'm going to do a Scarlett."

Gary looked at her, his face bewildered. "… Johansson…?"

"O'Hara, as in *Gone with the Wind*," said Angela, grinning. "I'll think about that tomorrow."

He laughed. "Oh, right. Do you want me to drop you off?"

"What? Oh! Yes – thanks, Gaz. I was forgetting I haven't got the car today. Driving to the coroner's with Patrick this morning seems a long time ago."

Madeleine, listening intently to her iPod, was just approaching the house as Gary and Angela drew up a short while later. She stopped and waited until Angela got out of the car. "Evening, Step-ma; how's it going?"

"Hiya, Maddie; we've made a start," replied Angela, turning back to the car and pulling her bag and briefcase from the back seat.

Madeleine bent down and grinned across at Gary. "Hi, Gary."

Gary leaned across the passenger seat. "Hi, Madeleine. How're you doing? What are you listening to?"

"I'm good, thanks. Vaughan Williams."

"Oh, really, which piece?"

"The 'Greensleeves' thingy."

"Ah! Love it; it's been ages since I heard that."

"Want a blast?" asked Madeleine.

"Yes, please." Gary leaned back again so that Madeleine could get into the car. Angela called out "Goodnight!" and got back a distracted "See you tomorrow", as Madeleine settled herself in the front passenger seat. Smiling, Angela shrugged and went into the house.

Patrick, examining a lasagne through the glass oven door, looked up and smiled as Angela came into the kitchen. She went over and dropped a kiss onto his lips.

"I hope you don't mind – I've invited Martin round for dinner," he said.

"Father Martin?"

"The very same."

"No, I don't mind – that's good."

"He called me today. He wants to ask our advice about something."

"*Our* advice?"

"That's what he said. He sounded a bit agitated, to be honest. So of course I said he'd be most welcome, and we'd been meaning to invite him anyway."

"Absolutely. It'll be a good opportunity for him to meet the returning prodigal."

Patrick laughed. "By the way, I thought I heard her voice in the street."

"You did. She's cosying up to Gary in the car. They're listening to some music."

Patrick raised his eyebrows. "I thought he seemed a bit… taken, the other night when he was here."

Angela nodded. "And she thought he was cute, if I remember."

Patrick looked at her. "Do you think…?"

Angela spread her hands. "I haven't a clue."

Patrick turned his attention back to the oven. "We'd better 'watch this space', then, hadn't we?"

Chapter Ten

The "space" didn't take long to be filled. Angela couldn't help being amused by the sheepish expression on Gary's face as he came into the house behind Madeleine a short while later.

"I've been invited in for a coffee, Angie. I hope you don't mind."

Gary recognized, as Madeleine didn't seem to, that having a junior officer coming in to her home on a social basis might not be what Angela wanted. She smiled to reassure him. "Not at all, you're very welcome."

"There's a murder all over the front page today; Kirsty somebody... Is that the one you had to go and see to yesterday, Angie?" asked Madeleine.

"Yes," replied Angela.

"What a stunner! She could have been a model."

"Which is probably the only reason she made the front page," said Patrick drily. "Sometimes I hate the way the media manipulates the news."

Madeleine looked at Gary. "The way the media carries on is one of Dad's soapbox things," she said. She turned back to Angela. "Will you be doing a press conference?"

"I wouldn't have thought so," Angela replied. "But you never know."

"OK." Madeleine's nose twitched and she turned her head towards the oven. "Hey, something smells good. I'm starving!"

In the kitchen, out of Gary's eyeline Patrick raised his eyes to heaven and gave a good-natured shrug. "It's very nearly ready and you'll spoil your appetite if you go drinking coffee this close to eating."

"Oh… er…" Madeleine managed to look a little abashed and threw a quick, questioning glance at Angela and her father.

Angela picked up the hint and grinned at Gary. "Do you want to stay to dinner, Gaz?"

"That'd be great, thanks. If you're sure it's no trouble. We were talking about music and Madeleine's got this CD that – "

"It's all right; you don't have to explain yourself. You two go and get comfy and have your chat about Vaughan Williams or whoever, and I'll call you when the meal's ready. We're going to be joined by our parish priest."

"Fortunately it's a big lasagne," said Patrick.

Gary and Madeleine disappeared into the living room. Angela went into the kitchen and shut the door behind her. "I must say your daughter's a smooth operator," she said. "If I was wearing a hat I'd take it off to her."

Patrick looked up from where he was pouring two glasses of wine and smirked. "She gets it from the old man; charm personified."

Angela laughed and embraced him. As she pulled away again she saw the newspaper lying on the worktop. Patrick followed the direction of her eyes. "It's true, though, about Kirsty, isn't it? Mind you, we saw that for ourselves at the mortuary this morning."

As the melodies of Vaughan Williams drifted in from the living room, Patrick paused, looking down at the headline story, his face sad. "Those poor parents," he muttered.

Angela hugged him again. "Come on, let's get the table laid," she said.

From his Richmond Hill penthouse, not too far away from Angela and Patrick's home, Nigel Summers gazed out into the evening. This window offered a vista across some of the most expensive real estate in the country, and beyond that gave glimpses of the river. He loved this view. For him it had come to symbolize everything he had achieved in life; and he had no intention of losing any of it. He knew his relationship with Kirsty could have done serious damage to his plans, and he felt very glad to have got her out of his life when he did. He admired her ambition, but she had no idea how to carry off the lifestyle.

She was shrewd, though, he had to admit. Especially if she'd managed to get Ian rattled in case she had some of his designs. Normally when Ian finished with a woman, he walked away without looking back, but from what Nigel could gather, he was still taking calls from her on the day she died. Nigel felt restless and uneasy; if he'd had his way, all connection with Kirsty would have been severed some time ago. Absently, as he turned the situation over in his mind, he drummed his fingers on the elegant French-polished console table. His gaze wandered from the view through the window to the silver-framed picture of himself with his mother; a similar photograph to the one on his desk at work.

Mother was always very understanding about his women; but he knew she wouldn't countenance Kirsty for a moment, and Nigel trusted her judgment implicitly.

Sinking into his sumptuous sofa, tastefully upholstered in top-grain leather, Nigel felt for his CD player remote and let flow a soothing surge of Sibelius. *Oh well,* he mused, *Let's hope the worst is over. If my name was going to come up in connection with that little trollop, it would surely have done so today when the police came to the unit.* But still his mind hovered stubbornly over the debacle of Kirsty, looking back now to that morning when the telephone call had come. He'd barely had time to lift the receiver to his ear when Ian spoke.

"Nigel, it's Ian."

And Nigel had been immediately alert, instantly detecting an indefinable quality in Ian's voice that did not augur well.

"Morning, Ian. Is there – "

"I won't beat about the bush. Something awful has happened over here... well, not over here exactly... it's just awful..."

Fearing that the call would go contrary to Ian's stated intention, Nigel interrupted: "What is it?"

"Kirsty."

"Yes? What about her?" he prompted.

"Bad news, Nigel; I'm afraid she's dead."

Nigel gasped. "Dead...? Did you... you did *say* 'dead', didn't you?"

"I did. But it gets worse. She was murdered."

"Ian! What on earth's happened... I mean... do you know anything about it?"

"The bare facts only, so far; it seems she was found dead yesterday afternoon by her flatmate."

"I... I... I don't know what to say."

"It doesn't appear to have anything to do with us, but the police might want to interview those who knew her..."

"Good grief, yes! Whether it's got anything to do with us or not, can't you just see the headlines?"

"Oh yes. *Ivano King girlfriend found murdered,*" intoned Ian.

"Exactly! Whatever shall we do?"

"We'll play it cool for a start," replied Ian. "There's no such thing as bad publicity. We can't be implicated. This isn't going to rebound on us. We can relax as far as that goes. The whole world loves a good murder, and it won't do any harm if Ivano King is seen to be a bit close to the edge. Nothing like a tragedy to set tongues wagging, and nothing like a bit of gossip to bring us to the forefront of minds that had almost forgotten us."

"You're right," agreed Nigel, beginning to rally from the shock. "On the face of it," he continued with a new note of optimism, "there's no need for me to be questioned at all. I haven't been involved with Kirsty for a while. I can rely on you to be discreet, I know – but you'll keep me fully informed, as things develop?"

"Of course," said Ian.

He'd spent most of the day on tenterhooks, half-expecting some plod to appear in the shop asking for "a word". He'd already worked out how to handle such an eventuality. "Of course I knew, Kirsty, officer. We had a little bit of a thing going for a while, but that's been all over for ages." Nigel had rehearsed the conversation. He'd be fully cooperative, his eyes wide, his face open and honest. He'd gloss over the fact that he was the one that dumped her. "Looking back, I think I just offered a stepping stone to something more high-profile, officer. She caught Ian's eye, and she was off. Well, you can't really blame her, can you? He's got celebrity status, after all."

Nigel heard no more from Ian until late that afternoon, when he called to say the police had been to the unit, interviewed the staff and seemed satisfied with all they had discovered. Nigel allowed himself a sigh of relief at this point.

As the Sibelius piece died away, the opening bars of Ravel's *Bolero* filled the room. He'd keep his act on the back-burner but it seemed less likely to be needed, after all. He remembered, with a profound sense of relief, the moment he had taken the opportunity to destroy any sign of a connection between them.

It was the day, not long after taking her to the *Passionista* party, he'd earmarked for telling Kirsty he couldn't see her any more. This had assumed an aspect of urgency when it had dawned on him that she had long-term plans for their relationship, which hadn't been his intention at all. Still new to her job and wide-eyed at the famous names and showbusiness connections all round her, Kirsty had seemed both star-struck and naive. He hadn't grasped the depth of her ambition. It wasn't just about him, it was about living in his world – a high-flying executive, celebrity-filled world. She saw modelling as the route to what she really wanted.

Kirsty wasn't sophisticated, but neither was she stupid. Some of the things she'd said about the hiring of the models, for instance, showed that she had a cunning grasp of matters which surprised and – if he was being truthful – worried him. It was then that he realized she could make life difficult. She had to go.

She'd taken his announcement badly. A look of shock had been immediately followed by the appearance of tears. Her deep blue eyes overflowed. She even looked lovely when she was distressed. "Why, Nigel, why? We're getting on so well. We're good together. I thought we had something special. I love you. I don't want to break up with you." Then she'd tried to seduce him out of his decision with sex; it was the only bargaining counter she had, really; it always came back to that. She seemed to think if a woman gave a man everything he wanted in the bedroom, he'd give her everything she wanted out of it. That was where she showed her naivety.

He'd benefited from that last session of love-making, though. She'd gone all out to impress; he could still become a little breathless at the memory. And then, unusually for her, she'd fallen asleep, which is when Nigel had found himself alone in his living room with her mobile.

He'd been aghast at what he found in the phone. She'd kept every text they'd ever exchanged, not that there were many. But even those few were too many. He was honest enough to admit to himself that here, he'd been the naive one. He located his own number in her contacts list and deleted it. He then went meticulously through the phone and got rid of every possible thing which could link them. When she woke up and realized he hadn't changed his mind, in spite of the good time she'd given him, she became tearful, and he knew he had to lay it on the line for her.

He'd played it straight. "Look, Kirsty, we've had a bit of fun; a laugh. But that's all it was, and it's over. It happens. Now, you've got a nice little job out at the unit. If you're sensible you'll just keep your head down and get on with it."

The flash of awareness in her eyes as she listened to him, affirmed his intuition about the cunning quality of her nature, but she covered it very quickly with a tearful look of resignation. He almost admired her. In that instant he could see she knew the score. If she made a fuss, she would suddenly find herself without a job. She wasn't the first woman who'd slept with her boss and had then become an embarrassment to be got rid of, and she wouldn't be the last.

Had he entertained any lingering doubts about his treatment of Kirsty, her subsequent history would have reassured him. Not a month had gone by before he heard the first whisper about her and Ian. Well, of course, she'd think she had it in the bag now – Ian, the man behind Ivano King. And if she fancied a bit of rough, there was always her regular boyfriend who, so far as he could tell, she kept stringing along. Nigel smiled, settling further into his sofa as he considered this. Oh yes, that young lady knew exactly what she wanted and she went straight for it.

He still hadn't got his head round her now being completely off the radar. It felt odd to think she'd gone. Happily, though, the police hadn't even cast a look in his direction. And he knew Ian wouldn't mention it. There was nothing left to link him with her at all.

Ian's Porsche glided smoothly to a halt outside his front door; he sat for a few moments staring absently at the street. He felt as though he had been at work for much longer than eight hours and was completely drained.

He'd had no deep affection for Kirsty and, in any case, considered himself in control of his emotions, normally. The traumatic effect of the day surprised him. Events themselves had been bad enough to begin with, but a couple of the tabloids had ferreted out his connection with Kirsty. Jenni had got rid of them efficiently, but he knew they would try again. He took a deep breath, exhaled slowly, and made himself relax.

He let himself out of the car and stood up, stretching his long form slightly to ease the residue of tension. A delightful breeze came towards him from the river and he stood for a moment without moving to enjoy its refreshing coolness. After a few moments he moved across to his front door.

The blow seemed to come from nowhere. One minute he was putting his hand into his pocket for his house keys and the next, something hit him in the middle of his back with such force that he was unable to prevent himself from sprawling across the pavement.

He was just about to raise himself on his hands and look round to see what had hit him when he felt a sharp kick in his side. He half-turned and saw the toe of a boot swinging straight at his head. Instinctively he curled himself into a ball, pulling his head into his hands. This action protected him causing the next kick to miss the target and catch his elbow. He let out a cry that was half-expletive and half-shriek of fear. Someone yelled "Hey!" and he heard feet clattering noisily from the direction of the river. Peeping from between his arms he saw a pair of legs turn and run away from the noise.

Coughing and spluttering he manoeuvred himself into a sitting position and looked round for his assailant.

There was nobody to be seen.

The owners of the feet, a young couple, reached him.

"Are you all right?" asked the man, squatting down to Ian's level.

"What happened?" asked his female companion, peering with a concerned expression into Ian's face.

"Well… I don't really know. It was all so quick. I suppose it was an attempted mugging." Ian reached across the ground to where his keys had fallen from his hand in the attack. He picked them up and allowed himself to be helped to his feet.

"Is there anything we can do for you?" asked the man.

"I think I shall be all right," said Ian. "I live just here." He looked at them. "Did you see who it was?"

"Not really. I saw you go down and heard you cry out, but it was all happening below the level of the car roofs."

"I think I saw someone running away, but nothing more than a shape, really," added the young woman.

Ian brushed himself down, and thanked the couple for their rescue and concern. He assured them no serious damage had been done. They obliged him with their names and addresses in case they were later needed as witnesses, and moved off to continue their journey. Home at last, Ian mixed himself a large gin and tonic before calling the police and gazed out into his garden. What a day! And what an ending to it!

A horrible feeling…

A few streets away, his assailant jogged to where he'd secured his bike, cursing himself and the two people who'd come running to the rescue. It wouldn't work, not in the street; even a quiet street was too public. He'd have to think of something else. He freed his bike, swung a leg over the crossbar and cycled off into the night.

Chapter Eleven

The conversation around the table drifted pleasantly and easily through a variety of topics, a good selection of jokes and a lively discussion about the relative merits of Chelsea Football Club over those of Arsenal. Cheerful and replete, as they poured the coffee to end their meal, Gary and Madeleine politely excused themselves to continue listening to the music of their choice in the living room.

Angela and Patrick turned to Martin. "You sounded a bit worried on the phone today," began Patrick.

Martin replaced his cup with thoughtful care into its saucer, weighing up what to say. "Yes. I had a disturbing experience this morning in the confessional."

"Oh, 'nuff said."

"Oh, nothing like that. I can share all of it and not break the seal. It wasn't confession. This young lady knew what she was doing and emphasized that she wanted me to tell someone about this. The trouble is, I haven't much to go on; but if what she said is true, it's very worrying, both from my point of view as a pastor, and legally."

"Tell us," said Angela.

Martin went quickly through the events of that morning. When he finished he sat back and gazed into two solemn faces. "What do you think?" he asked, after a moment.

Angela stood up. "I think I'd better get Gary in here," she said.

Gary came in, listened to the story, took notes and looked at Angela. "Do you reckon it's related to our current investigation?" he asked.

"I don't know," she replied, "but we'll have to throw it into the pot." She turned to Martin. "We're currently investigating the murder of a young woman. Did you read about it?"

"I think I did."

"There's a fashion industry angle to it, so, you never know, there might be a connection."

"Location, location, location," said Patrick.

"Mmm, that hadn't escaped my notice, either," replied Angela. "The murder took place in Roehampton and the episode in the confessional happened here in Richmond."

"It's only the other side of the park," he replied.

"We're talking about a very big park, but even so, I don't like this," said Angela.

"Me neither. I'm sorry," Martin grimaced. "I feel like an out-and-out coward, but I don't think I could have taken the bloke on; he was huge. Anyway, she told me to hide and I thought I'd better do as she said. If I'd tried anything on, I might only have made it worse for her."

"Yeah, if he's threatening to spoil her face somehow – I don't know, slash it or throw acid at it – that's scary," agreed Gary.

"Wherever the house is, it can't be all that far from the church," surmised Patrick.

"I've thought about that. I reckon it must be within a two-mile radius, three at the outside."

"Sounds reasonable, without knowing how long she was running," agreed Angela. "She sees an opportunity to escape and makes a dash for it. Obviously he sets off in pursuit but she doesn't know the area, I'm assuming that would be the case. She runs up one street and down another, finds a dead end or two, doubles back and ends up in his eyeline again and he gets to her, but this time they're near the church and she heads for safety. What was this word he said?"

"It sounded like 'asher'," said Martin. "I don't know if that's her name or an instruction in whatever language – well, Polish, I suppose. She said '*tak*' at one point, which I know is the word for 'yes'. That's more or less the extent of my Polish, I'm afraid."

"She didn't give you much to go on, did she? Understandable; she was stressed and scared. You mentioned she said 'I choose one with same name', when she spoke about looking for a designer. That's a puzzle. I suppose we can do a trawl of people in fashion with East European-sounding names."

"That's a bit of a hopeless task," said Gary. "The designer is the 'name', but there are multitudes behind them, aren't there? It could be any one of hundreds of people."

"You're right," agreed Angela. She turned back to Martin. "OK, I'll make the incident known to the local force, and put it through to Vice in case they can shed any light on it. And of course, I'll make sure our team are briefed and alert, just on the off chance there's a connection with our case." Angela looked at the young priest with a sympathetic smile. "Apart from that, I can't do much without more information, Martin."

"Thanks, Angie. I know there's not a lot to go on. I just keep thinking of that woman's face; the threat hanging over her... the things she – and the others – might be forced to do against their will. I know she said the others agreed, but surely under some very nasty form of coercion."

Angela nodded. "Sadly, it's a common story. Droves of them come over here from Eastern Europe, promised good jobs, only to end up in the sex trade. It's heinous." She looked at him. "I can't promise you anything, Martin."

"I know, but at least I've done what I could to help her."

"Do you think there's any connection with our case?" The question came from Derek at the following morning's briefing, once Angela had told them about Father Martin's experience.

"Well..." Angela ruminated on it. "On the face of it, no...

but... That's the thing. I keep thinking, 'but'. Here we've got an ambitious model killed in Roehampton, and now this other one running, terrified, into a church in Richmond. I think we'd be failing in our duty if we didn't keep this incident in mind. Unfortunately, that's about all we can do at this moment. Leanne, draw a balloon up here with the incident in it, so at least we've got it on the radar."

"Will do, guv," said Leanne rising from her seat and going over to the board. "Mind you, I reckon I could throw a bit of light on what that bloke said."

"Oh, really?" replied Angela. Leanne's surname was Dabrowska. Both her sets of grandparents were Polish and she was known to be fluent in the language.

"Yeah, it's quite a common diminutive of a longer name. You hear it all the time. Although it's pronounced 'asher' it's actually spelt A-S-I-A, like the continent. I know a few 'Asias' in the Polish community."

"Oh, that's helpful! Thanks, Leanne. At least this poor young woman has a name for us now. OK, what next?" Angela stood in front of the board staring at the photographs that were taken from Kirsty's dressing table mirror. They'd been taped up in the order they had been displayed, including the blob of Blu-tak under the final one where the missing photograph should have been. "This is irritating me," she said. "There *must* have been another picture there, and I think the murderer took it; but why?"

"Perhaps it's nothing to do with the case," ventured Rick. "Perhaps she took it down because she didn't think she looked good in the photograph."

Angela nodded, considering this. "OK, anything's possible, but I think we've got to assume the murderer took it because it was in some way incriminating. The thing is," she continued, "these first two are the normal girly pictures. Here she's somebody's bridesmaid, here she's on the beach. But the last two are completely different. She looks – oh, I don't know, she doesn't have the same feel about her. She's different, less natural; she's trying to impress, or something. She looks to me like someone with an agenda." Angela looked round at her team. "I'm sorry, can't you see what I mean? Do I sound daft? I can't think how else to put it. For my money, the missing photo belongs to the final two. She's at a party, but I get the impression it was a particular kind of party, not just a gathering at a friend's house."

"Hang on a minute," said Gary walking to the front and taking a closer look at the photograph. "Yeah," he said, after a moment's scrutiny.

"What?" asked Angela.

"Look," he said, pointing. "There's some sort of sign just on the edge of the photo. Er, it's the end of a word… er… STA. And I think that's an 'i' just before that, so it's a word ending in 'ista'."

"Oh yes," said Angela, peering. "You're right. It looks like a board attached to the wall."

"Like at those show-bizzy, fashiony-type parties."

"Oh yeah," said Leanne, "the sort of 'do' you get pictures of all the time in mags like *Hello* and *OK*, where they're launching something so all the celebs who turn up get photographed in front of the sponsor's logo."

"They have to earn their free champagne somehow," said Angela. "I think you're right, Gaz. That would account for the totally different feeling I get about Kirsty in these photos. Well done. OK," she turned round to the rest of the team. "Something-ista, anybody?" Most of them looked at each other in puzzlement and shook their heads. Leanne frowned in concentration. "Leanne, you at least look like it's not a complete mystery."

"Er, it could be *Passionista*. It's a fashion magazine," she replied.

"Ah!" said everybody else.

Leanne giggled. "If you lot could only see what you looked like just then."

Angela laughed. "It's a shame there was no photographer to record the moment – ah, hang on, that's *it*!" she exclaimed.

"What's *it*?" they asked, more or less as one.

"These types of events have an official photographer and probably also photographers from various magazines and newspapers in attendance, looking for stuff for puff pieces in the media, if nothing else."

"Yeah," said Rick, "but what Kirsty had were just snapshots, not glossies or anything like that. They just looked like the sort of thing you take on your mobile phone and print up later."

"Yes, but if there was a professional photographer there, he or she could have taken a shot at the same moment, or something very similar. We might at least get an idea of what the murderer might be trying to hide." Angela looked pointedly at Derek and Leanne in turn. "I'm looking at my ace researchers."

Derek grinned. "We'll get on to it."

"I want to know everything about this 'do' and see every available photo from it."

"Right, guv," replied Leanne.

"Oh good, a bit of progress, I hope," said Angela. "Now I need to set up another meeting with Darren Carpenter."

She went into her office, and was on the point of picking up the phone to do this when it rang.

"D.I. Costello?"

"Angie?" It was Jim speaking from the incident room. "Looks like somebody got missed out on the house-to-house."

Angela quashed the immediate judgment that rose to her mind and told herself that, no, Jim wasn't trying to get anyone into trouble.

"And you're telling me this instead of going and dealing with it because – ?"

"Got a bloke at the front desk who lives next door to Kirsty Manners and he's wondering why nobody's been to see him yet. Says he's got 'information pertaining to Sunday's incident'; I quote."

"Oh, don't tell me – 'I want to speak to the officer in charge.'"

"Got it in one, Angie," said Jim.

Angie sighed. "No worries, I'll talk to him. The rest of the house-to-house is underway, isn't it?"

"Yeah, all sorted."

"OK, put Mr Next-Door-Neighbour in an interview room. I'll be down in a minute." Angie left her office and headed downstairs, making a quick detour through the incident room to ask Gary to set up the meeting with Darren. Within a few moments, smile in place, she breezed through the door and found herself looking into the pinched features of Ronald Sanders.

Everything about him was thin. Thin hair clung limply to his head, his thin body sat primly upright on the seat and thin lips were pursed in an expression of disapproval Angela guessed was likely to be permanent. As she opened the door he was making a business of looking at his watch.

"I was wondering how much longer I would have to wait," he began in a grudging tone.

Angela had the distinct impression he was miffed by her prompt appearance. She sat down and opened her notebook. *I bet you always demand to see the head honcho in any given situation, don't you,* she said to herself.

Seconds later, Ronald Sanders confirmed this impression. "I asked to see the officer in charge. Is that you?"

Angela looked at him and cranked up the smile. *I'm the in-chargest you're going to get, boyo,* she thought. "I'm Detective Inspector Angela Costello," she said. "Chief Inspector Stanway is overseeing the whole operation but, for practical purposes, yes, I'm in charge."

"I have important information pertaining to the murder of my neighbour." He paused, his brow furrowed as if he wasn't sure a mere D.I. could be trusted with what he had to say.

"So I understand," she replied. She made a point of lifting up her pen and waiting.

Realizing that he wasn't going to get his chief inspector, Sanders gave a petulant little pout, shifted further forward in his seat and took a breath in order to give more weight to his words. "I think I may have seen the murderer."

Raising her eyes, Angela saw a look of smug satisfaction on his face. She nodded as if this snippet was no more nor less than she had expected. "Would you like to tell me about it?" she asked.

Disappointment that Angela didn't go running upstairs to bring the D.C.I. in on the interview showed clearly in his face and words. "Well, I... this conversation will be reported to the chief inspector, won't it?"

You need to get out more, she thought. "Word for word," she assured him.

Sanders made a final little moue with his mouth and capitulated. "I was waiting for a taxi on Sunday afternoon when I saw this person approach next door's front gate."

"What time was this, Mr Sanders?"

"It was thirteen thirty-five."

"You're sure about the time?"

"Perfectly, I was waiting for a taxi which was booked for thirteen-forty. I use this cab company all the time and they know my views on punctuality."

No doubt, she thought. "I see," she said, as she wrote. "OK, tell me about this person."

"It was a woman. A brunette."

"What was she wearing?"

"A rather elegant suit."

"What colour?"

"Hmm, dark. It might have been maroon but I couldn't swear to it."

"All right, what else can you tell me about her?"

"Well, it was all a bit odd. She passed my front window, and she slowed down as she got near next door's gate and veered towards it as if she were about to go in. Then the next thing I know, she'd picked up speed and was moving off up the road. I didn't think anything of that at the time. I mean, she could have been a stranger in the area and realized that she'd got the wrong house or, well, there could be several reasonable permutations on the theme. But then, blow me down; a moment later she was approaching the house again from the other direction."

"Did you manage to get a look at her face? I mean, would we be able to draw up a photofit?"

"No, unfortunately, she kept her face down. I presumed she just looked at the ground as she walked – as some people do. Anyway, she stopped by the gate again; and this time she pushed it open and went in."

"So, then what happened?"

Another disappointed look stole across Sanders's face; his allocated fifteen minutes of fame were coming to an end. "Ah, that's it, I'm afraid. Just at that moment, my taxi arrived. By the time I'd gone into the hall, got my coat and opened my own front door, she was nowhere to be seen."

What a bummer, thought Angela. "Had you ever seen this woman before, Mr Sanders?"

"No." He gave her a sharp, penetrating look. "Nor since." His expression lightened. "She hasn't tried to go back to the scene of the crime yet – but murderers do that, don't they? It's a well-known psychological fact."

"We don't know that she's the murderer," said Angela. But she had to admit, the situation did look strange. Perhaps this woman was accepted into the house in all innocence by Kirsty herself. She could even have been an accomplice to the man on the bike.

Angela made the arrangements for Sanders's statement to be typed up and saw to it that he was made comfortable and given a cup of tea while he waited to sign it. She went into the incident room and fed the new information into the computer. "Have we got another date with Darren Carpenter?" she asked Gary.

"Any time today would do for him," he answered.

Angela looked across at Leanne. "Anything back from the lab about Kirsty's secret files yet?"

"Not yet, guv; I phoned them earlier and they were hoping to have something this afternoon."

"OK."

"We've had something a bit odd in from uniform though, guv."

"Oh, really?"

"Yeah, Ian King was attacked last night."

"What?"

"Yeah. He was a bit shaken, apparently, but no harm done. He asked that you should be informed, though. In case it might be related to Kirsty's murder. He's worried that he might be next in line, and was asking for police protection."

"Oh no, I hope he's wrong. We're going over there anyway to see Darren, so we can go up to him after that."

"Shall I pass that message back to him, guv?"

"Yes, please, Leanne."

Less than twenty minutes later, Gary was steering the Homicide Assessment Team car past the Lebanese food wholesalers towards the sign saying Ivano King.

"Stop," said Angela suddenly.

"We're not there yet," replied Gary, stopping nonetheless, after a quick glance in the rear-view mirror.

"Sorry, Gary; still, let me congratulate you on your emergency stop." Angela grinned at him and then inclined her head out of the car to her left. "Do you see what I see?"

"It's a bike rack in a cage...? Oh yes, of course."

Secured snugly in its rack within the bicycle cage was an expensive-looking bike of a dull, reddish colour. It had white mudguards with strips of reflector tape added.

"Rust-coloured," said Gary. "Not what I'd go for."

"Yeah, but it's what Darren goes for, seemingly."

Darren led them through the despatch area and into his own tiny room, kicking the bottom drawer of his desk closed as he did so. He sat in his chair hanging his hands down between his muscular thighs, and looked expectantly at the two police officers.

"We won't take up much of your time, Darren," began Angela. "It's just that some information has come in that you might be able to help us with."

"Yeah?"

"A rust-coloured bike was seen outside Kirsty's flat on Sunday afternoon shortly before the time that she would have been killed."

Angela had kept her tone deliberately gentle, but it wasn't enough to prevent a spasm of pain flashing across Darren's face. His nostrils flared and tears sprung to his eyes. He lowered his head for a moment. When his gaze met Angela's again there was a puzzled look in his eyes. "So?" he murmured.

"I believe we've just passed your bike in the cage outside, is that right?"

"Yeah, probably."

"It's rust coloured, just like the one our informant mentioned."

Darren stared at Angela as if waiting for her to get to the point. *Good grief, this is like pulling teeth,* she thought. "Darren, was it your bike in the front garden of Kirsty's flat on Sunday?"

"Nah," he said. "My bike was at the gym. I was at the gym all Sunday afternoon. I told you."

"It's a bit coincidental, don't you think?" said Gary. "How many bikes of that colour do you suppose there are around?"

Darren didn't even bridle at the slight edge that Gary put into his voice. He merely shrugged. "Not many, but I've seen one or two about. It must be a coincidence."

Angela and Gary exchanged glances. "When you're at the gym, is your bike secured?" she asked.

"Yes, of course."

"With a chain?"

"Oh no, not at the gym. Tone lets me put it in the covered passageway. No one can get in to it from the outside."

"Where is this covered passageway?"

"At the side. It's a lean-to, really. Tone lets one or two of his special customers put their bikes there, out of sight of the road."

Angela quickly decided the next port of call would be the gym. "OK; so did you miss your bike on Sunday afternoon?"

"No, but I didn't check on it. I just left it there and came back for it later."

"Was it still exactly as you'd left it?"

Angela would never be able to swear to it but she thought for a second that the question caught Darren without an answer. He glanced away, then seemed to remember himself and looked back at her. His brow furrowed and he shrugged. "I didn't really take any notice. I mean, Tone might push it along a bit now and again to get to something, like, or somebody else might move it to make room for their bike. There's not a lot of space. It's only a tarted-up side alley."

"Yes, I get it," said Angela. "So you left your bike where you normally leave it and came back to it later when you were ready to go home, and that was that?"

"Yeah."

"OK, that's it for now," said Angela. "I believe a couple of our officers have already been to see you about your bike."

"Yes, they wanted to dust it for prints."

"It's a matter of elimination as much as anything else," explained Angela, wondering why she was bothering. The matter seemed to excite no emotion in Darren whatsoever.

"Sure, no problem," he replied.

"Right," replied Angela, standing up. "We just need a word with Mr King. It's back along that passage and up the stairs isn't it?" she asked, pointing.

"Yeah, but he's out."

"Oh, really?"

"Saw his car go past quite a while ago."

"OK, we'll catch him another time," said Angela. *At least he's not sitting around brooding about being the next victim,* she thought. She glanced back as she walked through the unit. Darren was staring intently down at the bottom drawer of his desk; at the back of her mind, she wondered why.

It was some moments, as Gary nosed their vehicle through the labyrinth of roads, before either of them spoke.

"Getting blood from a stone might have been a bit easier," began Angela.

"Darren? Yeah, not very forthcoming, was he?"

"I feel drained at the mere thought of ever having to interview him again."

"Yes, mind you, I don't think it's because we're the police. I get the impression he'd be like that with anyone... like... like..."

"Taciturn is the expression you're looking for," said Angela. "And I think you're right. Still, we can't all be stimulating conversationalists."

"And he's got plenty of brawn to make up for brains."

"That's not quite fair," countered Angela. "He's definitely not stupid."

They had reached the end of the estate by now, and Gary

slowed before pulling out onto the main road. "We'll have to file him under 'strong, silent type', then," he said.

"He certainly looks strong." Angela was quiet for a moment. "It wouldn't have been a problem, physically, I mean."

"What? Killing Kirsty? Darren? Yeah, no problem, I'd have thought."

"Hmm… I think we'll go to the gym. Let's check out this covered passageway where he keeps his bike. I'd like to see the layout. If he's such a good friend of the owner, a little chat could be very useful for all sorts of reasons."

"OK, have we got the address?"

"Drive in the general direction of Roehampton and I'll check it out on the Internet," replied Angela, pulling her mobile out of her bag.

Tony met them at the door. Standing about five ten, he wore a sleeveless T-shirt displaying finely tuned muscles on his upper arms. This, with his close-cropped hair, could have given an impression of aggressiveness, but somehow did not. Tony was affability itself. He showed them round, pointing out the particular apparatus Darren liked to use, confirming without being asked that Darren had indeed been there the previous Sunday, for most of the afternoon.

The covered passageway, when they got to it, looked a simple affair. Originally there had been an alley at the side of the building. This had been built over by, effectively, a lean-to. A glass door gave into the passage from the back of the club's reception area, with another door giving onto the street at the further end. Angela and Gary shuffled through the small area, easing their way past various bits and pieces of gym equipment to read a notice attached to the wall beside the street door, asking patrons leaving by this exit to shut the door firmly behind them.

"That's partly for insurance purposes," said Tony, seeing Angela take in the notice. "There's only a couple of people

I let store their bikes here anyway, and none of them would dream of not shutting the door properly. As you can see I've got some gym equipment here as well. Anything stored in here is completely safe. I can vouch for that."

"Yes, quite. So, really, there isn't any access to the club from the street by this passage?"

"No way. I wouldn't allow that. I need to be able to keep track. Everybody has to come through the main front door and sign in. Apart from the fact that it's my business, there are Health and Safety regulations to think about."

Angela nodded. She walked up and down the space and peered through into the gym and back to the passage's street door. "So," she said, coming through into the main building again, "this room is your reception and the refreshment area." She gazed over at the mass-catering coffee machines, the large urn and his selection of snacks arranged in a rack.

"Yes, that's right," said Tony.

"Hmm." Angela sat down at one of the tables. "You can't really see into the passage from this room."

"No, well, if you're sitting at one of those two tables at the back you can see into it a little way – " Tony stopped abruptly. There was a pause. Angela and Gary watched as something triggered a memory and a worried look stole across his features. His expression changed into one of diffidence and Angela moved in before it could become anything less than cooperative.

"Yes?" she asked, raising her eyebrows in encouragement.

Tony lowered his eyes. "Oh, nothing," he replied. "I was just remembering something."

You don't seriously think I'm going to let that pass, do you? No way, José, she thought. "About the bikes in the passageway on Sunday?" she asked. She was careful not to sound as though she was pouncing on the hesitant note in his voice.

Tony shrugged and feigned nonchalance. "It's nothing," he repeated. "It's just that I was talking to Sandra and she noticed Darren's bike out there."

"Did she not normally notice it?"

Tony cranked up the nonchalant attitude but his eyes didn't meet hers. "Yeah, yeah," he said. He then looked her full in the face and grinned. *Ah, you've found an explanation that you think will do,* she thought. "Yeah, but she's in love with Daz, ain't she? You know what it's like; she takes notice of the least little thing."

"So what did she say about Darren's bike?"

There was another inconsequential shrug. "Nothing, really; she just suddenly noticed it through the window. Come to think of it, she was sitting where you are."

Angela looked at Tony. His expression now was one that she'd seen many times on the faces of suspects, a whole variety of suspects, but always the same look: "Will she buy it?"

She decided to buy it for the moment. Tony wasn't going anywhere and she could come back to him. Since Sandra seemed to be at the heart of this mini-intrigue, she would speak to her. She thanked Tony for his cooperation and they left.

"Little bit of a mystery here," said Angela as she buckled her seat belt round her a few moments later. "I like to iron out the wrinkles as I go along."

"OK, so where to, then?" asked Gary.

"Hang on a tick," replied Angela, leafing through her notes. She found Sandra's mobile number and made a call. "Putney," she said a few moments later, as she put the phone back into her bag. "She's temping in an office near the High Street, and her lunch hour is due to begin in about ten minutes."

Chapter Twelve

It seemed Sandra's close proximity to a murder case had given her a frisson of celebrity status in the solicitor's practice where she was temping. When Angela and Gary arrived, the earnest young receptionist made no secret of the fact they were expected, showing them to a small room where Sandra would join them in a few moments.

It was closer to ten minutes before the door opened and Sandra appeared. "I'm sorry," she said, by way of greeting. "I had to finish an important letter to one of the clients."

Angela could hear a hint of hesitancy behind the seemingly reasonable sentence, and she saw guardedness around Sandra's eyes. "Not a problem," she answered.

Sandra came fully into the room and sat down on the only other vacant chair. "So you want to talk to me about...? Has something else come up?"

Angela and Gary noted the hesitation. *I bet "Tone" was straight on the phone to you,* thought Angela. *I'd love to know exactly what he said.* "Yes, we're just checking up on the business of Darren storing his bike in that lean-to at the side of the gym."

It would have been hard to miss the sudden tensing of Sandra's whole demeanour. She had enough sense to try to hide it behind a rather brittle smile, and she made a business of getting comfortable on the seat. "Yeah?" she asked.

Ten out of ten for sticking to a one-word answer, thought Angela. She could see Sandra gaining mastery over herself. *OK, let's make a pincer movement and see if I can approach from the flank.* "Did many of the clients store their bikes there?" she asked, assuming an innocent expression.

"Not many," replied Sandra, a smug look appearing on her face. "Daz is a favoured client; he's been going there so long, Tone's a friend by this time. He even runs some of the sessions, and helps out on reception sometimes."

"I get it. So Darren stored his bike there on Sunday afternoon?"

"Yes."

"Was it there all afternoon?"

"Yes," said Sandra firmly. Her voice was calm and level, but the guarded look in her eyes intensified.

"We were told you mentioned the bike while you were sitting at one of the tables in the reception area," said Angela, convinced Sandra already knew exactly what Tone had and hadn't said.

Her expression lifted a little. "Well, there you go, then," she said.

"Could it have been moved at any time, by anyone else, I mean?"

Sandra appeared to consider the matter. "Well, Tone might have moved it if he'd gone in there for something. He keeps some stuff in there. He could have pushed the bike along to get at whatever he wanted and then pushed it back further along than it was before. That would explain why I couldn't see it at one point and then suddenly noticed it."

"Right," said Angela. She made a note. She looked at Sandra and smiled. "Thanks, if we need to come and talk to you again we'll let you know."

"Of course." Sandra returned her smile, but there was no mistaking the relief in her face.

Back in the car Angela looked across at Gary, behind the wheel, as she pulled out her seat belt. "That's all a bit interesting, don't you think, Gaz? What did you make of it?"

Gary furrowed his brow. "Something's not adding up," he said.

"And what do you suppose that is?"

"They seemed to be a bit twitchy about where the bike was over the time of the murder."

"Hmm… that's what I thought; but to all intents and purposes it's completely innocent. Darren cycles to the gym and puts his bike where he always puts it, does his workout, probably sits about a bit, socializing, then gets out his bike and goes home again."

"So why are they uptight?"

"That's what I'm wondering. Right: Darren, Tony and Sandra; they've all got to be very big blobs on our radar."

"I reckon so," agreed Gary.

"OK, let's do that Virgin Mary thing until I've fed everything into the computer."

"Come again? The Virgin Mary?"

Angela smiled. "We'll ponder this in our hearts."

"Oh, right, for a minute I thought you were going to have me saying the rosary all the way back."

Angela laughed. "You can say whatever prayers you want, just so long as you don't close your eyes while you're doing it."

Everybody seemed engrossed with their computer screens when they arrived. Angela made a beeline for her two detective sergeants. "Rick and Jim, have you gone through the rest of the house-to-house enquiry?"

"Just doing it now," answered Rick. "It doesn't give us much. Most people seem to have been watching the telly, dozing, or out somewhere."

"Sunday afternoon, what can we expect?" said Angela. "Can you dig out the information on that woman opposite Kirsty's flat – the cake-maker who saw a cyclist arrive at the house?"

"Yep," said Jim, scrolling down. "Here it is. Mrs Sylvia Marchant."

"OK, go back to her and dig a bit deeper. I also want to know if she had any sort of relationship with either Kirsty or

Sandra. Anything from passing the time of day when they met in the street to being bosom pals."

"OK, Angie."

She headed back to a free console and sat down just as Gary's hand put a cup of coffee on the desk. "Oh, nice one, Gaz, thanks. What have I done to deserve you?"

"I know who to crawl to," he grinned.

"You'll go far, young man. OK, have you been pondering?"

"Yeah, it's possible that either Tony and/or Sandra *know* Darren went somewhere on his bike during the afternoon..."

"Right, and they're covering for him." Angela grimaced. "Hmm. That wouldn't make life too easy for us; they were almost smooth in giving their answers today. By the time it came to court they'd be completely twitch-less."

"Yeah, you're probably right. Mind you, that theory raises the question of why Darren..."

"Why he'd want to kill Kirsty? Yes, but if it turns out to be him he won't be the first to kill someone he loves. Oh, hang on, I've had another thought." Angela stared into the middle distance for a moment before looking speculatively at him. "We know Darren's a keep-fit fanatic, right?"

"Right; and he's into guns."

"Yeah, but forget the guns for a moment. How about this for a scenario? Darren comes to the gym, as per, and he gets stuck in to his session. So he's concentrating on the weights, and the treadmill and whatever else it is that he does."

"Yeah?"

"And he's pretty single-minded, is our Darren. That's the impression I have of him anyway; head down, eyes front, get on with the job." She looked at him. "Do you see where I'm going with this?"

Gary narrowed his eyes. "Er... Ah! Yes, he's so into his workout he wouldn't know if somebody *else* took his bike out for a while."

"Gottit!"

Gary beamed. "I'd say that's a definite possibility."

"Sandra's a tall, muscular woman. She could fit the bill as the person seen by Sylvia Marchant, and I don't think we'd have much trouble thinking up a motive for her."

"Yeah, and if we dig a bit we might come up with something for Tony."

"Hmm… they're definitely going to be revisited. OK, well that's good. That was bothering me, but I feel a lot clearer about the gym situation now."

Out of the corner of her eye, Angela could see Leanne and Derek coming towards her. She looked round and nodded them forward. "Yes? Have you got something?"

"Yes, guv," said Leanne. "The lab has got into those password-protected files." She waved some pages at Angela.

"Oh great; let's have a look, then."

Angela took the pages and laid them on the desk. The first few showed a series of sketches. Each one depicted a garment, drawn in clean economical lines. At the bottom of each page the initials "I. K." could be clearly seen.

"I suppose these are designs Ian King had been working on," said Angela, pointing at the initials. "The thing is, I wonder if he knew she had them on her laptop."

"It seems odd," agreed Gary. "I'd have thought dress designers were very cagey with their work – until it appeared officially, that is."

"Yes, me too. We've got to see him again, anyway, so we can let him know where we found these. What else have we got?"

She uncovered the next sheet and saw what seemed to be a page of letterheaded paper for a company. The paper was blank apart from a centred letterheading, *Massingham Models*. This company name stood out in large, bold, green, italic print. Underneath in smaller italics, but the same colour, followed the words, "address", "telephone number", "fax", "email" and "website" – but none of these were actually given. Beneath that came the words "company directors"; then, about halfway across the page, the name Kirsty Manners.

"Hmm…" said Angela. "How very odd."

"It's a funny sort of letterheading, that's for sure," agreed Derek. "No way of getting in contact with the company."

"And her name on the board of directors," finished Angela. "I keep hearing how Kirsty had told people that she was going to be 'someone'. She wanted a particular lifestyle. Maybe this is her sketching out a fantasy until the dream could come true."

"That could be it," agreed Leanne. "She might have been designing a letterhead for the company she hoped she'd run herself, one day. She was obviously trying to find out something about business; she visited the Companies House website quite a bit, didn't she, in her surfing?"

"Yes, but…" Angela laid the page on the desk. "I'm wondering, though."

"Guv?" said Leanne.

"Well, look where she's put her name. It's halfway across the page. What does that make you think?"

"It looks like she had the sense to realize she wouldn't be top dog – she would only be one of a board of directors. There's room for a couple of other names in front of hers," said Derek.

"That's what I was thinking," said Angela. She was silent for a few moments, going over in her mind everything she'd heard about Kirsty's ambitions.

"Perhaps the names would be added as her plans took shape," suggested Leanne.

Angela looked up at them both. "Chase this up. If Massingham Models actually exists, they'll be registered with Companies House and quite likely have a website. See what you can find out about them."

"OK, guv," said Leanne. "And you'll find there's even less on the other."

Angela glanced down at the last page and saw what Leanne meant. An A4 page with very little on it – just a series of numbers on one line at the top. Angela counted them. "Eleven digits beginning with 07; no prizes for guessing," she said.

"Mobile number, guv."

"Exactly. I'll tell you what. Before you look into this company, can you check up on all the telephone numbers we've got so far, from all the people we've spoken to, and let me know if this tallies with one of them?"

"OK, guv," replied Leanne. She and Derek moved away to get on with the task.

Angela switched on the computer. "OK, let's feed in the result of our labours this morning."

She worked silently. A quick and efficient typist, before long she pressed "save" and leaned back from the computer. "That's good," she said. "Things are moving. We've got a couple of promising lines to follow." Just at that moment, Leanne appeared by her desk again. "Ah, how'd you get on, Leanne?"

"Nothing doing, I'm afraid, guv. We haven't got this number anywhere on the system relating to this case."

"Oh, not to worry, thanks for trying."

"That's a nuisance," said Gary, as Leanne moved away. "It'll take a while to find out who it's registered to. We don't even know the network. Do you want me to get started, talking to the mobile phone companies?"

Angela smiled broadly at him. "Why do you want to make life so complicated? There's a much easier way to get the information we need."

A blush suddenly appeared and spread across Gary's face and he grinned sheepishly. "Ah yes."

Angela was still smiling as she picked up the desk phone and keyed in the number. After a moment or so, someone picked up at the other end. She could hear a conversation going on, and a male voice speaking, clipped and precise, with authority. Then he spoke into the phone.

"Nigel Summers."

Chapter Thirteen

Angela cut the line and sat with a puzzled look on her face.

"Anybody you know, Angie?" asked Gary.

"Somebody called Nigel Summers. We haven't come across that name so far, have we?"

"It doesn't ring a bell."

Just at that moment Angela saw D.C.I. Stanway coming into the room, and she stood up. "Good afternoon, sir."

Stanway returned her greeting as he stopped in front of the whiteboard, studying all the information relating to the case. "I've got an appointment tomorrow, so I'll miss most of the briefing in the morning," he said. "Will you bring me up to speed?"

"Of course." Angela went through the results of their work so far, finishing with the password-protected pages on Kirsty's computer.

"Oh yes; and what were they all about?"

"A few things, sir; she had copies of Ian King's dress designs."

"Oh, really? That's interesting. Should the office-junior-stroke-in-house-model have access to such things?"

"I wouldn't have thought so, sir, but we'll be speaking to Ian King again later. I presume you've caught up with the news that he was attacked last night?"

"Yes. I want you to keep a close eye on that, Angie."

"Absolutely, sir."

"What else did you find on the computer?"

"She had a letterheaded page for a company called Massingham Models."

"Which you're checking out?"

"Oh yes. And the telephone number of somebody called Nigel Summers."

Stanway smiled. "Ah, I'm ahead of you there, Angela. I took a look at the Ivano King website while the rest of you were doing all sorts of running around yesterday. He's a co-director with Ian King, but he's obviously the one with the business brain while his partner designs the frocks. Apparently he works from their premises in Chelsea, which I've no doubt is a very exclusive shop."

"Big bucks in all this, I should think."

"Oh, you can be sure of it."

"I wonder if he had a relationship with Kirsty as well."

"What makes you say that?"

"Well, I'm just thinking about what Darren Carpenter said when we first interviewed him. He knew that Kirsty was seeing Ian King, but he also thought there had been someone else before him; only he didn't know who that person was."

"Well, Nigel Summers's number must have been hidden in Kirsty's computer for a reason." Stanway smiled and raised his eyebrows and Angela realized she was being gently sent off to her next task.

"Yes, sir; I'll have one of the team ring and set up an interview."

As suggested by the address, the outlet for Ivano King in the King's Road, Chelsea, was very exclusive. A single, exquisitely cut suit formed the window display. Instead of a counter and a shop assistant, a young woman looking more like a receptionist sat at an antique Georgian desk. As Angela and Gary entered, she glanced up and smiled at them across the type of hush that can be produced only by fabric wallpaper and deep-pile carpeting. The two detectives were assiduous about wiping their feet thoroughly on the mat just inside the door. There weren't many other garments on display, but then Angela guessed that shoppers probably didn't come here "just looking".

"Good afternoon, we're here to see Mr Nigel Summers."

"Ah yes." The receptionist consulted a leather-bound book on the desk. "Detectives Costello and Houseman?"

Angela confirmed the identification, and the woman indicated they should each take a seat. She vanished into a room at the back of the shop, and they heard her mounting some stairs.

"So they own the whole building, then," surmised Angela.

"I bet it costs a bomb to keep going," said Gary.

Before Angela could reply, they heard footsteps descending the stairs; the receptionist reappeared, asking them to follow her.

The carpet pile was less deep up here, but Angela still felt her shoes sinking into it as she walked. Nigel Summers was standing up to greet them from behind a large walnut desk supporting one desktop computer and one laptop.

"Please sit down, Inspector," he said, indicating a chair in front of his desk. "Can I get you anything? Tea, or coffee, perhaps."

Angela sat down, declining his offer. Gary had already found himself a perch on one side of the room. "I just need to ask you a few questions," she began, "about Kirsty Manners."

"That was terrible, just terrible; what an awful shock." Nigel shook his head in horror as he slid onto his seat behind the desk.

"Yes, I can imagine," said Angela sympathetically.

"So," Nigel focused their conversation, "how may I help you?" His gaze was open and direct and his smile pleasant, but he'd picked up a pen and was tapping the end of it up and down on his blotter.

"Did Kirsty ever come here?"

"No, as far as I know she hadn't ever been in this shop. She would have no reason to. Kirsty was based at our unit in Wandsworth."

"Would she have ever been required to come here – with a message, say?"

"Once upon a time, Inspector, maybe; but in these days of texts and emails, it just doesn't happen."

Angela smiled. "What about if she wanted to buy some clothes?"

Nigel returned her smile. "Well, yes, but I know what we were paying her and I can assure you she wouldn't have been able to afford it."

"How well did you know her?"

Nigel thought for a moment. The pen tapped a little more rapidly.

"I saw her in passing when I went to the unit, of course. Well, to be candid, one could hardly help noticing; she was hotter than *Hades*. It's just dreadful to think of such a young life being destroyed."

Angela reminded herself that Nigel Summers was a company director in an industry with an ability to talk up its products *sans pareil*; by the same token, he could probably stonewall for Britain. It was time to cut across the preliminaries. "Had you been having an affair with her, Mr Summers?"

The pen stopped tapping and the eyebrows went up into the forehead. "An *affair*, Inspector? That's a bit of a leap from seeing her in passing, isn't it? What on earth makes you think Kirsty Manners and I were having an affair?"

You haven't answered the question and you've chucked the ball back into my court, thought Angela. *OK, let's bring up the heavy artillery.* "She had your mobile number stored in a secret file on her computer."

There was an involuntary movement from Nigel and the pen dropped to the floor. "Excuse me… ah… Oh, there it is." But it was too late. Angela had seen his true reaction. Though gone in a flash, it had unmistakably been, "Damn and blast the woman!"

Nigel scrabbled under his desk for the pen, sitting up again within seconds, smiling and urbane. He raised his hands in a gesture of surrender. "OK, I'd better come clean. I *did* have a bit of a fling with Kirsty; but it didn't last very long and, I can assure you, it was over and done with weeks ago."

Hmm, so Ian King had a dalliance, Nigel Summers had a fling and Darren Carpenter was in love, thought Angela. She considered her next question. Nigel must have taken her silence for disapproval because he spoke again. "She knew the score, Inspector," he said, unable to keep a defensive note out of his voice.

"The score?" asked Angela.

"You know, that that's all it was, just a fling."

"I'm not the arbiter of your morals, Mr Summers. What was she like?"

A puzzled frown creased Nigel's brow. "How do you mean, what was she like?"

"Just what I say; it's important to get as complete a picture as possible of Kirsty, and we can get this only from the people who knew her when she was alive."

"Ah yes, I see."

"So, what was she like?"

"Well, let me see now… If you'd asked me that before I… before we… before our… er…"

"Fling."

"Yes. Yes, I started off thinking that she was just about the most stunning-looking woman I'd ever seen. Then… after we… er… I amended my opinion to 'stunning airhead' but that didn't last long."

"Oh? So she wasn't an airhead. Was she bright, intelligent?"

"Er… no, not especially; well, that's not quite right. She was a long way from stupid. Cunning and calculating is more how I would put it. She had assimilated some fundamental lessons. She knew how to flatter, all right. If she was to be believed, I achieved a height of sexual prowess during our time together that even *I* wouldn't aspire to. And as for my job; Ian's lucky to have a man like me. How I managed to keep the label going was just amazing." An ironic grin appeared on his face. "I didn't enquire how she came to that conclusion. As you can probably imagine, she agreed with more or less everything I said. We could have carried on a bit longer if she'd kept to her side of the bargain – you know, I'd have bought her the odd expensive bit of bling and kept her in frilly knickers and we'd have parted amicably when I was good and ready. To be honest, I'm surprised she was still with us. Ian planned to take on an intern and I'd put him in touch with a likely candidate, but it didn't work out. So we kept Kirsty who was keen to learn about… well… about life lived at an executive level. She was very – er – what's the expression? Single-minded, yes, that's it. She knew exactly what she wanted and went straight for it."

"And what was that?"

"As far as I could tell, to marry well and live a life of luxury."

"Oh, not to be a supermodel?"

Nigel thought for a moment. "She probably started off with that ambition, but I think it changed. I can imagine her as the prettiest girl at nursery, in the class at school, at Girl Guides or whatever. She thought her looks were her passport to the good life, you know. If modelling was the route to take then that's the way she'd go. But to be honest, once she'd got her foot in the door she must have started to realize the prettiest girl in the class was now surrounded by beautiful women. And the fact is, Inspector, not every girl who makes it as a model has a face that one can even call attractive. I have to be honest; I realized that she wouldn't come up to scratch, socially, among my friends and acquaintances and dropped her fairly quickly, but she soon got her hooks into Ian; just so long as it was somebody of power and influence and earning a packet." Nigel smiled and shrugged. "I'm surprised she didn't bypass me and go straight for him in the first place, but maybe she didn't quite have the confidence at the beginning."

"So, you're saying…?"

"What I'm saying, Inspector, is that she was a gold-digger; very decorative to be sure, but that's what she was, nonetheless." The ironic grin reappeared. "And who says the young have no drive and ambition these days?"

"Quite. Did you know she had a regular boyfriend?"

"Oh yes. Kirsty was the kind of young woman who would always have someone simmering gently on the back-burner. Poor Darren, I couldn't help feeling sorry for him from time to time. She should have stuck with him, really. But there you go. She had big ideas."

"Do you own a bicycle, Mr Summers?"

"A bicycle?" Nigel's eyes opened wide in surprise at the change of subject, but he recovered quickly. "No. No, I don't. As a matter of fact, that's something I didn't ever get to grips with."

"Really?"

"Yes, I suppose I could learn easily enough, but it's not something I ever got around to."

"Ah," said Angela. "May I ask where you were at approximately three o'clock on Sunday?"

"Am I a suspect, Inspector?"

"It's a box-ticking exercise at this stage."

"OK." Nigel raised his eyes to the ceiling as he thought the matter through. "At three o'clock on Sunday I was probably just approaching the fourteenth hole at the golf club I belong to."

"I presume you weren't playing alone."

"No, there were four of us. Would you like their names?"

"Yes, please; my colleague will take them from you." Angela rose from her seat. "Thank you for your time, Mr Summers. I can imagine how busy you must be. I'm sure you're aware, as the investigation progresses we might need to see you again."

"Naturally, Inspector," replied Nigel, also standing up. "I'll be here if you need me."

Within ten minutes they were in the car from where Gary made a call to ascertain Ian King had returned to his office. They set off in that direction.

After a short while, Angela noticed that Gary seemed unnaturally quiet. "Wassamatta, Gazza?"

Gary grinned and threw a quick glance in her direction. "It's a bit, I dunno… it's all a bit depressing, isn't it?"

"What is?"

"Well, I suppose I can't talk. My life isn't lily-white, but some people seem to be such users, don't they?"

"You mean Kirsty trying to sleep her way to a rich lifestyle, and Nigel Summers and Ian King just using her for sex?"

"Yes."

"That's nothing new, though, is it?"

"No, but… at the end of the day, what was Kirsty going to get out of it?"

"She was going to get precisely nothing, Gazza; certainly not the rich, luxurious lifestyle that she craved. Unfortunately, I don't think she'd woken up to that reality."

"Poor thing."

"I don't know. She seems to have been quite ruthless in her own way. She kept stringing her boyfriend along as first reserve, remember. And as for Nigel Summers and Ian King, she just wanted them for what she could get out of them. There was no indication she actually cared for them as people."

"Yes. But it's all very superficial, isn't it? There's got to be more to life and relationships than that, hasn't there?"

"There is, Gary. There's a whole lot more."

Chapter Fourteen

Angela and Gary found themselves parking once again under the large, looping letters of the Ivano King label. Jenni appeared, ushering them into Ian's office.

"Ah good, the police," said Ian, jumping to his feet as they came through the door. He indicated chairs for them to sit on.

"We're calling about the events last night," began Angela, once they were seated. "I know these things are very upsetting, but we've looked through the police report of the incident and on the face of it, there's no reason to see it as anything other than a random attack."

"Oh, I'm sure that's not the case, Inspector," replied Ian. "It's shaken me up, I can tell you."

"No doubt," said Angela. "It's a frightening business, whatever the motive. Tell me, what makes you think it wasn't random?"

Ian looked, just for a moment, as if he thought the question a stupid one. "The circumstances are pretty indicative, I would have thought; the attack on me so closely following on from the murder of my very recent ex."

"You think whoever killed Kirsty might now be targeting you?"

"Isn't that the implication?"

Hmm, is that vanity or genuine fear speaking? wondered Angela, silently. "To be perfectly honest," she said, giving him what she hoped was a reassuring smile, "I would expect the two events to be totally unrelated. You've got a good address, a very nice car, and I can tell that's a highly expensive watch on your wrist. I wouldn't be at all surprised if your attacker put these things together and took a chance on your having something worth stealing. He didn't hang around once somebody set up a chase, did he?"

"Well, no, there is that," admitted Ian. "It was all very sudden and quite scary. I just assumed – "

"That's understandable," agreed Angela. "I think you're wise to at least ask the question. We're going to keep the matter on our radar, so to speak, just in case you turn out to be right. I know the police took a statement from you last night. Have you signed it yet?"

"I'm calling in at my local station to do that on my way home tonight."

"OK, Mr King, we'll make sure we have copies included in the file on the investigation into Kirsty's murder. I'm sorry we can't provide you with protection, but I'm sure I don't need to remind you to be careful and cautious."

"Absolutely!"

"Right, I think that's all we can do. Hopefully, nothing like it will occur again. If you see anybody behaving at all suspiciously, get in touch with your local police again. I'll make sure they alert us to any report from you."

"Thank you, Inspector." Ian stood up. "I feel a little better now and I hope you're right, and it was just a random event." He suddenly realized that Angela and Gary had remained seated. "Was there something else?"

"Yes; at least we think so. Kirsty had some protected files on her laptop and we're wondering about some of the documents we've found, now our experts have managed to break the password."

"Oh?" Ian sat down again.

"We found some designs with your initials on them." Angela took a photocopy out of her bag and showed it to him. It was a pencil drawing of a very smart trouser suit.

"Yes! I knew it! I just f – I just knew it! Thank God you've found them." Ian's expression was an odd mixture of triumph and fear. He took a set of keys from his pocket, selected one of them and unlocked one of the drawers in his desk. He pulled out a sheet of paper and turned it so the two officers could see what was on it. Angela and Gary were gazing at the same sketch of a trouser suit.

"Ah."

"Yes, 'ah', Inspector; this is from my new collection. I must ask you to immediately forget you've seen these."

"No problem, we won't be talking to anybody about them." Angela assured him. "How come Kirsty had them on her laptop?"

"That's a very good question, and one I wouldn't mind knowing the answer to myself. I can only imagine she went trawling through my computer when I wasn't aware." He flicked a glance across at them. "Asleep, maybe. There were one or two occasions when this could have happened."

"What would be their value to Kirsty, though?"

"Hmm, hard to say; she knew most of us are paranoid about our work and would be horrified at anybody seeing them until they appear on a catwalk. That's just the way we are. She might have thought it gave her a hold over me."

"But you split with her all the same. Weren't you worried that she would *publish and be damned*?"

"Inspector, I know a great many more people in this industry than Kirsty. She would soon have found every door slammed in her face. In any case, although we'd split, I made sure I left things a bit open, so to speak. Until I knew for certain what she had, I planned to string her along with the thought that we'd get back together again." Ian put the page back in his drawer and relocked it. "Calculating, I know, but you have to take precautions when there's a loose cannon about, and I couldn't be completely certain that she had my designs. Er – " He raised his eyebrows at them. "I do like to have control over all the copies."

"I'm sorry, I can't return them to you just at the moment. They might turn into evidence. I'll give you a receipt for them, though. We'll keep them perfectly safe."

Ian pursed his lips as though he might protest, but merely gave a curt nod. "OK."

Father Martin Buchanan closed the door of the presbytery behind him and gazed in both directions along the street. He had two things, some free time before Confirmation classes started and a plan. *To the right first,* he said to himself, and struck out. Martin tended not to wear clerical dress in his spare time, so he looked like any other thirty-something young man as he ambled along in sweats and trainers. He'd given a lot of thought to the frightened young woman in the confessional the day before, and the more he thought about it the less he liked it. Once he'd shared the story with Angela and Patrick he'd felt a bit better, but it still wasn't enough. Even though they'd reassured him about his actions, he still felt bad for ducking down behind the screen.

Somewhere in a house in one of these highly respectable suburban streets, one of his flock, kept against her will, faced who knew what awful threat for not complying with the wishes of her captors. She might even now be suffering a punishment for having tried to escape. Martin had decided to turn his private prayer into a walking event. He planned to trawl the streets around the church and see if he could find the house. They couldn't stay indoors all the time. What had the young woman said? "They want me do bad things, with mans – men, at parties." Unless the parties took place in the house itself, the women would have to come out, no doubt escorted by a hulking giant like Igor. And if they happened in the house, then guests would arrive. Either way, it would cause traffic. And he might just manage to pass at the right moment.

He knew it was a very long shot, and possibly naive of him, but he had to do something.

Eleanor and Jenni left the unit at the same time that evening, and made their way to the bus stop. They were both more tired than usual.

"This business about Kirsty is draining, isn't it?" remarked Jenni.

"You can say that again," agreed Eleanor. "It seems strange to be doing my normal work. I keep thinking everything should stop, and then I think, 'Why?'"

"I know what you mean. It's all a bit unreal. We'll have to get over it, though." Jenni looked at Eleanor, making her eyes big and round. "London Fashion Week looms."

"Aaaaaaaaaaaaargh!" screamed Eleanor, feigning horror. "Actually," she continued, "I'm quite looking forward to it this year. Ian's gone out on a limb with his new collection, and it'll be interesting to see the reaction."

"He's certainly had a bit more spring in his step lately," agreed Jenni. "I was getting worried. Some of our regular buyers haven't put in an order for ages, and I've seen a couple of articles in magazines where they've come right out and said he's lost his edge."

"I think he's got it back now," said Eleanor. "Some of this latest stuff is very exciting. I shall be after one or two pieces myself once they hit the high street."

Jenni looked across at her colleague. "I suppose that's all part of the transformation job you've done on yourself since your mum died," she said. She hesitated. "I think it's paying off," she ventured, wondering if Eleanor would pick up the hint and the conversation could lead into what was happening in Ellie's private life. Both Jenni and Raj had their suspicions about Eleanor and Ian, but they didn't feel free to ask.

Eleanor smiled back at her. "OK, I'll put you out of your misery. Ian and I are having a thing and it's been going on for about a month."

"I did wonder," replied Jenni, then she stopped. "A month… but wasn't he – ?"

"Yes, he asked me out before he'd dropped Kirsty, though that followed very soon after. It really put her nose out of joint, I can tell you. I know you shouldn't speak ill of the dead, but she behaved like a complete pig to me about it."

"I can imagine," said Jenni. "There was something quite feral about Kirsty, wasn't there?"

Angela invited Gary in for a coffee when they got home that evening. He still seemed a bit flat in his spirit; if Maddie was in, she would probably cheer him up.

In this she wasn't wrong.

"Hi, Gaz," she said, bounding into the living room ten minutes later, just as Angela was handing him a cup.

He brightened immediately. "Hey, Mads; how're you doing?"

"OK, thanks; I started looking for a job today. I wasn't expecting to see you back here so soon."

Gary's face took on a sheepish expression. "I think Angie's being a ministering angel."

"Oh, really?"

"He struck me as being a bit down," explained Angela. "I just invited him in for coffee."

"Oh poor you; wassup?" asked Madeleine.

Gary shrugged and the sheepish expression became stronger. "Oh, I just felt a bit fed up, that's all. It'll pass."

"The life goals that some people pursue can seem shallow and depressing to others," said Angela.

"I assume that's about the case you're on, so I'd better not ask," said Madeleine. "Anyway, it's nice to see you're a sensitive soul; that's good in a bloke," she added, and they all laughed. Gary looked for an instant as though he would have continued with the subject; instead he shrugged, got on with his coffee, and the conversation passed to other matters. But Angela remained curious and picked up on it again as she was showing him out about half an hour later.

"You looked as though you were going to say something else earlier, Gaz, when we were talking."

"Oh, it was only that I was thinking what a shame it is when a gorgeous woman loses her life so young."

"It's a shame when any young person dies, Gaz."

He smiled. "I'm being sexist, aren't I? It's a shame whether she was young and pretty or not."

Angela smiled. "Exactly; night, Gaz."

"Night, Angie," he replied, setting off down the path. "See you tomorrow."

She remained for a few moments in the hall after she closed the door behind him, a smile playing around her lips. The better acquainted she became with her detective constable, the more she warmed to him. She suspected consideration for Maddie's feelings had motivated his reticence earlier, and that pleased her. Perhaps he didn't want Madeleine to think that he had an eye for the ladies. Perhaps he was interested in Maddie. Angela wandered slowly back into the living room. *Hmm*, she thought to herself. *This could get interesting.*

As she entered the house that evening, Eleanor couldn't help glancing up at the ceiling, to her mother's bedroom. She immediately thought of Ian's visit on Sunday. It had been particularly good. Suddenly her memories of Sunday passed to an earlier moment from that day when she had acted completely out of character, and she moved quickly into the kitchen and began to get the things together for her evening meal in a brusque and angry manner. That was something she definitely didn't want to dwell on, thank you very much. She went cold and shaky at the very thought of it.

After her meal, however, she thought about the front bedroom again, with its still-very-obvious evidence of Sunday's activity. She hadn't cleared up in there at all and had no plans to do so immediately. *I'll just go up,* she thought, *and sit there for a while.* She couldn't have said why she did this, but she supposed that she wanted to savour the memory – the same room, the bed still in disarray, the empty champagne bottle and flutes abandoned on the night tables, and remember the time with Ian, remember she was desired. She didn't kid herself she was loved, and that made this affair a very bittersweet one.

Eleanor never had been one to harbour illusions.

The Tone-Up Gym reception area was empty when Sandra entered it that night. Tony saw her and raised his eyebrows. "I wondered if I might see you here tonight," he said. He lifted up a steaming jug of coffee and looked questioningly at her.

"Yes, please, Tone," she said, sitting down at the nearest table to the tiny counter. She let out a huge, heartfelt sigh.

"I can guess what sort of a day you've had," he said, putting a mug of coffee for each of them down on the table.

"It was awful," she replied. "Thanks for giving me the heads-up they might be on their way."

"Turned up, did they?"

"Yes. I reckon they must have phoned to say they were coming as they were driving away from you. They spoilt my lunch, really."

"How did it go?"

"Can't tell, really; they don't give anything away, do they? I don't get why they're harping on about me seeing his bike. All I did was notice the freaking bike in the lean-to and there's, like, this major enquiry going on. What's the bike got to do with Kirsty's murder, anyway?"

Tony took a sip of his coffee and looked at her with a thoughtful expression. "You've got to look at it from their point of view, Sandy. Darren must be in the frame for it, so they've got to check out his alibi."

"What's his bike got to do with his alibi? He was here all the time. I can vouch for that." Tony said nothing; he gave her a shy smile and let the silence lengthen. Light dawned for Sandra. "You thinking they don't want to rely on my word because of our relationship?"

"Well, I think they've got to rely on it, legally. But I'm sure they'll be looking for a way to crack it. It's what they do, isn't it? I mean, say for instance Darren was the murderer. He would have had to get over to your and Kirsty's place quickly and back again to the gym."

Sandra saw the sense of this and nodded. "The bike would have been perfect for that." She found herself suddenly having to fight back tears of frustration and anxiety.

Sensing the way she was feeling, Tony reached over, laying a comforting hand on her arm. "Don't worry, Sandy, it'll all work out. You'll see." The tenderness in his voice surprised Sandra, and she found herself having to work even harder to keep the tears at bay. "What does Darren say?" he asked.

"Oh!" Sandra's frustration and anxiety turned in an instant to irritation. "Sometimes I wonder if he's living on the same planet as the rest of us. All I get from him is, 'I ain't done nothing so I've got nothing to worry about.'"

"Did you tell him the police were asking about the bike?"

"Same thing, Tone: 'The bike was in the lean-to all afternoon wasn't it, so what's the problem?'" Sandra produced such a close imitation of Darren's voice that Tony let out a short, involuntary bark of laughter. She recognized the humour of the moment and grinned. The truth was, she'd become increasingly frustrated with Darren. He seemed not to be aware of her feelings at all, not to understand when she tried to talk to him. If only Darren could look at her with a gentle, caring expression, like Tony's right at that moment. She picked up her mug and tried to cut off that line of thinking.

Tony looked at Sandra for a moment, as if deciding whether or not to pursue the subject. Finally he spoke. "Why *did* you suddenly mention the bike on Sunday, Sand?"

She cast a puzzled glance at him and shrugged. "I dunno. I just saw it and mentioned it."

"If you remember," said Tony, carefully, "you said it hadn't been there earlier."

"Yeah, but that could easily be because it had been moved along a bit. You're always in there for stuff."

Tony looked at Sandra and slowly shook his head. "I don't think I went in there at all on Sunday."

A look of fear came into Sandra's eyes. "So… what are you saying?"

"I'm not really sure," replied Tony. The thought worried him, and the realization that he hesitated to share his growing suspicion with Sandra unnerved him even more.

Chapter Fifteen

Klara looked around and gave the ghost of a smile as Asia came into the kitchen. "Good morning," she said.

"Morning," replied Asia. She'd picked up from the television that English people mostly just said that one word.

"Have you any news?"

Asia shook her head. "No, I have to wait still. I have asked them all. They all say same, he very busy man. I have to be patient."

"But you met him once."

"Oh yes. He very nice. Say I very promising. Say he will help me." Asia deliberately made her voice sound cheerful. Her housemates had problems of their own. She faced the truth; all hope had evaporated of ever hearing from her contact, the man who had promised to help her get started in the English fashion industry.

Klara nodded. "You want coffee?" she asked. The door to the conservatory stood open and for one brief second Asia's heart leapt. It sank almost immediately as she saw the bulky form of Igor coming along the garden path towards the house. He veered off and went in through the French windows to the dining room.

Klara saw the hope flare and die on Asia's face. "He more careful now," she said. "Since Monday."

Asia raised her shoulders and let them drop again. Yes, it was now Wednesday. Not for the first time she realized how this incarceration could easily make her lose track of the days altogether. She thought again of her mad dash through the open front door, the sprint along the street, the feeling, the glorious, ecstatic feeling that she'd managed to get away. She'd do the same thing again without hesitation, but she didn't think she'd get another opportunity. She just thanked God it was Igor pursuing her. That was a blessing really. Igor hadn't been in a church in his life and didn't know the slightest thing about confessionals. If it had been Pawel, the whole story would have ended differently. He would have gone straight round to the other side of the screen and likely as not would have attacked that poor priest. Asia couldn't remember how many times she'd played that scene back in her head, though by now she felt convinced the effort had been wasted. She'd been too garbled, obscure, she hadn't given enough information, and her English was bad. Only the thought of the kindness and concern in the face of the priest kept her from despair.

As Klara pointed out, Igor's vigilance had increased; and if it wasn't him it would be Vladimir or Pawel. She hadn't wanted to make things awkward for the others, though. "If worse for you, I sorry," she said.

Klara shook her head, her eyes dull. "Is no matter; I obey, they not hurt me."

Asia nodded, knowing what Klara meant. It was a lie, though. "Maybe they don't beat you, but they hurt you all the same," she said softly.

Klara shrugged. "They keep promise, I get work. I work tonight."

"Tonight, what kind of work tonight?"

"Tonight, big fashion bash." Klara was obviously proud of knowing this word for a party. "Many peoples, much contacts, important for future career." Klara looked away. "We provide entertainment."

Asia picked up the kettle Klara had boiled and concentrated on pouring water into her cup, so Klara wouldn't see the pity in her eyes. They both knew what "providing the entertainment" meant. The only contact Klara would make that night would be of a sexual nature with whatever man she'd been offered to.

They both knew Klara wouldn't fight it. For a while, at first, Asia had wondered why; but only last week she'd seen traces of white powder around the nostrils of her friend, and knew the answer. No wonder her eyes were dull and the bloom had gone from her cheeks.

"When is next proper modelling job?" she asked.

Something of the old, carefree, hopeful Klara appeared in the other woman's eyes. "Soon," she replied. "They promise."

Asia cast her eyes down at her cup again. They promise. Poor Klara, she was so innocent, in her way. She thought back to the day she and the Russian woman had arrived at the house, both armed with bursting portfolios and relieved to think they had found reasonable lodgings while they pursued their dreams.

Klara's face fell again and she sat down at the little kitchen table. "When you first realize what goes on?"

"I suspect quite soon. I think, why always man in house like some… er…" Asia frowned as she tried to recapture the word eluding her.

"Bodyguard is word, I think."

"*Tak*, yes; then I realize, they not bodyguards, they just guards."

"They not make you go to provide entertainment now?"

"No, after first time when I refuse. My case different from you, they not have same hold. They leave me alone, but keep me here. Igor, Vladimir and Pawel, they not bosses; they taking orders from someone else. I think they don't know what to do with me." Asia got a grim sense of satisfaction from this, but it gave her little comfort.

"I remember that reception, our first one. I see – saw – you speaking with English lady."

Asia brightened at the memory. "Yes, she nice, take interest in my work. I show it to her from my phone."

Klara nodded, and both women were silent at the mention of mobile phones. These had mysteriously disappeared from their belongings, along with their passports, very soon after they arrived at the house. It was the same with the other girls. They didn't talk about it much among themselves but they all knew, they could all read the hopelessness in each other's eyes. There was no landline in the house. They were guarded all the time.

For Klara and two of the others the little packets of white powder had become the only form of escape.

"Jim, how are you and Rick getting on with this Sylvia Marchant who lived over the road from Kirsty?" asked Angela as soon as the team briefing had ended.

"We haven't managed to make contact yet, Angie," replied Jim. "She seemed to be out most of yesterday. We're going over there again this morning."

"OK. I've had a couple of thoughts about Kirsty's flatmate, Sandra, and that bloke that runs the gym."

"Tony something-or-other, yeah? Is this to do with what you were saying in the meeting, something dodgy about the bike?"

"That's the one. We've barely scratched the surface with those two. It's time for a bit of digging. For all we know, any one of them could have taken the bike out. They could be in it together and covering for each other, or not in it together and each trying to avoid letting the other know what they were up to. It's all up for grabs."

Angela turned to the more junior members of the team. "Leanne, Derek, have you managed to find anything about Massingham Models?"

"I got a number and tried ringing them," said Leanne, "but it went straight to voicemail; a message telling me to leave my name and number. Which I did," she added.

"Did you say you were from the police?"

"No, I just gave my name and my mobile number. I didn't want to alarm her."

"Good. Did you contact Companies House?"

"Yes. The only other information we could get was the name of the company director and one named shareholder."

"Yes?" she asked. "And they are?"

Leanne looked down at the paper in her hand. "Company director: D. M. Massingham, named shareholder: J. W. Massingham."

"Hmm… whoever the Massinghams are, they're keeping it in the family, aren't they?" Angela said, holding out her hand for the page.

"They seem to be, guv," agreed Leanne, handing the sheet over. "I tried Googling them. There was something about 'Massingham's girls' in one or two of the things I read, and they were related to fashion shows."

Angela took the page and tapped it against her lips for a moment as she thought. "Hmm, tell you what," she said, eventually. "I'd like to know a bit more about this before I go any further. Kirsty thought it was important enough to password-protect information about this company on her computer, so I want to proceed with caution. Trawl around and see what you can find out. Rick and Jim, you're still busy with Sylvia Marchant. Gary and I will concentrate on Tone-up Tony and Sandra."

As it happened, Angela didn't have to leave the building to speak to Tony again. She was just collecting her bag from her office when she received a call saying a Mr Chambers was in reception asking to talk to her.

Mr Chambers? Mr Chambers? she said to herself. Across the incident room she could see Gary in conversation with Derek. "Hey, Gaz, bring your notebook. There's a chap called Chambers downstairs asking to see me." Just at that moment she looked up at the whiteboard and saw, in the space between the names "Tone" and "Tone-Up Gym", somebody had squeezed in the name Chambers. "Ah! That's who it is. This is interesting."

"You were pondering about him in your heart, weren't you?" said Gary. "You know – the Virgin Mary."

Angela grinned. "I was indeed."

Tone looked up, a mixture of diffidence and embarrassment on his face when Angela and Gary entered the interview room a few moments later. They sat down across the table from him. "So," Angela began. "What may I do for you?"

"I've been thinking about what you were asking me yesterday; about this business of Darren's bike."

"Yes?"

"Well… I think there would have been a gap."

"A gap?"

"Yeah, in the timing. I think there might have been a space when the reception wasn't manned. On Sunday, I mean." He looked at them and leaned back slightly in his chair.

"How long a gap are we talking about, Tony?"

Tony fixed his eyes on the surface of the table. His hands clenched and unclenched compulsively. "Maybe half an hour, or even a bit more," he said eventually.

"At what time?"

The eyelids remained resolutely lowered. "About a quarter to – ten to three."

"And when did you and Sandra have the conversation about seeing the bike in the lean-to?"

Tony looked up; the worst was over. "Twenty past."

Exactly the period covering the time of the murder. Angela and Gary made a point of not looking at each other.

"How can you be so certain about these times?" Angela asked.

Tony was more relaxed now. "I'm guessing at the time before three, but I don't think I'm far out. I'm sure about the end time because I had someone booked in for quarter past. It was a new client looking for a personal trainer, and when he arrived the first thing he did was apologize for being late, so I automatically looked at the clock."

"I see; and is the reception area generally left unattended?"

"Not often, but lately it's been the norm round about that time on a Sunday. I always go out for my ciggie then. There's a little room behind the counter in reception."

Angela was no smoker, but she was reasonably certain it didn't take half an hour to smoke a cigarette. Something of this thought must have shown in her face, because Tony continued.

"The thing is, I'm a personal trainer as well, and that's how I'm building up my client base. And I only had this one client booked in for last Sunday afternoon."

"I see," said Angela but she didn't, quite. "This timing still isn't clear to me. The reception was empty for…?"

"Sorry, yes, I'm not explaining this very well. Sunday afternoons I generally know exactly who's there and who isn't. If anyone goes into any of the rooms, there'll be someone there I can trust. Darren or someone'll be in the weights room, for instance, and there'll be Sandra, or another person I know well, doing cardiovascular stuff. I mean, anyone coming into the club won't get very far without being noticed and challenged."

"Isn't that still risky, though? Didn't I notice a till on your counter?"

"Ah no, when I'm out the back I can see the till and the counter from where I sit. It's just that I can't see the front door and that whole side of the room where the lean-to is."

"I'm still not sure why it takes half an hour to smoke a cigarette."

"It doesn't," replied Tony. "But I take a bit longer, specially lately. It's a chance to chill out, to have a think. I only opened the gym a couple of years ago, and I've been working flat out to build it up the way I want it. Now it's taking shape I let myself relax a bit here and there."

"OK. So, what was said about the bike, exactly?"

Tony took a deep breath as he marshalled his thoughts. "It was nothing really. Sandy just said, 'Oh there's his bike,' or something like that, and I said, 'Where else would it be?' and she said it hadn't been there earlier. That's all it was."

"Could the bike have been moved along at all?"

"I suppose so."

"Did you move it?"

Tony swallowed. "I didn't go into the lean-to at all on Sunday afternoon."

Angela looked across at Gary's notebook and watched him write down the details of the conversation. She gave an infinitesimal nod and turned back to Tony. "Do you have any idea why we asked about the bike?"

Tony shrugged. "No, but you *did* ask about it, and Sandra seemed to think it had been moved. Then I thought about my ciggie routine and realized maybe it was significant."

"OK. Thank you very much for coming in to see us, Tony; you've been helpful."

"Sure, no problem. Is that it, then?"

"Yes, for now," said Angela, standing up. "We'll get someone to type up your statement so that you can sign it."

"Will it take long?" asked Tony, rising as well. "Only I've left the gym locked."

"Don't worry, one of our officers can bring it to you tomorrow for signing."

"Thanks. She couldn't have done it, you know," he said abruptly.

Angela raised her eyebrows. "She?"

"Sandra. She's solid gold. She just wouldn't. It's not in her. Nor him, he's all right, just a lump of fitness, really. I mean, I know he's into guns but he hasn't got a malicious bone in his body – Darren, I mean."

Angela smiled at him. "Thanks, Tony. Let's hope you're right."

Back in the incident room, Angela stood over Gary's shoulder as he typed in the latest information. "It seems as though this bike was used in the murder, isn't it?" he remarked as he tapped the keys.

"It's looking like a contender. By the way, I haven't seen the forensic report on it yet."

"Oh, you're right. I'll get on to it."

"My impression is that Tony didn't notice the bike at all on Sunday and would never have picked up on this if Sandra hadn't said, 'Oh look, there it is.' On the other hand, I could be wrong. We have to put Tony in the frame with the others."

Gary stopped typing and looked a question at her.

"Think about it, Gaz. If the reception stood empty for about half an hour, give or take, then nobody was there to clock Tony. We've only got his word for it that he was chilling out in the little room behind the counter."

"You're right. Say the perp did use the bike to whip round to the flat and kill Kirsty. How much time do you reckon that needed?"

"No much. It would take little more than two minutes to cycle from the gym to the house. Kirsty lets him in."

"Or her."

"No – if it was Sandra she can let herself in."

"It could have been another woman."

"Yes, of course. But, whoever, I get the impression they wasted no time on pleasantries. The attack came from behind, so it took her by surprise. It would have all been over in a matter of moments."

"Easily, I'd think. If this is how it happened, Kirsty could have been dead within ten minutes of the murderer cycling away from the gym."

"Then the bike has to be returned to the gym and put back

into the lean-to. This is where he or she took a big risk. They couldn't know they wouldn't be seen wheeling the bike back, through the reception." Angela sat down. "Hang on, let's think about this," she said. "At the start of the enterprise, Matey comes into an empty reception and goes into the lean-to."

"Does he/she come in from the street or from further into the gym?"

"Either. Let's say 'he'. He wheels the bike out through the lean-to front door. Ah!" Angela's eyes lit up and she raised a finger in the air.

"Oh yeah!" said, Gary, picking up the thought. "He leaves the lean-to door on the latch."

"Absolutely," said Angela, remembering the sign by the lean-to front door asking patrons to make sure they shut it behind them if leaving that way. "When he comes back, he doesn't have to come into the main reception at all."

"And the timing fits in with the estimated time of death."

"Yes. He still took a chance, but a much smaller one than we originally thought. And, of course, the perp knew there'd be a bike."

"Or a strong possibility of one being there."

"That's right. So – who've we got in the frame?"

"Tony, as you've pointed out, Darren and Sandra – and I suppose, other members of the gym."

"Yes, we'll need to obtain a full list of the membership and find out exactly who came in to the club on Sunday afternoon. That'll be a job for our D.C.s, I think. We can't rule out the possibility of a house-to-house in the vicinity of the gym, although the question they will have to ask is a bit of a no-brainer."

Gary grinned. "Did you see an athletic-looking person wearing gym clothes cycling away from here on Sunday afternoon?"

"Duh!" said Angela, putting a finger to her lips.

Chapter Sixteen

Immediately after lunch, Leanne appeared in the doorway of Angela's office. "Hi," said Angela, looking up at her. "How are you getting on?"

"I've just been talking to the director at that company – Massingham Models – guv."

"Oh, that's good. What have you found out?"

"It's run by a Mrs Massingham, She phoned in response to my voicemail message."

"Oh right; and what did Mrs Massingham have to say for herself?"

"Nothing yet, guv. She sounded a bit bewildered when I said it was to do with one of our investigations."

"Bewildered, eh? Did you tell her we'd like to pay a visit?"

"Yeah, but she wants to come here. She said it would be more convenient. Shall I arrange a time with her?"

Surprised that the woman thought the effort of a journey more convenient than receiving a home visit, but glad of the time it saved, Angela looked at her watch. "OK, let's say three. Thanks, Leanne."

"Guv." Leanne left to make the phone call.

Mrs Massingham, in her mid to late sixties, from her beautifully cut and styled hair through the flawlessly applied make-up to her expensive, elegant suit, looked every inch a successful company director. She arrived a few minutes before three. Angela remembered Leanne's use of the word "bewildered", and set about putting Mrs Massingham at her ease. "I expect you're wondering why we wanted to see you," she said, as she sat down at the table between them.

"I'm completely intrigued," replied Mrs Massingham. She raised an enquiring eyebrow in Gary's direction as he sat beside Angela and opened his notebook. "Am I being interviewed, er… er… officer?"

"I'm Detective Inspector Angela Costello, and this is Detective Constable Gary Houseman. Don't be alarmed, Mrs Massingham, it's just that the name of your company has appeared in the course of one of our investigations, and we're hoping you might be able to help us."

"'Helping the police with their enquiries'," quoted Mrs Massingham. "When I hear that on the news, I always wonder if it's a euphemism for the police grilling a suspect."

Angela smiled. "Not at all. We'd better take some details first. You're Mrs D. M. Massingham?"

"Dorothea Millicent, if you want the full name. I suppose you want my address as well?"

"Thank you, yes," said Gary, noting all the information as she dictated it in her well-modulated, cultured voice.

"Are you familiar," said Angela, once Gary finished writing, "with the name Kirsty Manners?"

Mrs Massingham's brow furrowed as she considered the question. "Yes… I… I'm sure I've heard that name recently. I just can't think in what connection."

"Kirsty was trying to break into modelling. She was killed on Sunday afternoon at her flat in Roehampton."

"Ah yes! That's it. I remember reading about it in the papers. Poor thing."

"Yes, she was. Did she have any connection with your company?"

Mrs Massingham's expertly arched eyebrows went up towards her hairline. "With Massinghams? Well, I suppose she may have approached us at some time. It's conceivable we could even have her photo on our system – but I have never put her forward for any work. I would remember that."

"A document relating to Massingham's was found among her personal effects."

"How extraordinary!"

"Could she have applied to your company for a job other than modelling, perhaps?"

Dorothea Massingham gave a gentle laugh. "We're a very small enterprise, two men and a dog, if you see what I mean."

"Two men and a dog," repeated Angela, considering the comment. "I believe the named shareholder is a J. W. Massingham?"

"My husband, Inspector. As someone several years older than I, having already retired, the role of company director no longer appealed to him. When I started the agency, he preferred to take on a supporting role."

Angela smiled at Mrs Massingham, wondering why she'd launched herself into an explanation about her husband's status in the company. She decided it must be a generational thing, and to respond in kind. "That's good," she said. "Some men would have had a problem with it, wouldn't they? Especially men of a particular, er… "

"Age group? I dare say you're right. Not Jeremy, though."

"Then is there any possibility Jeremy would know the name Kirsty Manners?"

"Not a chance, Inspector," Mrs Massingham responded swiftly and decisively. "If this young woman – or indeed any young woman – applied for a position with Massinghams, it would be I who dealt with it. We have not been advertising any secretarial positions. I assume you have in mind that Kirsty Manners may have applied for an office job?"

"Yes, that or… well, anything, really. I was just following a trail." *Which unfortunately seems to have come to a dead end,* thought Angela. "Right. Well, I can't go much further with this, then; but if you come across the name Kirsty Manners in any of your business papers, or any connection comes to your attention, I'd be grateful if you'd get in touch. Let me give you my card," finished Angela, fishing in her handbag.

"Certainly, Inspector. If I can help in any way – "

"Ah yes! There is one thing. May I have a copy of your letterheaded notepaper?"

"Letterheaded...? Yes, of course. I'll fax you a page."

"Would you also drop a hard copy in the post for us, please?"

The sculpted eyebrows rose once more, and a good-natured smile appeared on Mrs Massingham's face. "I don't see what – still, mine not to reason why. I'll attend to it immediately on my return."

"Thank you very much. You've been most helpful." Angela went to the door, holding it open for her to go through first.

Mrs Massingham gave a small laugh as she allowed herself to be escorted along the corridor. "I'll take your word for that, Inspector," she said, as she disappeared through the front entrance.

"Hmm..." Angela closed the door slowly behind her.

"Angie?" said Gary.

"I dunno, Gaz. Did you get a funny feeling about that woman?"

Gary shrugged. "I could tell she was nervous. I thought she was uncomfortable about being in a police station."

"So why volunteer to come in? We could have gone to see her. Never mind. Perhaps I'm being overly sensitive. Come on – let's see what the others have been up to."

Angela and Gary got back to the incident room just seconds after Rick and Jim.

"Hi, guys," she said. "Any luck with Mrs Marchant?"

"Not as regards the bloke on the bike," replied Jim.

"Person on the bike," corrected Rick.

"Yeah, person; well, her story hasn't changed from what she told the house-to-house lot. Person and bike as per description turns up a little before three, possibly goes into house where Kirsty lives, is gone by three. And she didn't really have any relationship with Kirsty. She think she nodded 'good morning' to her once in the newsagents, that's all."

"I don't think it's going to get any better than that, Angie," said Rick.

"No, I suspect you're right. And we've only got the next-door neighbour's account of this woman who was seen earlier – " Angela stopped abruptly and everybody looked at her. "No, we haven't," she said.

Several pairs of bewildered eyes turned towards her, which made her laugh. "You should see your faces."

"Has a witness slipped off the radar, guv?" asked Derek.

"Nearly, I think." She looked at Leanne. "Leanne, remember telling me the house-to-house had thrown up information about someone on a bike, and a woman in a dark suit?"

"Yes, guv."

"And afterwards Jim called and told me Ronald Sanders was in reception, asking why nobody had been to see him yet and asking to speak to – " Angela spread out her hands.

Her prompting was rewarded with a small chorus of " – the officer in charge", followed by a communal: "Of course!"

"Good-oh; that means someone from the house-to-house had already mentioned this woman. Check it out, will you?" she said to Jim and Rick. "Whoever it is might have got a better look than Sanders did. The timing is a bit earlier than the murder, but we don't know the circumstances. She could still be the murderer."

"Or in on it with the perp, maybe," suggested Jim.

"Possibly," agreed Angela.

"We'll get onto that," said Rick. "How did things go with Massingham Models?"

"I've now spoken to the director, a Mrs Dorothea Millicent Massingham. She didn't know Kirsty, apart from reading about the murder in the papers, and can't think why we've found a connection."

"Did you tell her?"

"Oh no. This trail needs a bit more work on it yet. Hello," she said, breaking off as she saw Gary coming across the room towards her with a paper in his hand. "What's that?"

Gary handed it to her. "It's the report on the bike from forensics. They found a clear thumbprint and some fingerprints on the crossbar of the bike." He mimed the action of picking up a bike by its crossbar to a chorus of "Aaaaaaaaaaaaaaah" from everybody in the room.

"Our hypothesis is looking more and more likely, isn't it?" suggested Angela. "If I wanted to take a bike quietly, I think I'd be inclined to pick it up and carry it rather than wheeling it away, wouldn't you?"

"Oh yeah," agreed Gary. "Unfortunately, the print isn't known to us."

"Don't be downhearted. It might become known."

"Needles and haystacks come to mind," said Rick.

"You might be right," said Angela. "Never mind, Gary, it's a hoop we have to jump through; feed the information into the computer and that's another box ticked. I'm presuming they found loads of Darren's prints as well?"

"Not as many as you might think. They reckon he wiped the bike down on a regular basis, which is why, they think, this one is so clear."

"Hmm. I'm not surprised. He looks the sort of bloke who'd take really good care of his stuff. The other thing to do is make sure we've got Tony Chambers and Sandra Hodges's prints."

"Yeah," said Gary. "I'll get on to it."

Dorothea Massingham hurried up the garden path and entered her house. She'd managed to maintain her sangfroid throughout the interview with D.I. Costello, but anybody seeing her at this moment would have recognized her agitation. Her natural pallor had gone, replaced by a bright red spot on each cheekbone, completely negating the effect of the blusher she'd put on before setting out. She had been thinking she'd make herself a cup of tea, but as she closed the door behind her she knew she would opt for a stiff drink instead.

But she was nothing if not efficient. She went into the office and faxed a copy of Massingham Models letterheaded notepaper to the number on Angela's card. Then she took the same sheet, put it between two pieces of cardboard and slipped the whole thing into an envelope. It would go into the postbox when she went out later. She'd been planning a quiet evening in, but that would have to change now.

She poured herself a gin and tonic and sat down, sipping it slowly. After a few moments, feeling much calmer, she picked up the telephone and dialled a number.

When the phone was picked up at the other end she spoke before the person could even say "hello". "I've just come back from a most interesting chat with a Detective Inspector Costello."

She heard an intake of breath at the other end of the line, but didn't wait for any speech. "She seems a nice woman. I'd probably take to her if the circumstances were different... astute, gets to the point, doesn't miss much."

There was silence at the other end. She raised her eyebrows. "However, it looks like *I* might have been missing something; what do you think?"

After a few seconds there was a mumbled response.

"Indeed we *will* have to talk," she said, "and very soon. I shall see you later." Dorothea put the receiver down without even saying goodbye.

Chapter Seventeen

"You're being niggled at; I can tell," said Patrick as he laid the table that evening. Angela had managed to get home in time to do the cooking and she now came into the dining room with the sugar bowl in her hand.

"What?" she asked, putting the bowl on the table.

"Well, for a start," replied Patrick, picking it up again immediately. "Do you intend for us to sprinkle this on our steaks?"

Angela blinked. "Oh. I'm just not with it." She took the bowl and disappeared into the kitchen, returning a few moments later with a tray bearing two steak and salad meals and the salt and pepper pots.

"By George, she's got it," said Patrick, sitting down. "It looks lovely but the state you're in, I'm a bit hesitant about taking the first bite."

Angela put down the fork she had just picked up, and looked questioningly at Patrick. "Did you say something, darling?"

He grinned. "Yes."

Angela sat up straighter, picked up her fork again and started on her meal. "I'm sorry, Paddy. It's just that something is niggling at me."

"No! Really?" he said in mock disbelief. "What is it?"

"Well, I interviewed a woman today and it's been on my mind ever since."

"Oh?"

"Yes. When you were in the police, did you ever find yourself being led in interviews?"

"Rather than doing the leading, you mean? I had plenty of suspects who would lead the interview if I gave them the chance, and tell me only what they wanted me to hear, but that comes with the territory. It could even be useful to – er – get an angle on where he or she didn't want me to go. You can learn quite a bit that way."

"That's exactly it! I've had that before in an interview and I play it by ear, depending on the circumstances. But I was puzzled by this woman today."

"Can you put your finger on what it was?"

"No. If I could answer that, I don't think I'd feel so niggled at. It's not as if this woman is a suspect. She's only got a marginal connection to the case – from the looks of things."

"But you're left with this impression."

"Yes, there was some tension in her that didn't sit with the whole interview."

"If she's got something to hide, she should have made more of an effort to relax. She's a blob on your radar now, isn't she?"

"Yes, of course she is. That's it; I'll do a bit of digging tomorrow. More than likely I'll find I can cross her off my list." Angela's face cleared and she laughed. "Right, sorted, I can enjoy my dinner now."

"That's a relief; I was beginning to wonder what I might end up with for dessert." They heard the front door open as Madeleine came home. "In the dining room!" Patrick called out.

"Evening, peeps," she said, appearing in the doorway.

"Hi, Mads," replied Angela. "Your steak's in the oven. I've only just served so there's no need to reheat."

"Thanks, Angie," said Madeleine. She joined them after a few moments with her plate in her hands, and sat down at the table. "Look what I've done," she said, holding out her arm. There was a long tear in the sleeve of her blouse. "I'm really cross about it. I put it on for an interview this afternoon, but I particularly wanted to wear it tonight. I think I ripped it on a door handle. Fortunately I'd already had the interview."

"How did it go?" asked Patrick.

"I felt it went pretty well, but you know what it's like; got to play the waiting game now."

"Indeed. Shame about the blouse, though, it's a very smart one," he said.

"Yes, elegant is the word I would use. I hope I can get it invisibly mended," replied Madeleine.

"What are you doing tonight?" asked Angela

"Gary and I are going out for a drink."

"What, my Gary?"

Madeleine laughed. "He's not yours, but I know what you mean. Yeah, that's the one."

"He's kept that very quiet! Not that I asked him what his plans were for this evening."

"I think he tries to keep home issues out of the workplace."

"Very wise," said Patrick.

"Bit of a bummer about your blouse, though," said Angela. "I tell you what – I've got a similar one. You can borrow that if you want."

"Oh yes, I know the one you mean. If anything it's a slightly better quality than this. Thanks, Angie. I'll just get it out ready," she said, heading for the passageway.

"There, that's sorted," said Patrick with a smile. "Angie... Angie... darling?"

Angela jumped. "What! Sorry, Paddy."

"Oh, no..."

"Sorry, Pads. It's not the same thing, though. Something Maddie's just said put an idea into my head."

"An idea about what?"

"That's just it, I don't know 'cause it flew straight out again."

"It'll come back when it's ready. Make a little note in your notebook and forget about it. I don't want you niggled all evening." He raised an eyebrow. "Nibbled maybe."

Angela smiled and winked at him as Madeleine came back into the room.

"OK, folks, what have we got?" asked Angela the following morning as she stood in front of the team.

"We've got a bit more on this woman in a dark suit, but not much, Angie," said Jim.

"Spill the beans."

"Well, we went to this other neighbour, a bit further up on the other side of the road. She saw the woman outside the victim's house and gave virtually the same description as Ronald Sanders."

"What did this neighbour say?"

"She says the woman went up to the front door and rang the bell. She presumes the woman went into the house but didn't actually see her do so."

Angela thought for a moment about the account from Ronald Sanders and this new information. "Oh, it's a blooming nuisance, this! We've got two people seen at the house, they quite likely gained access, but nobody saw either of them leave. Did this other neighbour give the same time frame as Sanders?"

"Yeah," said Jim. "About twenty to two, she said."

"Hmm, that tallies; and the person on the bike is later – much closer to three – the time of the murder."

"They could still be connected though, couldn't they?" said Derek.

"Absolutely; well, keep digging everybody," said Angela. "Rick and Jim, take Tony Chambers's statement to the gym and get him to sign it. I know it wouldn't normally be your job, but I want you to push a bit about Sunday afternoon. I don't think he's a man with an easy conscience and you might come up with something." She turned to Derek. "Did a fax come in from Massingham's yesterday after I'd left?"

"Got it here," he replied. "The page we took from Kirsty's computer is with it."

"Ah great, thanks, Derek." Angela took the two sheets of A4 paper. Superficially they looked very similar but a second glance showed that the font wasn't quite the same. And of course, Kirsty had added her name to the one on her own computer. Leanne, passing by at that moment, stopped and looked.

"No prizes for spotting how many differences there are between them," said Angela.

Leanne laughed.

"The interesting thing is how close Kirsty's version is to the real thing. She'd obviously had either possession of, or a very good look at, the real letterheaded notepaper at some point."

"It's not exactly top secret, though, is it, guv?"

"No, that's true, but we haven't come across any other connection between Kirsty and Massingham's. She might have applied to them for work once, Dorothea Massingham said she wasn't on their books as such, but her photograph might be on their system."

"That's another box that needs a tick, then."

"Yep," said Angela and moved towards the door. On her way back to her office she ambled past where Gary was sitting. "Enjoy your date last night, Gaz?"

He looked up at her and gave a sheepish grin. "I didn't say anything because – "

Angela waved away his words. "Gary, you don't have to consult me about your social life. Did it go OK?"

Gary relaxed. "Yeah, it was good. We only had a drink and walked along by the river, but – what?"

Angela was frowning. "Sorry, Gaz. It's just that talking about last night has reminded me of something that was said at dinner. It struck me at the time, but I can't think why – and the memory is still eluding me."

"Oh, it drives me crazy when that happens! Never mind. If you don't think about it, it'll probably come back to you."

"For sure. In any case, something needs looking into that was nibbling away at me last night too."

"Nibbling?"

"Niggling; I mean niggling."

Angela smiled at him and continued on her way leaving Gary looking after her, rather puzzled. She didn't turn back; she knew she was blushing and didn't want him to see it.

She sat staring at her console for a long while. She closed her eyes and let her mind wander back over the interview the previous afternoon. At this stage she didn't want to look through Gary's notebook. She had good recall and within a couple of moments she could visualize Dorothea Massingham seated opposite her in the room downstairs. It was a whole package with that lady. She presented exquisitely to give a particular image – elegant, intelligent, sophisticated; then why the jarring note? Angela felt certain that something in the whole scene didn't sit right. She saw herself asking Mrs Massingham if her husband, Jeremy, would have known Kirsty, and suddenly she knew what she was looking for. "Not a chance, Inspector," Mrs Massingham said. She'd said it so quickly – too quickly. Angela had the definite sense she'd been headed off at the pass: "We're not going down that road" was the message.

That led Angela on to wondering why Mrs Massingham had been so firm in asserting it was more convenient for her to come to the station rather than have the police visit her in her home. Generally speaking, people coming to police premises was feasible enough. Already, Ronald Sanders, Kirsty's neighbour, and Tony Chambers of the gym had turned up to volunteer information. But why should it be more convenient than a home visit?

By now Angela definitely smelled a rat. Was Mrs Massingham trying to keep a distance between the police and her husband? Given Kirsty's track record it could be that Jeremy Massingham knew her not only socially or professionally but in the biblical sense, which could explain Dorothea's reluctance to speak of her.

Chapter Eighteen

Leanne was just putting the phone down when Angela appeared by her desk.

"How are you getting on?" she asked.

Leanne beamed up at her. "I managed to find out one thing. The official photographer at the *Passionista* party was a chap called Leon… er…" Leanne flicked back a page or two in her notebook. "Leon Rushton. He's got his own studio and website and it looks like he does a lot of fashion photography."

"Promising; will you set me up with a meeting?"

Tony Chambers was just being called away to help someone with their session when Rick and Jim arrived at the Tone-Up Gym. They assured him they were happy to wait, and each accepted a cup of coffee.

They took advantage of the opportunity to familiarize themselves with the layout as they'd heard it described at the briefings. They sat where Sandra had sat when she remarked on Darren's bicycle, and inspected the lean-to and realized how easy it would have been for someone to go into it, take Darren's bike, leave the front door on the latch, and replace it through the same door, all without being seen from the reception.

"It would have taken a bit of nerve," opined Rick, sitting down with his coffee, "but I think our bloke's got that, hasn't he?"

"I reckon so," agreed Jim, strolling around the little reception area, peering at posters and looking at the noticeboard. "He cycled up to Kirsty's gate in broad daylight and left the bike in the front garden while he did the deed."

"Allegedly," cautioned Rick.

"Yeah, OK." Jim joined his colleague at the table. "The thing that's always struck me is the risk he took. The bike could have been stolen while he was inside with Kirsty. I mean, it's a valuable bike."

"Probably wasn't too bothered."

"He was bothered enough to take it back to the gym. That must have been part of the plan."

"True; we don't know that he didn't put a lock on it, though."

"Maybe; in any case, he had to take a bit of a risk at some point. If we're assuming the cyclist is the guilty one then it looks like he wanted to put Darren in the frame."

"Could still turn out to be Darren."

"OK, but if it was Darren he wouldn't come on his own bike, would he? That would be stupid. I mean, the neighbours in Kirsty's street didn't strike me as being that much concerned with each other, but the ones that take any notice were used to seeing Darren's bike there."

"Yeah, so someone else used his bike to point the finger at him."

"I reckon so; unless of course, it's a double-bluff."

"Could be, but if it wasn't him it's got to be someone who knew where he stored his bike at the gym, and how easy it could be to get at it if you just knew the system."

"So we're looking for someone who knew the system here."

They both looked up as Sandra Hodges entered through the front door, just as Tony returned from one of the inner rooms.

"Hello," began Sandra, her brow creasing into a frown. "Weren't you with the police at my flat last Sunday?"

"That's us," confirmed Rick, standing up and flicking open his police ID. "I'm Detective Sergeant Rick Driver and this is D.S. Jim Wainwright."

Jim nodded. "Is this where you work?" he asked Sandra. Even as he said it, he remembered Angela reporting that she and Gary had interviewed Sandra Hodges at some solicitor's place in Putney.

"No, I'm not working today. I had a casting this morning. For a modelling job," she added as she noticed a puzzled look on Jim's face. "I've just come here to hang out." Her eyes flicked across at Tony behind Rick and Jim and a small smile appeared fleetingly on her face.

"They want to ask some more questions about Kirsty," said Tony.

Sandra's expression changed to one of peevishness. "OK, I'll go and do some weights or something," she said, her voice tight.

"Actually, it would be helpful if you stay," said Rick. "We would have tried to see you as well later."

Sandra couldn't hide her sense of satisfaction. Fully mollified, she sat down. "Sure," she said, with an attempt at nonchalance.

Rick and Jim took out their notebooks.

"We're trying to fill out our picture of Kirsty a bit more," began Rick. "You know, her likes and dislikes, what sort of person she was."

"For instance," Jim went on, "we've heard about how she had plans to 'be somebody'. Do you know if this was just a pipe dream or did she have something specific in mind?"

"D'you know…" began Sandra, then stopped and thought for a moment before starting again. "OK, if you'd asked me that question when she moved in with me, I'd have said she relied on her looks and just hoped to sleep her way to a fortune, if you know what I mean?"

Both the detectives nodded. "And now?" asked Jim.

"She'd started to wake up, I'd say. She was already going out with Daz when she moved in, but there were a couple of blokes in the background – Kirsty was that kind of woman.

She seemed to need the reassurance of knowing that she could pull, right?"

"I get you," said Jim.

"She was quite open about her love life at first, but as time went on she got more cagey. The other men disappeared off the scene, I think."

"But she still didn't limit herself to Darren?"

"Oh, no way! That was when I got the impression she'd started dating some kind of high-flyer."

"What made you think that?"

"Partly because she wasn't so open, I suppose. But she was obviously going out somewhere and I didn't think it was with Daz."

"She always went for blokes with money," said Tony.

"Yes, Tone's right," agreed Sandra. "Once she started with this new bloke, though – the one I'm saying is a high-flyer – she seemed to begin to realize it isn't just about money. You know, like, in the top echelons of society, you can be poor and still be one of them. She started to see you needed something money can't buy."

"Class," supplied Tony.

"That's it," agreed Sandra. "I don't think she was ever going to cut the mustard, but she wouldn't have accepted that. I think, going out with this *whoever-he-was* gave her ideas. The other blokes seemed to float off into the ether and Darren, as far as I could tell, became the man on the back-burner. I never said as much to him because I didn't want to upset him, but I think he had a pretty good idea."

"So," said Rick. "You think she was using this new man to climb up the social ladder."

"I think so. Because she'd twigged that for some men she'd need more than good looks."

"How did you make that out?" asked Jim.

"I noticed that she was – well, not exactly nervous but anxious to please. No, not that; anxious to get something right; that was it."

"Well, that's normal when you're dating someone, isn't it?" asked Jim.

"This is Kirsty we're talking about," Sandra reminded him. "She never had to try too hard; blokes flocked to her like bees round a honeypot."

"Can you give us an example of this trying 'to get something right'?" asked Rick.

"Well, for instance, she got all dressed up to the nines one night – let me see, this would have been a couple of months ago. She came into the kitchen to ask me if I thought her outfit was right for a posh restaurant. In fact she looked a bit tarty, and I told her so; I mean, that's what friends are for. I said if it was a really classy restaurant she'd do better to look a bit more... erm... demure."

"Demure?"

"Yes. I don't think she entirely got the point, but she changed into something else; and, to be honest, she looked a lot nicer. Anyway, I'd already gone to bed when she came home, so I didn't ask her how it went until we both got in from work the evening after. She surprised me by saying she'd realized I was right. The clothes she'd changed into were a lot more suitable and... how did she put it? Oh yeah. 'The outfit was commented on favourably.' That was it."

"Anything else?" asked Jim.

"Actually," said Tony, "I noticed her attempts to change her image as well."

The policemen's eyes turned towards him. "In what way?" asked Rick.

"Well, she wasn't an out-and-out Cockney. She spoke what they call Estuary English; but I noticed she tried to alter her accent a bit here and there, and she definitely began making an effort not to drop her 'H's. She used to join me sometimes in my little cubbyhole back there for a crafty fag. She didn't want Darren to know she smoked, because she didn't want him going on at her about it. Darren's into health in a big way."

"So what did you talk about on these occasions?" asked Jim.

"That's where she surprised me most of all. At first she chatted on about other people who came here, and keeping fit, but then it changed. She started asking me about the business side of running a gym. Once she grasped that if the gym is registered as a company – which it is – then I have to be on the books at Companies House as much as a big conglomerate or a bank, well, then it was all about that. She wanted to know every detail about how you got registered and what's involved – all that sort of thing."

"Did she say why she was interested?"

"I asked her that. I said, 'What? Are you thinking of going into business, then?'"

"And what did she say to that?"

"She didn't really give me an answer. She just said you never know what might happen, and she just wanted to find out how it all works."

"And that was it?" asked Jim. "Nothing more along those lines?"

"No; she came back to the subject a few times but it was only to go over the same ground, make sure she'd understood it right."

"OK," said Rick, consulting his notes. "And we've heard somewhere along the line that she might have been frightened of Darren."

The spontaneous reactions of both Tony and Sandra gave lie to this. Their mouths dropped open and they started forward in their seats.

"What?" exclaimed Sandra, disbelief etched into every line of her face.

"It's just something that someone put forward," replied Rick.

"No way!" asserted Sandra. "She could twist Darren round her little finger."

"He's a powerfully built bloke, though." Jim was determined to pursue it to the bitter end. He and Rick hadn't actually met Darren, and were working solely from Angela and Gary's description, but Sandra and Tony didn't know that. "I would think twice about getting on the wrong side of him," he continued.

Tony shook his head with a smile. "Daz is a gentle giant," he said. "Wouldn't hurt a fly. And he was absolutely besotted with Kir – " He broke off and smiled a little sheepishly at Sandra.

"It's all right," said Sandra returning his smile. She came round to stand behind him and rested her hand on his shoulder. "It doesn't matter any more."

Tony half-turned to look up at her, and grasped her hand. They remained in that position and looked at the two policemen. "That's right, it doesn't matter any more," said Tony.

"In any case," continued Sandra. "Darren was here all Sunday afternoon, but you lot already know that."

"Don't forget what I said about when I was having my ciggie break, Sandra," said Tony.

"Oh yeah, of course." She turned to Rick and Jim. "I'd be very surprised if it was Darren," she said. "But, like… I assume he was here all the afternoon because he normally is. That's his routine."

"But you weren't watching him the whole time."

"Well, no. Obviously he went to the loo now and again, and got himself a drink. But that would have been all. And Tony's right, he's obsessed with Kirsty. I thought we were getting it together, but I can see now that I was fooling myself. It just wasn't going to happen. Not with her around."

Jim raised his eyebrows as he noted this. Looking at him, Sandra realized how it might sound.

"I mean," she said, a hurried, nervous tone in her voice, "I was already beginning to realize that, and accept it. I was OK with it; not a problem."

Rick caught Tony flashing Sandra a look which he interpreted as, "Don't protest too much." Quickly glancing at Sandra he managed to catch a glimpse of an answering nod.

She took a breath. "It's like Tony said," she continued in a level voice. "Daz is a gentle giant, really. He's probably a borderline stalker but he wouldn't harm her."

The two policemen nodded, closing their notebooks to indicate they'd had all the answers they needed for the moment. They thanked the pair for their time. As they left the premises, Rick glanced back and saw Sandra sitting down very close to Tony. The way she leaned in to him and his arm snaked around her neck left no room for doubt about their relationship.

"That was a bit useful," said Jim as they reached their car.

"Too right," agreed, Rick. "I wonder how they'll take it if we come back and ask Tony where Sandra was or Sandra where Tony was."

"That's it," said Jim. "You can include Darren and say any one of them could have disappeared for fifteen minutes or so, and none of the others would have been any the wiser."

Ian had learned caution. He parked as close to his front door as he could, and checked the street before getting out of the car. He continued to look all around as he crossed the pavement, making sure he had the key ready in his hand to slip straight into the lock. Once inside his flat, the chain went on and he breathed a sigh of relief. A few days had passed since the attack but he wouldn't forget it in a hurry. He went over to the window overlooking the street in front of the building His stomach knotted itself into a tight ball. Yes, there was someone out there. He couldn't see the person standing near the lamp post, but their elongated shadow was thrown along the pavement. This made the second night he'd been aware of the presence outside.

After mixing himself a salad and putting a ready-meal into the microwave, he checked again. He saw a tall shape wheel a bicycle from behind a nearby tree and ride off.

He cycled home, aware of the frustration building up inside him. He wasn't sure how much more of this he could take. He was going to have to do something soon or he'd burst. But he realized now the man's own area wasn't the right place. He needed somewhere familiar, a place he could act with confidence. It was a big job he was planning; he had to be in control throughout.

Chapter Nineteen

Father Martin turned left out of the presbytery. It was now Friday morning, a fine, bright day and he had just enough time for what would be his third investigative walk before an appointment with an engaged couple to discuss their wedding plans. His two previous walks didn't lead him to the right location, as far as he could be aware, but hadn't dimmed his hope of success. People had to come out from their houses sometime. You just never knew. He had his rosary with him today, and he set off along the road fingering the beads in the pocket of his jogging bottoms.

He rounded a corner and stopped dead in his tracks.

Immediately he berated himself and began to walk again, knowing he had to walk past showing no interest, and he might very well be wrong. He moved forward at the same steady pace, telling himself to stay calm even though his pulse raced.

Two men stood outside a house about halfway along the street. They were very big, with close-cropped hair. Something about the stance of one of them reminded Martin of the shape he'd seen briefly through the glass panel in the confessional door. He drew level with them. He heard their conversation, in some unknown language. He passed on, not hurrying or looking back.

When he reached the end of the street he went through a pantomime of not being quite able to decide which way to go next, before turning round. His little act had been unnecessary; the men had now disappeared. He gazed along the other side of the street. *Now, doesn't God just go before me,* he thought. *Katy D lives along here.* He crossed the road and approached a house nearly opposite to where he'd seen the men, and rang the bell.

Katherine Devine, bespectacled, middle-aged and a stalwart member of the charismatic prayer group, opened the door and beamed when she saw who was standing on her front step.

"Martin!" she exclaimed delightedly. "This is a nice surprise. Come in." She turned and led the way into her front room. As he followed her in he saw what a good view she had of the houses over the road. "Take a seat, Father M," she said. "What can I do for you?"

Martin sat down. "Well, this might sound very odd, Kate," he replied, "and believe me I'm not being a nosy parker, but I'm wondering about the people who live in the house nearly opposite you." He pointed. "The one with the blue door."

A sudden silence settled in the room. Katherine looked at Martin with an expression on her face that made him think his quest hadn't been in vain after all. "You know," she said after a moment, "once or twice I've wondered about that house myself."

"Ah," he said. "In that case, I've got a bit of a story to tell you."

Leon Rushton was up to his neck with preparations for a fashion shoot when Angela and Gary arrived to interview him. He greeted them at the door of the Whitechapel studio to which they'd been directed. "Hi. You the cops?" he asked. Angela introduced herself and Gary. "Come through," he said, turning and leading the way into the studio proper. He had an egg salad sandwich in his left hand, and picked up a polystyrene cup of coffee from the reception desk with the other as he went. About £3,000-worth of long-lensed camera was slung over his right shoulder. He was a tall, lanky man with a pleasant, smiley face. "I hope you don't mind if I get on while you're talking to me," he said.

"Not at all," replied Angela. "Thanks for sparing us the time."

"Well, I suppose I'm not, strictly speaking," he grinned. "But deadlines are necessary evils and we're already late on this one." He pointed to a couple of chairs. "Park yourselves there for a minute, while I see where we've got to."

Angela and Gary found themselves sitting to one side of two large arc lamps mounted on stands and pointing to a blank, white space. Several racks of clothing in plastic covers lined the opposite side of the space, and in one of the remaining corners, rather huddled together, five girls sat while a small team of hair and make-up artists got them ready.

"Cor," said Gary. "They're all so lovely! You can see what Kirsty was up against, can't you?"

"And this lot have the necessary height," agreed Angela.

"Yeah, they must all be nudging six foot," agreed Gary, casting an admiring glance at several pairs of long, smooth legs.

Just at that moment, Leon came back to their side of the room with a fold-up chair in his hands. He pulled it into shape and sat down. "OK, how may I help you?"

Angela took out some photocopies of the snaps found in Kirsty's room, and handed them to him. "The originals of these are part of an investigation we're dealing with at the moment."

Leon took them and immediately identified the event. "Oh yes, that was the *Passionista* bash; quite a while ago now, I think. Do you need me to check my diary?"

"Yes, please. We'll make sure we take all the details we can before we go, but do you recognize the woman in those pictures?"

Leon held his hands out in an apologetic gesture. "Really sorry – in my job…" he cast a hand back to indicate the women on the other side of the room. "It's just that I photograph so many; you can imagine how it is – oh, but hang on. Is this the woman who turned up on the arm of Nigel Summers?"

"It's possible," said Gary.

"I remember him being a bit peeved. Arm candy's supposed to stay on your arm, isn't it? But she struck out on her own a bit. I seem to remember seeing her in conversation with one or two of the other women there."

"Why would that annoy Nigel Summers?" asked Angela.

"Oh, it wouldn't have been that so much; I think she was found trying to get into a back room where she hadn't been invited. Some things in this business are a bit delicate, aren't they?"

Angela and Gary turned enquiring looks onto him and Leon gave them a disarming smile. "Me, I keep my head down and my eyes on the job. But let me give you an innocent example. Supposing you took your date to a showbusiness party and he or she went around asking the celebs for their autographs."

"I don't think that would be quite right," said Angela.

"Spot on; it isn't. You have to know how to behave in different situations and I don't think this girl did. In any case, I've run into Nigel a few times since and she wasn't with him. Oh wait! The police – asking about…?"

"Yes," said Angela. "She's now dead; murdered."

"Oh my, yes – I did hear about that. I'm sorry. I should think that's the last thing Ian King needs right now. He's having a tough enough time as it is at the moment."

"Oh, really?" asked Angela in her most inviting manner.

"It's no secret; he's had a couple of very bad years. The word is, he's lost his edge. We'll have to see what sort of reception he gets for this year's collection. But as for your enquiries, I don't think I can be much help to you." Leon's attention was distracted by a woman coming up to him. He turned towards her. "Sure thing, Bethany," he said. "I'm all ready, just waiting for the word. Are the two in the swimsuits sorted?" Bethany, with her back to Angela and Gary nodded, saying something they couldn't catch. "What?" exclaimed Leon, in an amused tone. "You're not serious? Stacey and Tr – ? Oh. OK." He yelled across the open space. "Right, girls! Stacey and Tracey – can we have you in the swimwear now, please?"

He turned back to the police officers as Bethany hurried away. "Sorry about this, time's money and all that."

"Not a problem," replied Angela. "We won't keep you any longer. I'm just wondering if it's possible to have any of the pictures you took at that party."

"Easy-peasy; you can have the lot. I produced a couple of sets and the magazine only wanted one. I can get them biked over to you later."

"That would be brilliant. Thank you," said Angela, taking a card out of her bag. Suddenly Bethany appeared at Leon's side again, muttering something in a worried whisper.

"Oh no!" said Leon. "Just what we need." He turned to Angela. "Minor crisis, I'm afraid. The swimwear is stuck in traffic in a taxi coming up from Wapping."

"Oh dear," commiserated Angela. "And time's money."

"Yeah," he said, and turned back to the assistant. "OK, Beth, darling, get them into the next looks. We'll do the swimwear later."

Bethany ran off again and Angela stood rooted to the spot. After a moment, she became aware that Leon was looking expectantly at her. "Er, hello?" he said.

She blinked. "Sorry." She gave him her card.

"Right," he said. "They'll be with you later today."

"What did you just say?" asked Angela.

A bewildered look appeared on Leon's face. "I said they'll be with you later today."

"No, before then."

"Er, the swimwear is stuck in traffic?"

"No – looks, you said – "

"Oh that. Yeah, I just told the girls to get into the next looks; we'll go back to the swimwear once it arrives. No biggie."

"I don't get this, 'looks'."

Leon grinned. "It's just trade jargon for the clothes, the

outfits, the designs, whatever. Here." He reached into a large holdall containing what looked like photographic equipment, and pulled out a pad. He flicked open the pages and Angela could see a different design on each one. This is an old one from last year, but it's what's known as a 'look book'."

"That's very, very enlightening," said Angela. "More than you could possibly know." She slung her bag across her shoulder. "Thanks for your help, Leon," she said, moving towards the door. "I look forward to getting the *Passionista* prints."

They were on the pavement before Gary spoke. His voice was excited. "Looks! So that woman in the confessional – "

"Absolutely, Gaz; she wasn't in the least bit worried about being disfigured. She's a dress designer. She must have come over here with a portfolio of 'looks' hoping to break into the industry."

"They must be good."

"Quite. Somebody thought they were worth stealing."

Chapter Twenty

Angela phoned the office as Gary started the car and pulled away from the kerb. Derek answered. "I want you to add a new note to the board," she explained. "It might be window dressing, but possibly not." She quickly told him what they'd learned from Leon Rushton.

"Got it, guv. Where are you off to now?"

"We're on our way back by a circuitous route. We're going to try to catch Nigel Summers in Chelsea, then his business partner in Wandsworth. I just want to take the questions a bit further – see if I can rattle their cages a bit."

"OK, guv. See you when you get back."

Angela finished the call. "Did you pick up on that other little matter of interest when we were with Leon Rushton, Gaz? No, turn here; the City'll be clogged up with traffic. Head for Tower Hill and go along Lower Thames Street. We can drive more or less all the way to Chelsea along the side of the river."

"OK," replied Gary, swinging the car round to the south. "Do you mean that comment he made about Ian King having lost his edge?"

"Yes. He said Ivano King has had two very bad years, yet Nigel Summers still operates from that very expensive place in the King's Road."

"Good point. What's more, the carpet looked very new to me and classy as well. And the place in Wandsworth was firing on all cylinders, wasn't it?" agreed Gary.

"Yes, it was; none of the sense of gloom you get when people are worried about their jobs."

"Could be toughing it out, keeping up appearances. I wouldn't be surprised if one or both of them have plenty of dosh."

"You could be right but the question still has to be asked. Or maybe it's the Financial Investigation Unit that'll be asking."

"Are we calling them in on this, then, Angie?"

"It's a possibility. If I put it to Stanway he'll want some concrete evidence."

"Ah, hence the cage-rattling."

"Exactly, Gazza."

Nigel Summers's expression seemed more guarded than at their previous interview with him. But any irritation or annoyance he may have felt at their unannounced visit was hidden by the time his receptionist showed them into his office after a short delay. He had only one computer, a desktop, in operation today.

"Sorry to bother you again, Mr Summers, but I'm afraid investigations throw up all sorts of questions in the most untidy manner."

"Not a problem, Inspector. How may I help you?"

"It's just that a clearer picture of Kirsty is emerging, and it seems she was developing quite a lively interest in how business works. Since you're the business side of Ivano King…" Angela's voice tailed off when she saw Nigel nodding at her with a resigned smile on his face.

"Yep, you've got it. It wasn't just business, though, Inspector. She was curious about all sorts of things, most of which were none of her business. To be honest, she was a snoop."

"Really?"

"Oh yes. I think she thought knowledge was power; well, it can be sometimes but not with Kirsty; I wouldn't expect her to be discreet about having inside information."

"She doesn't seem to have told anyone about having some of Ian's designs, though."

"Yes, Ian told me you found some of his looks on her laptop. He was mightily relieved. I would think she imagined having them gave her some kind of hold over Ian, which is what she wanted. And you're right. She doesn't seem to have done anything with them; we would have heard otherwise."

"What about other aspects of your business?"

"Which other aspects?"

"The normal business side of things; you're effectively a clothing company, so stock, orders, invoices, all that sort of thing."

"She would have picked up quite a lot of the normal day-to-day running from her work at the unit, that's true. You'd need to speak to Jenni to find out if she poked her nose in where it wasn't wanted."

"Could she have learned anything about hiring models from Jenni?" Angela couldn't swear to it, but she thought Nigel tensed for a second.

"The invoicing is done through Jenni, but either Ian or I do the actual negotiating. We prefer it that way."

"What agency do you use?"

He was fiddling with his pen again. She remembered the mannerism from the first time she'd interviewed him. "We mostly use the same one; Massingham's. We find them very reliable."

"Yes, we met Mrs Massingham the other day. From Kirsty's personal effects, it's clear that she had some interest in the agency."

"You surprise me. But I suppose it's not impossible. They're a modelling agency and she was trying to make it as a model, in theory at least."

"Would Kirsty have ever had access to your computer, either here or at your home?"

"Absolutely not!" He looked horrified at the idea before adding, "Not that she would have found any reference to Massingham's in any of my files, because there isn't any."

Why are you twitchy about this? thought Angela. "There must be something if you hire models from there, surely?" she asked.

Nigel's mouth suddenly formed a thin tight line. He was piqued to be wrong-footed. "Yes. OK, I might have their number, but for everything else you'd need to speak to Jenni." Angela decided to take the finality in his tone as her cue to depart.

"Thank you very much for your time, Mr Summers," she said, rising.

"Not at all," replied Nigel. "Happy to be of help."

"Not much doing there," commented Gary, as he belted himself into the driving seat.

"Apparently not," agreed Angela. "But you never know. We dropped a pebble into a pool. Logic dictates that some ripples must be produced. We still need to know why Kirsty fancied herself on the board of Massingham Models."

"She was well deluded if she thought her beauty could swing her a job like that. Her mum and dad didn't do her any favours, bringing her up to believe stuff like that, did they?"

"You're right. You can't blame any parent for thinking their children are the bees' knees, but it sounds as though in this case they got a bit carried away. The first interpreters of the world, for all of us, are our parents – or whoever brings us up – and if they feed us a load of hogwash it's very hard to do a rethink when our experiences don't meet the expectations they planted in us." Angela glanced across at Gary. "Father Martin would say she'd been badly catechized."

"*Catter* what? Oh, is that to do with the catechism, like, religious teaching?"

"That's what I like to see, a detective who can follow a trail."

Gary laughed. "Yeah, but we've got no indication that Kirsty was religious in any way."

"It's not just about religion. Think of it as teaching. Everybody gets taught *something*. If you're brought up to believe that the sun shines out of your eyes and you can have everything you want just for the asking, then that's what you've received and you'll try to live by it."

"Oh, I get it. Yeah, Kirsty was definitely going nowhere fast. The bloke in the unit at Wandsworth had the angle on that, didn't he? You know, when Jim was reporting on his interview with him and he talked about one of their dates happening in a suburban backwater. Then it was probably back home to bed without even a 'How was it for you?' the next morning."

Angela laughed. "I think you've hit the nail on the head, Gaz. This is what Ian King calls a dalliance. Well, maybe Kirsty learned about Massingham's from him. OK, let's go, young Houseman. I'll phone him as we go."

"You don't want to just turn up, like we did with Nigel Summers?"

"I don't think it would work. I expect Nigel's already rung Ian and told him about our visit *and* mentioned that we've shown an interest in Massingham Models. Ian could decide that if we're on our way to him next, he might suddenly discover pressing business elsewhere. Ringing ahead will make that more difficult."

However, it didn't seem that Ian was trying to avoid the police. They hadn't been on the road for more than five minutes when Jenni rang back in answer to Angela's request to say Ian would be happy to see them just as soon as they got to the unit. Twenty minutes later they parked under the now-familiar sign and through the glass panel in the front door could see the office manager waiting for them.

Ian was doing something at his computer when Angela and Gary were shown into his office a few moments later. He clicked the mouse a couple of times and turned away from the screen with something of a flourish. "Right, Inspector, you wanted to see me again." He spread his hands to indicate the two chairs on the other side of his desk. Angela and Gary sat down. "I don't flatter myself that you've come because of my report from last night."

"Your report from last night?" asked Angela.

"Yes, I saw someone watching my flat. Whoever it was left wheeling a bicycle. I phoned the local nick, as requested, but since nothing happened I suppose it's not very high on your scale of things to follow up."

Although she knew somebody on the team would have logged this report and added it to the file, Angela fought down a sense of irritation with herself for not having checked through everything. "I'm sorry," she said. "I haven't been in the office very much. I'll make sure I read it when I go back."

Ian waved away her apology. He'd dispensed with casual today and was wearing a superbly cut charcoal grey suit with royal blue coordinates. Angela could imagine Patrick looking just as good in the same clothes. Her mind drifted a little. It had been quite a while since Paddy had bought anything new.

Ian shot his cuffs, rested his elbows on his desk and steepled his fingers. "So what can I do for you?" he asked.

Angela dragged her mind back from the contemplation of getting Patrick out of tweed and into charcoal. "Oh, it's just that one or two more things have come to light we think you might be able to help us with," she began.

"OK, fire away," he said.

"Would Kirsty have known of Massingham Models?"

"Oh, I expect so. She could hardly work in the office here and not hear of them. She probably sent them photos at some point, trying to get on their books."

"Nothing else?"

"I don't see what else there would be, not for Kirsty anyway, Inspector."

"She didn't, for instance, have any involvement in the company?"

Ian's eyebrows shot up into his forehead. "Kirsty, involved in Massingham's? Not to my knowledge. How very odd."

"Odd? Why?"

"It just seems strange to think of Kirsty being involved in any sort of business. What do you mean by 'involved'?"

"That's just it, we don't really know. The thing is, along with some of your designs, which you already know about, we found a copy of Massingham's letterheaded paper on her computer."

"Really?" Ian laid his hands flat on the desk and produced full-on puzzlement. "How weird!" There was a brief silence and when Angela didn't rush to fill it he continued, "I'm completely stumped." He thought some more. "I can understand why she'd want to have my designs on her computer. Obviously I'm not happy that she did, but it makes sense. I'm sure she thought it would give her a bargaining counter. But letterheaded notepaper – this is completely bizarre, Inspector."

Angela cast her mind back over the picture of Kirsty at the *Passionista* event. "Do you think Kirsty could have tried to pass your designs on to someone else?"

Ian took a very deep breath. "That was my biggest fear. When you have as high a profile in this industry as I have, you can be sure there's someone out there who'd love to bring you down."

"Yes, I can imagine. Who would she have passed them on to?"

"That's a good question. She networked where she could, but I don't think that amounted to a great deal and I wouldn't think she'd made any likely connections."

"I remember you saying that she talked about her friends. Could you get any idea about them? Did she mention them much?

"Oh, Inspector, does the Pope have a balcony? Kirsty's friends were her main topic of conversation."

"What sort of things did she say?"

Ian shook his head as though trying to rid it of confusion. "You're asking me something, there. I remember a lot of 'he saids' and 'she saids' interspersed with a great deal of babble." Ian smiled. "I tuned in only occasionally, I'm afraid."

"Do you know who her friends were?"

Ian raised his shoulders and let them fall again. "I don't. I expect she had one or two she'd been at school with. I suppose she met others wherever she was working before she came to us. And she went to some gym on a regular basis. I'm sure she must have made some there."

"She didn't tell you any names?"

"I think her flatmate was Sandra and somebody called Tony was one of her friends at the gym. That's about it; sorry."

Angela nodded. She was being pointed back to the gym again and she wondered if this entire visit had been a waste of time. Even as she had the thought she dismissed it. The whole business of the designs on Kirsty's computer and her interest in the modelling agency made her sure there must be something more here to be ferreted out, but she couldn't identify exactly what it was.

Hmm, she thought, *there's definitely something not quite right here, something I'm not getting, but I don't know what questions to ask to flush it out.* She stood up. Gary did likewise. "Thank you very much for your cooperation, Mr King. If I need clarification about anything else, I'll be in touch."

Ian managed, more or less, to hide his relief that Angela was leaving. He rose with a smile. "Certainly, certainly; anything I can do to help."

"There's more there," said Angela as Gary drove them away a few minutes later.

"I'm sure you're right, Angie but…"

"Yes. *But.* I was stumped. I suddenly felt I'd reached a dead end."

"There's something I don't really get, Angie."

"Yes, what?"

"This letterheaded page; I mean, this business of 'fleshing out a fantasy'. I don't get that."

"Oh, I do, Gaz. I remember Patrick telling me once, when Madeleine was about twelve and really into schoolgirl stories, she decided when she grew up she wanted to be the headmistress of a girls' boarding school. She designed the whole place, right down to the sports pavilion. She could even have told you the names of the school houses. I can remember doing something similar when I was a kid as well."

"Yeah, but not at twenty-three, surely?"

"Depends on the circumstances, I would have thought. A lot of athletes do it, apparently. They visualize themselves making the winning run or whatever. It's called Neuro-linguistic programming."

"Oh, I think I've read about that."

"Yes, there is one question I wanted to ask and didn't."

"What's that?"

"I'd like to know where I could get a suit like that one he had on. Patrick would look great in it."

Gary laughed and slowed down to negotiate a roundabout.

When they got back to the incident room, tiredness was etched on the faces of all the team and Angela didn't need any hints to realize they were all hoping to be dismissed for the weekend. She couldn't help but sympathize as she took them all through a case conference that made sure they were up to speed on every development. "Our best bet is still this cyclist who turned up just before three o'clock," she finished.

"What about this woman?" asked Jim. "Any joy there?"

"Not so far; I've interviewed Dorothea Massingham," said Angela, "but I don't think she's the one we're looking for. In any case, her connection is very tenuous."

"Didn't that bloke Sanders describe her suit as elegant?" said Jim.

"Yes, he used that word." Angela made to move across the room. She hadn't been listening closely to Jim as he spoke, but his words suddenly registered. She stopped and stood very still, as though in a trance.

"What is it?" asked Rick.

Angela blinked. "I'm not sure. What Jim said reminded me of what my stepdaughter said last night, which has made me think of something else."

"What was that, then?" asked Jim.

"Ah, that's a good question. When I've remembered *that* I'll let you know." Angela gave herself a slight shake and grinned round at the question on the faces of each of her team. "Sanders didn't strike me as being a fashion-conscious person; quite the opposite, in fact."

"Perhaps he thinks any jacket and trousers that match is elegant," suggested Rick.

"Oh, no, I think he was a bit more aware than that," protested Angela. "Never mind. It's one of those niggly things which I'm sure will come back to me later. When it does, I'll let you all know. Look, it's late, we're all tired. Well, I know I am. Let's call it a day. Unless there's some sort of a breakthrough, I'll see you all here first thing Monday morning."

Angela didn't make it out to the street without interruption. The desk sergeant was in conversation with a motorcycle courier just as she was coming through the front entrance.

"D.I. Costello," called the sergeant. "This one's for you; could you sign for it, please?"

"What on earth's that?" she asked, coming over and looking at the bulky envelope with her name on it in large felt-tip letters. Then she saw a sender's label in the top-right hand corner: Leon Rushton Photography. "Oh great," she said. "Yes, I know what these are. We've all knocked off for the day now, but I'll take them home with me so I can have a look tonight."

Chapter Twenty-one

"What's that?" asked Patrick, coming along the passage from their kitchen to greet her, twenty minutes later.

"It's a set of photographs which might turn out to be evidence; one or two of them, anyway."

"Oh, really? Where were they taken?"

"At a fashion magazine reception a little while ago. Our victim was there, and I'm hoping for a snapshot the same as, or very similar to, one that was removed from among some others in her bedroom." She grinned at him and planted a kiss on his mouth. "I'm working on that theory, anyway. The courier arrived at the incident room just as I was leaving to come home and I couldn't be bothered to take them back upstairs." She took the package into the living room.

"So did she get copies of the photographs for her bedroom, then?"

"No, I don't think so. The photographer only just about remembered her, which I don't think would have been the case if she'd contacted him for pictures. Besides, the ones stuck round her mirror looked like nothing fancier than printouts of phone snaps. I'm hoping that among these professional shots will be some from the same sequence – so we can get a match with what's there and identify what's gone missing."

Patrick raised his eyebrows. "You're an intelligent woman; there must be some reason why you don't just check her mobile for photographs."

Angela smiled and nodded. "Oh yes, Paddywack. We haven't found her mobile phone."

"Ah! And how do you know a picture was removed from her bedroom?"

Angela explained about the Blu-tak in the space left by the missing photograph and Patrick listened thoughtfully.

"Ah." Patrick looked at the ceiling and placed his index finger on his forehead. "Leaps to obvious conclusion: the murderer took it because it might lead you to him/her."

Angela laughed. "I can see why you made it to D.I." She handed the package to him. "Here, park these somewhere, please. I'll go and get started on the dinner."

"OK, may I have a look?"

"I don't see why not. You know what the dead woman looks like."

Patrick sat down on the edge of an easy chair, pulling the coffee table towards him, when the doorbell rang.

"I wonder who that is," said Angela making her way to answer it. "Oh hello, Martin," she said, as she opened the door to find their parish priest standing on the front step. Martin was beaming at her, and almost hopping from one foot to the other in overflowing excitement. "You're looking very pleased with yourself," she added. "Come in."

"Yes, thanks, I will," he answered, stepping into the hall. "I think I've found her," he blurted out, unable to contain his news a moment longer.

"What? Found her? Oh! You mean that woman who came running into the confessional."

"Yes. I hope so, anyway. If I'm right, she's in a house nearly opposite Katy D, who's on high alert, by the way, and says the police are welcome to use her front bedroom to maintain surveillance."

"Oh, wow! You have been busy," replied Angela. "Come in here, Martin; have a seat."

Angela led him into the front room. Patrick looked up from

a spread of photographs. "Hi, Martin; did I hear that right? You've found that poor young woman?"

"I think so," he answered. "Of course I could be wrong, but I was passing a house today – "

"Near where Katy D lives," said Angela.

"Yes, actually we've got two or three parishioners along that street but the others are out at work all day." Father Martin filled them in on his adventures of the day.

"That's really brilliant, Martin," said Patrick, as he continued to sort the photographs into groups. "Well done for turning detective. Let's hope you're right." He looked up at him, across at Angela and back to Martin. "Of course, the police will have to approach cautiously. We've got an awful lot of people from Eastern Europe in England these days, and I should think a good few of them are big, chunky guys."

"Oh, I know it's not conclusive," agreed Martin. "But the interesting thing is that Katy has wondered about the occupants of that house for a while."

"Oh, really?" said Angela. "Well, that's something to be going on with. We can certainly take a look."

"Good," said Martin. "Katy's a sensible woman and not at all fanciful…" Martin drew to a halt, his eyes on Patrick, still bent on his task. He frowned as Patrick laid a photograph on the pile and then his eyes widened in excitement.

"*That's her!*"

Patrick clicked his tongue in sorrow. "Yes, that's Kirsty Manners, the victim. She really was a looker, wasn't she?"

"No!" shouted Martin. "Not her; the other one."

Patrick held up the photograph so that they could all see it. It showed Kirsty standing beside an attractive blonde woman.

"Do you mean…?" began Angela.

"Yes, exactly," said Martin. "That's the woman who came running into the confessional last Monday."

A brief, stunned silence reigned in the room for a moment or two until Angela broke it. "Are you sure?"

"No doubt about it," said Martin. "I'd recognize that face anywhere. She's certainly good-looking enough to be a model."

"As it happens, you don't have to be good-looking," said Angela, taking the photo from Patrick and scrutinizing it. "Well, not for the catwalk, anyway; that's something I've learned from this investigation. Actually, you know," she laid the photograph on her lap, "presuming they're both standing on the same level, they look to be roughly the same height, which makes her too short for modelling." Angela turned her gaze to Martin. "She didn't say she'd come here to be a model, though, did she?"

"Er… Well, I assumed that was the case." Martin screwed up his face as he thought back to the previous Monday. "Um… I jumped to that conclusion."

Angela grinned at him. "If I remember correctly, you reported her as saying she'd come here for the fashion industry."

"Yes, that's it! You're right. Modelling wasn't actually mentioned, now I come to think of it."

Angela turned the photograph around so Patrick and Martin both had a clear view of it. "OK, what do you see?"

"Two young women at a social event," said Martin.

"Dressed up to the nines, full make-up, hair, the works," added Patrick.

"Posh social event," amended Martin.

"What else do you see?"

"Other people milling around. It's a regular party scene," said Martin.

"And just off to one side there's a large board with letters 'ista' on it," said Patrick. "Do we get a prize for this?"

Angela laughed. "Nope. What I'm looking at is that they've both got mobile phones in their hands."

"Who doesn't have a mobile phone in their hand these days?" asked Martin.

"Ah yes, but a mobile phone represents the freedom to communicate, independence."

"And you haven't found Kirsty's," said Patrick.

"Quite."

"Oh," said Martin. "And that other young woman certainly didn't have any independence last Monday."

"Precisely. I bet she hasn't got access to her mobile now. What's more, I've learned a little bit about this do from the photographer; Kirsty was meant to be there in a decorative role only."

"Oh – arm candy," said Patrick.

"Exactly how it was put to me earlier," agreed Angela. "She caused some annoyance by going off on her own, networking and generally snooping around. It sounds like she was a bit too curious for her own good."

"Which might be why she's now dead," suggested Patrick.

"Yes," said Angela with a grim expression. "Let's come back to these phones. I'm assuming these two women hadn't met before, but I can't be sure about that."

"In any case, they struck up enough of an acquaintance to swap numbers, from the look of things," answered Martin.

Angela was silent as she stared into the middle distance. Eventually she spoke. "I wonder if that's all they were doing," she said.

Later that evening, after Martin had gone back to the presbytery and they'd eaten, Patrick picked up the photograph and sat gazing at it as Angela brought their coffee into the living room. "Bit of a breakthrough, this," he said.

"Oh yes, I've called the team in for tomorrow morning and started setting up surveillance procedures. It won't be a full day, Pads. I just want to get everything in place."

"Yes, of course," he answered. "Katy's going to find her home life disrupted for a while. Let's hope it doesn't go on too long."

"Oh, amen to that. She's a good sort, Katy, and she has a strong sense of civic duty."

"What did you mean earlier, when we were talking about them swapping mobile phone numbers – and you wondered if that was all they were doing?" he asked.

Angela sat down and took a sip from her cup. "We've already found some designs from Ian King on Kirsty's laptop. What's to say she didn't also have them on her phone?"

"Showing them to the other woman?"

"Yes, something like that. I haven't thought it through yet, but I'm getting a clearer picture of Kirsty. She liked to be on the inside of things. That's why she poked her nose in where it wasn't wanted."

"A worry for people with something to hide."

"Yes, but I don't think she wanted to be a threat to anyone. I think she just wanted to muscle in and be part of what went on behind the scenes. She didn't want to simply turn up for jobs and be told 'wear this, wear that', 'stand like this, stand like that'. She wanted to be somebody of more consequence than that."

"A dangerous path to tread, though," Patrick pointed out. "Usually, whatever wheelings and dealings are going on backstage, so to speak, are already under someone's firm control. The territory is marked."

"Oh yes. She was a silly woman playing with fire, and she'd already become a liability."

"So Ian King and his partner loom large in the frame."

"Yes, they've got to, haven't they? The problem is with opportunity; they both have solid alibis."

"How solid?"

"A round of golf for Nigel, and an afternoon session in bed with his girlfriend for Ian."

"Ah, tricky. Who else have you?"

"Eleanor Chandler, the head stitcher, is a possibility – although she's the alibi for Ian. Kirsty made life difficult for her because she – Eleanor – supplanted Kirsty in a relationship with Ian."

"Not a strong motive for murder, I wouldn't have thought."

"No, I agree. I need to dig a bit more there. The flatmate, Sandra, had motive, means *and* opportunity – as did Tony, the bloke who runs the gym; well, I don't know about motive for him, but he certainly had the means and opportunity. I can't discount Darren, because you never know what unrequited love will do to someone, and he most certainly had the opportunity and the means."

"Bit of a conundrum you've got there, sweetheart."

"Yes, and I still don't know if it all really ties up in any significant way with this woman from the confessional, apart from her being photographed at a party together with Kirsty. It could be a complete coincidence." She sighed, suddenly feeling quite exhausted.

"I'll tell you what you're going to do," said Patrick.

"What?"

Patrick leaned back and drew her into his embrace. "You're going to enjoy your coffee, then later on we'll have a wee dram of something and listen to some music."

She smiled up at him. "Then what?"

"Ah, then I suggest we get an early night. We can do something to take your mind off your work problems completely."

Angela nuzzled her forehead contentedly against his chin. "Sounds like a plan."

The plan worked. Angela appeared in front of the rest of her team the next morning feeling completely refreshed.

She pinned up the photograph of Kirsty with the unknown blonde and looked around at her team. "Sorry to get you all in on a Saturday morning, but this new development is too important to be left until Monday."

"Not a problem, Angie," said Rick, speaking for them all. "Looks like a breakthrough."

"I hope you're right," replied Angela. She pointed at the photograph. "This was taken at a magazine bash a while back," she said, "giving us a concrete link between these two individuals. Kirsty Manners, here. And *this* woman came running into the parish of the Immaculate Conception asking for help, last Monday. We think that she and some other women may be held against their will, at this house." She tapped the address, now displayed alongside, and explained the sequence of events that had brought it to prominence. "We've got the help of some uniformed officers, but I think we need to stay very hands-on."

"We'll end up spread a bit thin if we're on watch all the time, Angie," Rick pointed out.

"Especially if it drags on," added Jim.

"Yes, I'm aware of that," replied Angela. "And, of course, we can't be entirely sure this is the actual house. Father Martin didn't get a really good look at the man in the church, so we've got to keep up all the other lines of investigation. Derek and Leanne, I'd like you to go and camp out. You won't find it unpleasant; Katy makes a nice cup of tea and I'm sure you'll find her willing to help, but take in your own food; she's a busy lady and it's not fair to presume on her hospitality. Jim and Rick, I want you checking in with them as much as you can. We need to know what's going on, if anything, and we want pictures – as many as we can get."

"All the comings and the goings," said Jim.

"Not just that, the surveillance location is nearly opposite the house, so you might get a sight of someone inside one of the rooms. Just go for it. I want to know if a curtain so much as twitches."

The team nodded and murmured acquiescence.

Chapter Twenty-two

Twenty-four hours later, as the front door downstairs banged shut, Derek drank the cold dregs of tea and put his cup back in its saucer. "That's Katy back from Mass. What are the odds she'll be up here with another cuppa in a minute?"

Leanne laughed. "I'm not betting; I'll lose."

They'd arrived after lunch the previous day and taken Angela's instructions to heart, coming loaded with supplies of food. Katy Devine wasn't under Angela's authority, however, so she had included them in her calculations for the evening meal. Derek and Leanne found the appeal of their shop-bought sandwiches faded very quickly compared with the aroma of a fried liver and bacon dinner followed by lemon meringue pie. And not an hour passed in which Katy didn't pop upstairs to ask if they were ready for another cup of tea. A full English breakfast had arrived the moment they'd come to take over from the uniformed officers who'd stood watch overnight. By this time the sandwiches had dried up on a shelf in the corner.

Leanne flipped through the overnight notes. Two men and three women had been seen to leave the house at nine o'clock. Photographs were taken, but they weren't very satisfactory. The car taking them to wherever they went had blocked the view and the chances of seeing anybody's face. The observers were merely left with the impression that the women wore elegant evening clothes. The party had arrived back around four o'clock. Only pictures of their backs as they disappeared into the house had been possible.

Leanne turned a page, read a note and looked across the road. "Oh," she said.

"What?" asked Derek.

"There's a note here about all the curtains being pulled back in the upstairs front room at ten o'clock last night."

"I saw that. I thought it strange as well. Weren't they all out at that time?" said Derek.

"They can't all have been, can they?" replied Leanne with unassailable logic. "OK, we'd gone off duty by nine, but three women and two men were seen leaving the house."

"So that can't be everybody in the house."

"You got it, Sherlock; somebody must have been left behind."

"Who amuses himself or herself by opening the curtains, nets and all."

A silence fell on the room. Leanne and Derek stared at each other for a few moments.

Finally Derek spoke. "Lee, babes, what would you do if you were being held in a house against your will? You're fairly feisty, remember; you've already tried to escape once."

"I think I'd do every little thing I could to draw attention to myself. I'd…"

"Yeah?"

"Well, if the only thing I could do was to draw the curtains in one of the rooms looking out onto the street, I'd still give it a go, and…"

"Yeah?"

"I'd stand in the window if I could."

Instinctively they both looked across the road. At that moment the house looked a perfect picture of suburban respectability. The nets covered the windows and the heavy curtains were drawn back exactly as one would expect at this time of the morning. They could see nobody.

Just at that moment there came a gentle tap on the door and Katy put her head into the room.

"Now," she began with a cheerful smile, "I'm sure you're both ready for a nice cup of tea."

"Yes, please, Katy," answered Derek with enthusiasm. They'd all arrived at first-name name terms very soon after being installed in the cheerful little bedroom with its single bed, wardrobe, dresser, desk and a couple of chairs. It wasn't a Spartan room by a very long way, but it was entirely without decoration or ornament and both the officers surmised that it had been occupied by a male.

"That's good," said Katy. "I'll just get the kettle on. And I've got a nice piece of lamb for lunch. Do you both like mint sauce?"

"That would be really marvellous, Katy, thank you."

"My pleasure," beamed Katy, as she withdrew.

"Katy!" Leanne called after her.

Katy's head popped back into the room. "Yes, dear?"

Leanne nodded in the direction of the house across the road.

"The overnight notes say all the curtains were drawn back in that upstairs front room at ten o'clock last night."

Katy pushed the door back and came fully into the room. "Well, d'you know, that's one of the first things I noticed about that house. The curtains are sometimes all drawn back and sometimes they're pulled across at the oddest times of the day and night."

"Have you ever seen anybody inside the room?" asked Derek.

Katy shook her head. "No, I can't say I have. Mind you, I did see them being drawn back once, but the person kept behind the curtains as they came across, if you see what I mean, so I couldn't see who was there. Is it important?"

"We're not sure," replied Leanne. "We've got to take notes of everything, though."

Katy sat on the bed. "Yes, I suppose you must. Whoever pulled those curtains looked in a great hurry, I can tell you that much."

"Oh, really?" asked Derek. He and Leanne exchanged looks. Leanne pulled the notes towards her and picked up a pen.

"How could you tell that if you couldn't see the person?"

Katy thought about this for a minute. "It was the impression I formed. When I looked, one side was already drawn to the middle and the other side came across really quickly. I remember wondering if they were in a hurry to do something in secret."

"Is that the only time you noticed any movement in that upstairs room?" asked Leanne.

"Yes. I'm sorry I can't be more help," answered Katy, after a moment's further reflection, with a regretful look on her face.

"Not a problem," Derek reassured her with a smile. "Every little helps." He looked around the room. "Leanne and I have decided this was probably a boy's room," he said.

Katy beamed fondly. "Yes, my son. He moved out to get married in March of this year."

"So, have you got an empty nest now?" said Leanne.

"I have! I'm not really used to it yet. I'm gradually finding more and more things to keep me busy, but it still seems strange without Ally. He's my baby," she grinned, "all six feet, twelve stone of him."

"Ally?" Derek sounded a little puzzled. Ally sounded like a girl's name to him.

"Alistair," explained Katy. "My husband's family are from Scotland, so we decided to give a nod in their direction with regard to names, when Ally was born. We called him Alistair Ian."

"I didn't know they're Scottish names," said Leanne.

"Oh yes," said Katy. "Very much so; Alistair is the Gaelic for Alexander and Ian is John."

Leanne didn't answer. A thoughtful look had appeared on her face.

"There you go, you learn something new every day, don't you," said Derek, as if to fill the silence.

"Yes, you do," said Leanne slowly, still following her own train of thought.

Katy slapped her leg and stood up. "Well, this won't get the dinner cooked, will it? And I mustn't distract you like this." She made for the door. "I'll be up shortly with that cup of tea," she promised as she disappeared through it.

"Are you all right, Lee?" asked Derek, once the door had closed.

Leanne frowned. "Mmm," she said. "I didn't know that Ian was a version of John."

Derek shrugged. "I've never really thought about it. Why? Does it matter?"

"It might. Didn't this young woman talk about coming to a designer of the same name?"

"That priest thought so, yeah, though it sounded like he had a bit of trouble making out everything she said."

"But he definitely thought she was Polish, didn't he?"

"Yes. Why? What's that got to do with it?"

"It's just that I think I might have an angle on this."

Derek smiled. "Oh yeah, Miss Dabrowska. You would have if anybody would."

"Yep," replied Leanne. She made up her mind. "I know Angela's probably busy cooking her Sunday lunch right at this moment, but I think I'll give her a call."

"If it seems that important, go for it," said Derek. "Here, let me take over anyway. You've been sitting in that spot since we arrived, and it's about time I did a stint."

Lunch being in Patrick's hands, Angela was just standing back to admire her newly appointed sewing room when Leanne's call came through. Patrick brought the phone upstairs and stopped on the threshold. "My goodness, you have been busy," he said. "I hope you're not going to disappear up here, buried under piles of material. I don't want to become a sewing widower."

Angela laughed. "That's not going to happen, darling. But I am looking forward to making a few things for myself. Who's on the phone?"

He held out the mobile. "Leanne, from Katy's house."

She frowned. "I hope it's important. I did tell them that I wanted to know if so much as a curtain twitched, but I didn't mean it literally."

Patrick covered the phone with his hand. "Leanne's a bright lady," he said. "She wouldn't call you for something trivial."

Angela took the phone from him. "You're right, I'd best take it."

Later, she was very glad she did.

The next morning, Angela had just finished telling the team it had been a quiet Sunday with nothing much to report except some oddity about whether or not the curtains were drawn, when her mobile sprang to life. Leanne's number appeared on the screen. "Yes, Leanne, anything happening?" she asked.

"Guv, two men and three women left the house about ten minutes ago. Soon after they went, all the curtains, nets and drapes, were pulled back in the upstairs room and there's a young woman standing in the window looking out into the street."

"Picture?"

"Yes, Derek's taken several. He's zoomed in as much as he can, but she's obviously still in a bit of shadow. We think there's a good chance it's our girl from the *Passionista* party, though."

Angela punched the air and gave a quick look round at the team. She could see them all interpreting the conversation for themselves and beginning to move. "Load it up to your laptop and whizz it through to my email, please, Leanne. I want to send one to Father Martin, for confirmation."

"Already done, guv," replied Leanne, as a gentle beep told Angela her phone had mail.

Oh, thank you, God, for Leanne thinking on her feet, she thought. She opened up her email and gazed at the image. It definitely looked like the woman from the party.

"Right, everybody," she said. "We might be on the money with this, but I do want to get Father Martin's say-so first. He's had the best close-up look at the woman so far." She brought up Martin's contact details and forwarded the picture.

"That'll only take a few minutes, won't it?" asked Jim. He was hovering by the door, clearly wanting to get moving.

Angela looked at her watch. "Bit longer, I'm afraid. He's probably just begun celebrating Mass. Not to worry, he'll pick up his messages as soon as he's finished. It will give me the chance to bring D.C.I. Stanway in on it." She beamed around at them all. "Get on with whatever you can."

"Ah, Angie," said Stanway, as she walked into his room a few minutes later. "Got any progress to report?"

"It's looking very much like it, sir," replied Angela. She held her phone out to him to show him the photograph Leanne had taken.

"Oh yes, the same woman as you have on the board in the incident room," said the D.C.I. "Have you sent it to your priest?"

"Yes, sir."

"And does he confirm it's her?"

"I haven't heard back from him yet, sir, and I don't expect to for a while." Just at that moment her phone rang again. It was Derek this time. "Excuse me, sir," she said, putting it to her ear. "Yes, Derek?"

"The others from the house have come back, guv. We saw the car turning the corner, 'cause you can see that end of the street from here."

"And?"

"And just about the same moment we saw the car, we looked and the curtains came across the window again."

"Oh, bingo! Sit tight, Derek. I'm with D.C.I. Stanway at the moment." She cut the connection and looked at her boss. "It looks like we're in business, sir."

Stanway picked up the phone on his desk. "I'll get the back-up sorted, Angie. I'll meet you at my car in five minutes."

By the time Stanway joined Angela, she had alerted the rest of her team. Twenty minutes later saw the D.C.I.'s car nosing its way past Katy's house, looking for a parking space between the sleek vehicles belonging to this quiet, residential street.

Derek stood well back from the window in the front upstairs bedroom, his phone to his ear. "That's the house, guv," he said, watching their car glide past the blue door.

"OK, thanks," said Angela. Stanway drove on a little further, finding a place to pull in at a discreet distance. In the rear-view mirror, Angela saw two more vehicles turning into the street. One, a patrol car containing Jim, Rick and Gary, stopped near the corner, out of sight of anyone in the house. The other, an unmarked police van, drove right on by to a space several cars beyond Stanway's. Angela knew six uniformed police officers sat inside, all eagerly awaiting the word to go.

Angela and the D.C.I. got out of the car. "How are we going to play this, sir?"

Stanway smiled. "This is a sedate street in an affluent neighbourhood. We'll play it the way the locals would relate to. We'll knock on the door and make a polite enquiry." Even so, he took a walkie-talkie out of the pocket of his anorak. "Of course, we'll stay in touch with the troops just in case it all suddenly becomes not so respectable."

Angela grinned. Just at that moment her mobile buzzed and she took it out of her pocket. Martin had sent her a text. *Yep, that's the one; am approaching Katy's house now.* She looked up and sure enough there he was walking along the street. Wearing clerical dress this morning, he looked like a priest and not a jogger. He gave her a wave and turned in at Katy's front gate, a member of the clergy just paying a parish visit.

Stanway watched him disappear through the front door. "Can't be avoided, I suppose. It would have been impossible to keep the lid completely on this, not with Leanne and Derek in the house."

"He has a pastoral concern, sir. It was to him the woman ran for help."

"Yes, of course," replied Stanway. He seemed to pause for an instant and square his shoulders before starting off again. "OK, let's get going," he said, leading the way towards the blue door.

They were still about twenty yards from the house when Stanway stopped and turned to Angela. "Leanne – she's got Polish grandparents, hasn't she?"

"Yes, sir."

"Does she speak Polish?"

"Yes, sir."

"Good. Get her out here with us. We might need an interpreter."

Angela phoned through. By the time they reached the gate, she could see Leanne heading down Katy's front path.

Stanway stood back to let Angela precede him. "I'm right behind you, Angie, and the back-up can be here in ten seconds."

"Sir." Angela walked up to the front door and rang the bell.

Chapter Twenty-three

Nothing happened at first, so after a few moments Angela rang again. They waited a little longer, straining their ears for any sound from within. She had just lifted her hand to ring for the third time when they heard a key turning in the lock. They looked at each other. *Locked from the inside,* thought Angela. The door was pulled open to reveal a giant of a man with a close-cropped head, dressed in black jeans; his pristine white T-shirt stretched across powerful looking pectoral muscles. His unfriendly gaze moved slowly over each of them. Angela experienced a slight shiver.

"I help you?" he asked in some unidentifiable accent. His words belied his expression; he didn't look in the least as though he wanted to help them.

"I hope you can," began Angela in a businesslike tone. It was obvious the man's mother tongue wasn't English, but she decided not to speak slowly for him; she wanted the advantage. She held up her identification. "I'm Detective Inspector Angela Costello of the Metropolitan Police; this is Detective Chief Inspector Stanway and Detective Constable Leanne Dabrowska. We have reason to believe a young woman is being held in this house against her will."

The giant took his time computing this sentence. At no time did he appear fazed or worried. Finally he shook his head and gave a small, somehow unpleasant, smile. He clearly wasn't troubled by their appearance on the doorstep. "Is not so," he said.

The amount of time he'd taken coming back with his answer had given Angela the opportunity to construct her next comment.

"In that case, you won't have any objection to us taking a look, will you, sir?"

It didn't take as long for him to deal with this. He pushed his bulk more squarely across the front entrance. "Is not good time; my girlfriend sleep." He spoke with finality. Angela could see she was dealing with a bully. She'd always believed it best to let bullies know, right from the outset, you weren't going to be intimidated by them. In her experience it saved a lot of trouble in the long run. She took a step forward. "We've received a report from a concerned member of the public," she said. "May we come in?" She didn't bother with *please*; if push came to shove, Stanway had a warrant in his pocket.

A look of surprise dawned on the man's face as she moved towards him, but just then a door further down the corridor opened and he half-turned. "Klara!" the man called and Angela sensed both warning and menace in his voice.

A female shape appeared in the dimness of the hallway. She was very tall with long blonde hair. It was immediately evident she was not the woman from the upstairs window. She said something in a half-asleep voice. The three police officers could only make out the final word, "Igor."

Angela pounced on the name. "Right, Igor," she said to the man, continuing her move forward. "We just want a few words. We won't take up much of your time." She crossed the threshold quickly, followed by Stanway and Leanne. The first door on the right stood open and she went through it and found herself in a comfortable sitting room looking out onto the street. A three-piece suite was grouped around an empty fireplace. A few books and some ornaments were arranged on the shelves, one in each alcove either side of the fireplace. A couple of upright chairs primly guarded a folded table by the back wall.

Angela sat down in one of the single armchairs. Stanway, close behind her, took the other one and Leanne headed for the sofa. With a face like thunder, Igor followed them into the room. Angela suspected he was much more used to people cringing before him rather than barging past. She took her notebook and a pen out of her bag. "May I have your full name, please, Igor?"

Igor narrowed his eyes at Angela as he subsided onto one of the upright chairs. He jerked his head to Klara, now standing in the doorway, and said something to her. She looked hesitantly round at them all, took a step towards him, rested her hand awkwardly on his shoulder and looked down at him with the most unconvincing smile Angela had ever seen. The man tugged at the girl and she perched herself half-on, half-off his lap. Angela would have been willing to lay odds that what he'd said had been along the lines of, "Come here and pretend to be my girlfriend." She cast an enquiring glance at Leanne who correctly interpreted the look and shook her head. "Russian, I think, guv," she said, under her breath. Angela nodded.

She opened her notebook and tapped a fresh page with the pen. "OK, may I have your full name please, Igor?"

"Igor Dimitri Zolnerowich." Like Angela he made no attempt to speak slowly. He looked at her with an unpleasant smile as he rattled off his name.

Angela saw he was playing her at her own game, which amused her. "Would that be the usual spelling?" she asked. She sensed rather than saw Stanway and Leanne quickly hide smiles, but Igor saw them clearly and his eyes darkened as he guessed they were sharing some English joke. The woman suddenly jerked and winced, causing them all to look at her. As she settled again on her unlikely perch, her eyes glazed over and she stared out of the window.

So you express your chagrin by pinching the lady, thought Angela. *Not nice.* "OK, Igor, thank you," she said, writing, phonetically, what she could of the name. "Now is this your girlfriend – Klara, is it?"

"My girlfriend, *da*." Igor hugged Klara closer to him but his eyes never left Angela's face, which meant that he wasn't looking at Klara. As she wrote, Angela looked up briefly and saw Klara's eyes fixed on her with an intense stare. She held the other woman's gaze briefly.

"How many other people are living here?"

"Six; three mans, three womans."

"We'd like to talk to them."

"No possible, sleeping," answered Igor, with finality. He kept his eyes fixed on Angela, bold and intimidating. Out of the corner of her eye, Angela could still see the intense gaze of the woman on his lap.

Stanway cut in. "The thing is, Mr Zorrovitch – s'cuse the pronunciation – we have to take these matters very seriously. As I'm sure you're aware, you're living in a very nice borough of mostly affluent middle-class people…" Stanway got into his stride and continued with what Angela suddenly recognized as his speech to the Neighbourhood Watch committee given at a fundraising dinner earlier in the year.

He was doing it for a reason. He leaned forward in his seat, casting a slightly dismissive gaze to Angela on his right and Leanne on the left, engaging Igor in a clearly man-to-man manner, and began spouting what she knew could become a lengthy analysis of local crime statistics. It worked. After some more of Stanway's monologue Igor's attention diverted, with a puzzled frown, to the D.C.I., allowing Angela to look Klara fully in the face without Igor noticing.

The minute she saw she had Angela's attention, Klara raised her eyes slowly to the ceiling. Then she repeated the process to make sure she was understood. Angela nodded; a barely noticeable gesture. Klara gave the merest of smiles and seemed to relax.

Stanway recognized what had happened. He cut off the exposition on summertime pickpocketing in the riverside pubs, and went straight into the matter in hand without a pause. "So anyway, Mr Zorrovitch, we'll have to talk to your housemates. Please, just call them in here."

Igor looked at him, uncertain of what he was dealing with. He hadn't picked up most of what Stanway had been saying, but he recognized there'd been a change of tack and could tell they were now back on course.

"Your housemates, Igor," repeated Angela. *I applaud you for having a stab at the surname, sir,* she thought, *but I'll stick with what I know, if you don't mind.*

"They sleep."

"Then wake them up."

Igor looked at the three officers. "No – you make me?" His smile was contemptuous. He was baiting them.

Stanway beamed at him. "No, I won't make you." He cocked his thumb behind him to the street. "My officers outside will be the ones to make you." He took the walkie-talkie out of his pocket and it cackled into life.

Igor understood that without a problem. He stood up, unceremoniously unseating Klara, and stomped over to the window. It didn't take him long to locate the van outside and he had no trouble assessing how many men it could hold. He barked an order at Klara and she went out of the room. Seconds later they could hear her knocking loudly on a couple of doors and calling out to people.

Five minutes later, two more men and two more women had joined Igor and Klara in the front room. The men, in T-shirts and jeans, were cast very much in the mould of Igor. They looked questioningly at him and threw wary expressions towards the police officers. The women, another blonde and a brunette, were tall and slim, like Klara. There was a glassiness in their eyes and Angela thought she could detect faint traces of what could be white powder just below the nostrils of one of them. As the room filled up, Igor spoke rapidly, no doubt giving them a rundown of what was going on.

"So," said Angela, looking at them. "You three men are living here with your girlfriends?"

The two men who'd just walked in suddenly became alert and each grabbed hold of the nearest woman. One said "*da*", the other said "*tak*", and they nodded their heads in a helpful manner.

"A more unconvincing set of 'couples' I've yet to see," said Angela, sketching quotation marks in the air. "Are you telling me there are only three women living here?" This was met with more "*das*" and "*taks*" and nods, even some smiles this time. They'd switched on full cooperation mode.

The most cooperative, however, was Klara. She hung back behind Igor, and when Angela asked for confirmation that only three women were living in the house she held out her hand and raised four fingers.

"We think differently," said Angela. "And while we've got you all gathered here, we'll put this to the test." She looked at her young colleague. "Leanne."

"Yes, guv." Leanne went into the hallway and stood at the bottom of the stairs. She took a deep breath, opened her mouth and beginning with the name "Asia", let out a very long, very loud, stream of something in Polish. One of the two newly arrived men started forward and shouted at her. Stanway put out a hand to stop him and spoke rapidly into the walkie-talkie. The man shrank back and began speaking in a low voice to the others. In the brief silence before the sound of the back-up team came tearing up the front path, a distinct noise came from somewhere far above them. They could all hear the muffled sound of someone banging and calling out.

"She's up there, guv," said Leanne, just as Stanway opened the front door and police officers overran the house.

It didn't take long. Leanne raced up the stairs ahead of the back-up team, and it quickly became obvious the missing woman was locked in the attic. In his haste to get her out of sight and answer the door, Igor had stashed the stepladder behind the nearest bedroom door, leaving it easily available to be run up against the loft hatch. When they pushed up the trap door, the tear-stained face of the woman from the photographs appeared over the hole. Leanne called up to her in Polish, gently explaining who they were. When she realized rescue had arrived, the tears began all over again, this time in relief and happiness. She was helped through the hole and down the ladder, shaking and sobbing and all the while being comforted by Leanne.

She clung to Leanne all the way down the stairs, out along the front path and into the street, where she finally stopped and looked around.

A small crowd of curious onlookers had gathered, all wondering volubly what could possibly be going on. Only two bystanders – Katy Devine and Father Martin Buchanan – waited in patient silence as the scene unfolded before them.

As she looked up and took in the crowd, Asia finally caught sight of a face she'd seen before; she recognized the priest from the confessional into which she'd run during her mad dash for freedom at the beginning of last week. Martin smiled and raised his hand, half-benediction, half-wave. Whether she was just glad to see a familiar face or had guessed he was instrumental in her rescue remained unclear, but it didn't matter. She let out a loud cry as she flew across the road and into his arms.

Chapter Twenty-four

As the brouhaha of the police raid died down, Angela spotted Rick, Jim and Gary coming towards her along the pavement. She beckoned them over to join her, Leanne and Stanway.

"Looks like a good result," began Rick. "Do you want us in there, sir?" he asked Stanway, nodding towards the house.

"Probably, but let's get these people sorted first," replied the D.C.I. As he spoke, the three men, now handcuffed, were led out and taken along to the police van.

"What is it, wrongful imprisonment?" asked Jim.

"For starters," said Stanway. "But from the look of a couple of those women, we might find something other than damsels in distress. Did you notice the traces of white powder on the face of one of those women?"

"I did, sir," said Angela.

"Hmm. Yes. Well, who knows, we might find more of the same inside." As Stanway spoke, Martin led Asia back across the road to Angela.

"I expect you have some questions for these women," he said.

It was Stanway who answered. "I think we'll let them recover a bit from their ordeal; especially this one," he said, looking at Asia. He smiled gently at her. "Miss – er?"

"My name is Asia Krol," she told him. "I am very thanking you for rescue me."

"All part of the service," beamed Stanway, and when Asia looked puzzled, he added slowly, "I'm very happy to help you."

"Ah!" Asia smiled and nodded.

Stanway indicated with his hand to where the other three women were standing, of whom only Klara looked fully aware of her surroundings. "Will you wait there with your friends?" he said in the same slow voice. Asia nodded and moved towards the others.

"Mind you, I'm not sure how much of an ordeal it was for the others," he said to Angela. He looked towards the police van and back to her. "Are we looking at 'disorderly house', do you think?"

"I wouldn't think so, sir. Going on what Martin could glean at the beginning of last week, along with the comings and goings observed from Katy's bedroom, I would think they were being taken out to parties and gatherings to be used as high-class prostitutes."

"That ties in with what she said on Monday," agreed Martin.

"Hmm. So I suppose the 'boyfriend' pantomime was exactly that. They wouldn't really have got a look-in," said Stanway.

"No, sir; they would have been under very strict orders not to – er – handle the merchandise."

Stanway nodded and looked at Angela and Leanne. "Well done, the pair of you," he said. "Very well done."

Leanne and Angela smiled. "You deserve congratulations, too, sir. I think that was a good bit of teamwork in there," said Angela.

Stanway beamed. "That's what it's all about, eh?" he said.

"Yes, sir," replied Angela. "I remember that speech."

Stanway gave a smirk. "I cut it down considerably for the Neighbourhood Watch do. I could have spun it out for twenty minutes."

"It did the trick, all right."

Stanway nodded. "OK," he said. "The work goes on. We need to put these women somewhere until we can talk to them."

"The nuns attached to our parish run a hostel for students," said Martin. "It's nearly empty at this time of the year. I can arrange rooms there for the time being."

"Some of them might also need a detox programme," said Angela.

Martin nodded. "The sisters will know how to access one. All sorts of problems turn up at that hostel."

"Excellent," beamed Stanway. "Leanne and Derek, you get that sorted with the, er, Father here. Get the women settled in. Make sure they understand someone will be coming to talk to them tomorrow, then come back and join us at the incident room." He turned to the others. "OK, let's follow that van and get started with these men. A search team will be here to go over the property any minute, and they're best left to get on with things on their own."

"Yes, sir," replied Angela. "I'll just thank Katy for her cooperation and the use of her house."

"Absolutely. Make that on behalf of us all, Angie."

Within fifteen minutes, Katy and Father Martin sat comfortably in her living room, reliving all the excitement over a cup of tea, a search team had started a painstaking examination of the house with the blue door, and the street had emptied of all visible signs of police presence.

A very palpable sense of euphoria and self-congratulation pervaded the incident room later that day. Jokes and light-hearted banter went back and forth between the team as they settled down. It was still going on when Angela took the case file from her office and joined them. Jim, Rick and Gary shared in the pleasure of a successful outcome but bemoaned the fact that they weren't really needed during the event.

"I was hoping to rush in there, throw a woman over my shoulder and come running out," joked Jim, "so I'd be a hero and you could all give me a pat on the back."

"We'd have to give you oxygen, more like," countered Rick. "Apart from the one we already knew about, they're tall girls, aren't they?"

"Yeah, they looked more like they could pick *us* up and carry us," laughed Gary. "When they're not strung out on something or other, that is."

Silence suddenly reigned in the room.

"Yes," said Angela, after a moment. "I know we all feel good about the rescue, and it's only natural to have a laugh and a joke, but what was happening to those women stinks."

"Yeah," said Gary. "They might have an addiction now that they didn't have when it all started."

"You can't be sure of that with the fashion industry," countered Rick.

"That's true," agreed Angela. "Still, let's not wallow, chaps and chapess, we've got work to do."

"Yes, we don't really know if this gets us any closer to Kirsty's murderer, do we?" remarked Rick.

Angela cast a glance at the picture of Kirsty and Asia on the board. "We'll know more tomorrow," she replied, "after we've spoken to that poor woman they shoved in the loft."

Rick nodded. "Asia, isn't it? I bet she'll have a better night's sleep than she's had for some time."

The others were nodding and agreeing with him when Angela spoke. "Yes, Asia," she said, giving it the correct pronunciation. Leanne looked up, caught her eye, and they exchanged smiles. "Leanne's been educating me about Polish names and how they get changed into pet names. But I'm sure you're right. She should sleep very soundly tonight. Well, let me just say it definitively, once and for all. Congratulations, everybody, on a job very well done today. It went much more smoothly than we'd a right to hope for. But we need to get back to the task in hand. Jim and Rick, I want you to take those men." She looked at a page on her desk. "I gather two of them are Russians and one is Polish."

Rick and Jim looked pointedly at Leanne.

"No," said Angela. "I want Leanne to go with Derek and speak to the women. Gary and Derek, get a couple of interpreters in. The men can stew overnight and you can get started first thing in the morning. Oh – please will you arrange for a Russian interpreter for the women, at the same time? I wonder if those ladies who looked so spaced out today will be ready to talk to us after a night's sleep, or just desperate for their next fix."

"That's a point," said Gary. "I wonder if they're even aware they've been taken from a bad place to a good one."

"We'll find out tomorrow," said Angela. "Leanne can interpret for Asia. That's one lady who knows exactly where she is."

"Going through an interpreter with these blokes might make it more difficult to tell if they're stonewalling," remarked Jim.

"Oh, I think you'll get the measure of them once you've got into the interviews," replied Angela. "But honestly, I doubt they'll be able to tell you much. I'd lay odds they're hired for their muscle and probably get their orders and their wages from a go-between. Whatever racket's going on, they won't know who's behind it."

"So, do we try to find out who is pulling the strings, or pass it on to Vice and Narcotics?" asked Gary.

"Good question," said Angela. "Let's run with it a bit more. We need to do the first interviews at least." She looked across the room. "Leanne, can you and Derek find out who owns that house? They might know what's been happening there or be completely in the dark, but it's as good a place to start as any."

"Will do, guv," replied Derek.

"Jim, Rick, even though we're not handing it over yet, get through to Vice and Narcotics. Bring them up to speed, and see if the address is on their radar."

"OK," said Rick. Angela stood staring into space, a small frown on her face. "Got nothing to do?" he joked.

"I wish!" replied Angela. "I could really do with sitting down quietly to let my mind wander over all the facets of this case. All the different threads are floating about in my head, confusing each other. Unfortunately, this afternoon's events won't write themselves up, and I want the report finished before Stanway asks for it." She picked up the loose-leaf case file. Just as she raised it in the air to emphasize her point, the telephone rang on the desk behind her. The shrilling made her jump, and the file flew from her hand, pages scattering everywhere across the floor.

"Oh, no!"

Gary ran forward. "Don't worry, Angie," he said. "I'll get this; you answer the phone."

"Thanks." Angela turned and picked up the receiver. "D.I. Cost – oh; yes, sir, right away." She put the phone down and turned back to the room. "Hang on to that for me, Gaz. Stanway wants a word."

D.C.I. Stanway turned from the contemplation of the roses on his windowsill with a beaming smile on his face as she entered the room. "We're getting mentioned in despatches, so to speak," he said.

"Oh, really, sir?"

"Yes, the assistant chief commissioner has heard about the operation over the weekend, and the rescue today. She has asked me to extend her heartfelt thanks and congratulations to everybody involved."

"Oh, great, sir; I'll pass that on. They've all been a bit hyper since we got back, but they're calming down now."

"That's understandable; but yes, must get the noses back to the grindstone. You'll need interpreters for the interviews. I mean, I know they all speak English to a degree, but we want to make sure everything's clear."

"I'm on to it sir. Gary and Derek are making the arrangements. Jim and Rick can make a start on those three men first thing."

"What about the women?"

"I've asked for a Russian for the three models, but Leanne can deal with *Panna* Krol."

"Panna? I thought her name was Asia."

Angela grinned. "*Panna* means 'Miss'. I've had a potted language lesson from Leanne over the weekend."

"Oh, right. Well, you seem to have it all under control, Angie. I'll leave you to get on with it."

"Thank you, sir," replied Angela, but she didn't get up from the chair.

Stanway raised his eyebrows at her. "Is there something else, Angie?"

"Yes, sir. My mind is becoming cluttered with issues around this case and I'd like to go over them with you. Do you have a few minutes?"

The D.C.I. looked at his watch. "Not right now. I was due at a meeting two minutes ago. In any case, I know you. The stuff you kick upstairs to me is usually very relevant, quite likely off the beaten track, and will most probably take more than a few minutes." He smiled. "I don't expect the meeting to last all afternoon. I'll call you when I'm back."

"Thank you, sir," replied Angela. She got up and made her way back to the incident room to find most of the team either working at computers or talking into telephones. Gary, however, sat perched on the corner of a desk holding the now tidied-up case file in his hand.

"Ah; thanks, Gazza," she said, going over to him. "The sooner I get started on this report, the sooner it's finished." She reached out to take the file from his hand, but he resisted, holding onto it by one end, an odd look on his face. "Gaz, I need this," she said, pulling gently at it.

"Yeah, but I want to show you something."

"Oh, what?"

"As I was picking up those papers – the witness statements and stuff – I noticed something funny."

"Ha ha, or peculiar?"

"Peculiar."

"OK, want to come into my office? You can tell me there." Gary nodded and followed Angela to the door.

Leanne put down a telephone and called across the room. "Guv?"

Angela paused and turned towards her. "Yes, Leanne?"

"I've just been speaking to the Land Registry. The house we raided today is owned by somebody called Massingham."

The room went quiet. Everybody stopped what they were doing and looked at Leanne.

Chapter Twenty-five

Angela looked at Gary. "Will the peculiar thing keep for a minute?"

"Yes, it will."

"OK," she said, moving across to Leanne. *Don't jump to conclusions, Angie,* she admonished herself. *Check the facts first.* "Is it a 'D' Massingham, Leanne?"

"No, the initial's 'J', guv."

"Ah!" Angela brought a chair over and sat beside Leanne. Gary came and stood behind them. "Bring up the interview Gary and I had with her," she said.

Leanne did so, and together they read through the account. The report was as innocuous as Angela remembered the occasion to be. Dorothea had mentioned her husband, but made it clear the agency was her baby. She'd said "the role of company director no longer appealed to him".

"OK, we need to check this out to make sure we're talking about the same family of Massinghams. I think it must be; it would be too much of a coincidence otherwise, but we have to be sure. We might have a direct link between Kirsty's murder and a drugs and prostitution racket, and we can't afford to blow it."

"No probs."

"Assuming he's Dorothea's husband, the contact details should be the same for them both, but I suppose it doesn't automatically follow. In any case, find out what you can. Then get hold of her and ask if I can go and see her this afternoon."

"Will do, guv."

Angela got up and turned to Gary. "OK, Gaz; my office," she said, leading the way.

"Right, what's this 'thing', then?" she asked, as he passed her to enter the room.

"Look," he said, taking out two pages from the file and laying them side by side on the desk. "I noticed it as I was collecting up all the pages when they fell."

Angela walked over to her desk. "What am I looking at?"

"You get three guesses."

She laughed. "Do I indeed?" She looked from one of the pages to the other and cast a puzzled glance up at Gary before scrutinizing them again. "OK," she said, after a moment or two. "I give – oh no, I don't! At least I don't think I do." She stretched out a finger to a place at the bottom of the right-hand page and then moved the same finger to point at something on the other sheet. She looked up at Gary with an enquiring glance.

He smiled. "That's it, Angie; what d'you think?"

Angela nodded her head slowly. "I think I'm looking at something very odd that requires an explanation," she said. "Well done, young man. You can have a boiled sweet."

"Coo, fanks, Miss," he beamed.

"I can check this out tomorrow. It won't take long." She tapped the page on the left. "In the meantime, you work back through the formatting on this one and see if anything's been cropped off or airbrushed out. If you have a problem with it, ask the lab."

"OK, Angie. I think my IT skills are equal to that."

"Good-oh," she smiled at him. "Now clear off, Houseman. I've got a report to write."

Left alone, Angela got stuck into her task. After half an hour she felt pleased with her progress. As she sat back yawning and stretching, Leanne's face appeared in the glass panel of the door. "Come in, Leanne!" she called. "Mission accomplished?" she asked once the young woman was in the room.

"Yes, guv, she's on her way here."

Angela looked up in surprise. "Did you say I would go and see her?"

"Yes, but she says she's out and about this afternoon and it would be just as easy to pop in here."

Angela frowned but nodded. "Hmm, that could be true. But more likely she just doesn't want our plod footwear on her shag pile. Ah, well. What have you managed to find out about her husband?"

Leanne frowned. "Well, that's the really funny thing."

Angela looked at her with an amused, quizzical expression on her face. "What is it with the younger members of my team and 'funny things' at the moment? I presume it's the same Massingham on the letterhead as owns the house."

"Yes, guv, it is. But it's really fun – er – strange."

"Yes, what is?"

"He's been dead for the last eighteen months."

Angela stared up at her junior officer. "This is all getting very murky. I think, on reflection, I won't ask her about the house and what happened there this morning. It would be better to wait until we've got a full report from the search team, anyway. I'll stick to what you've just found out and see where we get with that."

Dorothea Massingham duly arrived and was put into an interview room. Angela and Gary entered. Angela beamed warmly at her. She wanted her completely at ease. "I'm so sorry to have to bother you again," she began. She noted again the woman's perfectly coiffed and made-up appearance. She certainly knew how to put her best face to the world. Angela didn't miss, though, that the air of tension had intensified; she noticed an ever-so-slight tightening of the lips.

"Not at all, Inspector, think nothing of it. I'm only glad I was in the vicinity. It was very convenient to pop in."

"That's good; well, it's just a small matter. Since talking to you yesterday about your company I've discovered that the named shareholder – "

"Ah yes! I know what you're going to say and you're right." She paused and sudden tears sprang to her eyes. She clenched her lips together for a moment to gain control of herself. "I'm sorry, Inspector."

"Please don't be."

"Thank you. Yes, I know it's irregular. I have to be honest and admit it's partly laziness." Mrs Massingham stopped and looked Angela full in the face. "I presume we're talking about the fact that my husband is still listed as the shareholder?"

"Yes, considering…"

Mrs Massingham nodded. "Considering he died over a year ago; yes, I do see why that would puzzle you. I'm sorry if I've created a… what do they call it? A red herring in your investigation."

"Yes, it's just that these little discrepancies loom large. They acquire a greater significance than they need to, perhaps; but there it is."

"I do see that, and I'm sorry for wasting your time. As I say, it's partly laziness but mostly the difficulty of…" she turned a regretful smile upon Angela, "… the difficulty of letting go. It only seems like yesterday that he and I… that we were…"

"I understand," said Angela. The previous interview had proved good training for her. A quick learner, today Angela could pinpoint the precise instant Dorothea Massingham set about deflecting the thrust of the conversation. She leaned back in her seat listening, all sympathy, as Dorothea talked fondly of her husband and how things had been during those last months of waning health. Nodding here and there, adding the occasional comment, Angela allowed herself to become a quasi-grief counsellor. She didn't mind. She knew the next step to take, and could afford to be patient. It served her purpose that Mrs Massingham should be completely relaxed.

Twenty minutes later, Angela was walking slowly back towards the main entrance with her. They stood together in the reception area, Mrs Massingham fulsomely thanking Angela for her understanding attitude. Angela looked up, nodded and said, "Sir," as Stanway came into the building. Stanway dipped his head in response, cast a casual glance of scrutiny at Mrs Massingham, and made his way to the front desk. He collected his messages and stood waiting for Angela as she saw Mrs Massingham off the premises.

"You wanted a word, Angie?"

"Yes; your office or mine, sir?"

"Mine's closer," he replied, turning and leading the way along the corridor. Once inside his office he hung up his coat and popped out to the fountain in the corridor for a glass of water. Angela sat in front of his desk and marshalled her thoughts. "Right, go for it, Angie," he said, coming back in.

"The fashion industry is a very rich one; a good designer can make absolutely thousands in a year."

"I can't think why." Stanway cast a brief glance down at his own clothes. "I've had this suit for the past five years and it's still as good as new."

"Yes, but you're not a *fashionista*, are you, sir?"

"A what? Oh, never mind; I'm sure I won't be any the wiser if you tell me."

Angela smiled. "The thing is, Ian King, from what I've heard and read, has had a couple of very bad years. From what I can gather, he's lost his edge. His last two collections barely raised a blip on fashion's horizon. We're talking about one of the top designers, somebody with celebrity status – so he must have lost quite a bit of face as well as a fortune."

"And?"

"He's going full tilt showing his next collection at the London Fashion Show this year. I've been to his Wandsworth office, where the clothes are made, and it's all business as usual; a full staff doing all their regular stuff. I've been to their outlet in Chelsea, too. Very swish, sir."

"You'd expect that, in Chelsea."

"Yes, the decor looked expensive, and I wouldn't be at all surprised if it's fairly recent. And I expect they used an interior designer who I'm certain wouldn't have come cheap. A glance through the glossies shows he's been keeping his profile high on the social scene, too."

"Champagne, caviar and all sorts of substances they'd probably prefer the police not to know about."

"Exactly, sir. Keeping up this kind of lifestyle takes a very great deal of money."

"And you're wondering where it might have come from."

"That's it, sir."

Stanway steepled his fingers and rested his chin on them as he digested this. Angela waited patiently through his "hmm-ing" and "hah-ing".

Eventually he spoke. "You don't have a business brain do you, Angela?"

"No, sir; I'm a policewoman. I have an enquiring and suspicious mind."

He grinned and nodded. "Quite."

"It's just that you can't make nothing from nothing, sir. I'm wondering if there's enough reason to ask the Financial Services Unit to take a look at their books."

Stanway thought for a moment. "Hmm, I can have a word with them, Angie; see what they think."

"Thank you, sir." Angela paused. "There's another small thing that's just come to light. Of course it might be nothing but while you're talking to the FSU – "

"OK, let me in on it."

Angela quickly went through what she'd learned about Massingham Models. Stanway listened closely and nodded. "So, what does your suspicious policewoman's mind make of this business?"

"These facts have only come to light in the past couple of hours and I haven't really had time to consider them properly; but I think that, unlike me, Dorothea Massingham *is* an efficient businesswoman. Leaving her husband's name on the list of shareholders isn't an oversight or the result of her grief."

"What do you think it is, then?"

"A calculated risk. She needs a name on the letterhead. It's most unlikely that anybody's going to run a trace on him. They'd just see the director and the named shareholder, as required by law, and think, 'That's all right, then.' There would be no grounds for further investigation."

"Ye–es, so it's a low risk; but all the same, why take it?"

"Yes, that's the puzzle isn't it?" Angela lapsed into thought. Stanway waited and after a few moments she spoke. "Well, she described the workforce of the company as being two men and a dog, so I know she's not a one-woman band, though – " Angela stopped.

"Yes?"

"I should think running a modelling agency can be quite an undertaking. I got the distinct impression she's not alone in the enterprise; but that was when I thought she meant her husband."

"And now we know she's not talking about her husband?"

Angela smiled. "The people she's actually in business with don't want their connection with the company to be known."

"Exactly! Yes, I'll flag that up as well and pass on the details. We can't be too careful. Yes, a word with Fraud, I think." He picked up the telephone.

"Thank you, sir." Angela got up and moved towards the door. "OK, back to the team, see what they're all up to."

"Yes indeed." Stanway looked at her before dialling. "By the way, what on earth was Dottie Finch doing here?"

"Dottie Finch, sir?"

"Yes, I got to know Dottie very well when I was a young constable. A lady of the night; used to get pulled in regularly, along with her colleagues – though, mind you, Dottie always looked smarter than the others. I said to her one day, 'Dot,' I said, 'you've got a good brain in your head. Why do you settle for this?' She took my words to heart but not in the way I meant. Would you believe it, the next time I had to arrest her she was done for running a brothel," Stanway gave a laugh, "and running it very efficiently, I believe. Last I heard, she'd struck lucky and nabbed herself a rich businessman."

"Sir, I don't know any Dottie Finch."

"Yes, you do."

"Er…"

"That lady you were speaking to when I came in."

"That was Dorothea Massingham, sir."

"Ah." Stanway gave her a big smile. "Dottie Finch, as was. I would have recognized her anywhere. This is becoming very interesting, Angie." He smiled into the middle distance as he cast his mind back. "I must say she's scrubbed up very well. I always knew she could."

Angela came back and sat down again.

Chapter Twenty-six

"Indulge me, sir, while I say this slowly."

Stanway grinned. "Go on, then."

"One of the documents on Kirsty's laptop has led us directly to a woman, Dorothea Massingham, who runs a modelling agency, often used by Ivano King, a company about whose funding we have questions."

"Very succinctly put, Angela."

"And it now transpires this same woman, an ex-tom, once ran a brothel."

"That's right. Interestingly enough, you don't seem to see it so much these days, but there was a time when the word 'model' was a euphemism for 'prostitute'; a bit before your time, Angie; you'd see it on the shop doorways and in the small ads. Well, you still get it, of course, but not nearly so much."

"Yes, sir," replied Angela, only half-listening to him as she tried to gather up the strands of the investigation. "Sir, that house we raided today – when Asia first ran into the confessional last week, she told Father Martin she came here for the fashion industry."

"Ah yes! I remember you telling us at the briefing. I know where you're going with this. She'd ended up expected to do 'things' with men at parties, didn't she?"

"And she said that 'the others' went along with it. I wonder how she got away with not complying."

"They had to hang on to her, I suppose. She probably knew too much."

"Which is probably why they stuck her in the attic when we came calling."

"Oh yes, we'll see what Fraud make of it. Always leave the expertise to the experts. That's what I say."

"Yes, sir."

"You'll need to revisit everything you've got so far – not a bad practice, in any case – and see if, how and where this new information fits in." He cocked his head to one side and smiled at her. "I thought I'd save you the trouble of saying it."

"Sir?"

"That's the answer to your next question about how to proceed."

"Nuh-uh, that wasn't going to be my next question. I'd already asked that and answered myself."

"Oh, really, and what did you tell yourself?"

"What you said, sir."

Stanway laughed. "So what questions had you moved on to?"

"The ones you'd expect, really. How much did Kirsty know about this and, if she did, was she aware of the full importance of it?"

"And how had she reacted to it?"

"Yes; this casts a whole new light on that sheet of letterheaded paper, doesn't it? Was she trying to muscle in? Was she trying a spot of blackmail, even?"

"And was she killed because of it? Those are the very questions. Getting the hang of this job, aren't we?"

Angela smiled. "I believe so."

"OK, Angie: all joking aside, I'll point Fraud in your direction once I've made contact."

"Thank you, sir," she replied as she left his office.

Back in the incident room, Angela quickly brought the rest of the team up to speed.

"If that turns out to be what it looks like, and Kirsty was trying to muscle in, she was playing a very dangerous game," said Jim, after Angela had finished speaking.

"No argument there," agreed Angela, "but let's not become too blinkered. Fraud enquiries apart, our main task is still to find the murderer, and the most likely candidate is still someone who left a bike outside her flat the Sunday before last."

"Which brings us back to the gym," said Rick.

"Indeed it does. Tell you what, Rick and Jim, go back to her flatmate, Sandra, and Tony who runs the gym. We can be a bit more focused now. Tony and Sandra are on our suspect list and we haven't pushed them far enough yet."

"We can harp on about Kirsty's ambitions to start," suggested Rick. "They'll think we've got nothing new and they might relax and let out something without meaning to."

"Exactly, we need to chip away at them a lot more; and Darren. I've also got an idea about this 'lady' seen outside Kirsty and Sandra's flat."

"You think it might have been Mrs Massingham, guv?"

Angela nodded. "We've only got a sparse description, but I reckon Mrs Massingham would fit that."

"Along with millions of other ladies," said Jim.

"Yes, but we've now got reason to believe she might have been an interested party. She claimed not to know Kirsty when I first spoke to her, but I'm not relying on that."

She turned to Leanne and Derek. "Will you find out what you can about Mrs Massingham? We know she has a record and was known to the police in former days as Dottie Finch, so start there."

"Will do, guv."

"I want to go and see her, and I want a bit of background first."

"I bet she'll ask to come here, same as before," said Gary.

"She's not going to get the chance. Our next interview will be on her turf but my terms. OK, everybody, let's get going."

Within two minutes Rick and Jim had set off on their errand, while Leanne and Derek disappeared in the direction of the kitchen to make a cup of tea before getting stuck in to their tasks. Angela and Gary were the only two people in the room.

"Are you and Maddie planning any more dates?" she asked.

He flicked a glance towards her, slightly apprehensive. "I was planning to phone her later," he said.

Angela smiled. She detected a worried note in his voice. "It's all right; I'm not going to pump you for all the juicy details, and I'm most definitely not reporting back."

He relaxed visibly. "Yes, it's very early days, but the signs look promising."

"That's good." Angela made her way into her office, an amused smile on her face. She turned her computer on and set about revisiting all the evidence they'd collected so far.

An hour and a half later, she and Gary sat in the car in a quiet street in Kingston, looking at a house a little distance away on the other side of the street.

"OK, let me just see what Leanne managed to dig up for us," said Angela, taking some A4 pages out of her bag. Derek had presented them to her just before she and Gary set out.

"She's pretty good at research, isn't she?"

"Leanne? Yes, she's very efficient. I wouldn't be surprised if she ends up in somewhere like FSU."

"FSU?"

"The Financial Service Unit; Stanway tends to call it Fraud but it's not just the old Fraud Unit, its remit expanded when it changed its name to incorporate financial investigation. I tell you something, I wouldn't want them beavering away in my bank account!"

Gary laughed. "They'd be lucky to find anything in mine."

Angela looked at him with a grin. "Go Dutch next time."

"It's OK, I'm exaggerating."

A faint blush had appeared on his face. Angela cast a very brief glance across at him. *It's not something they teach you at police training college, Gazza, how to date your D.I.'s stepdaughter,* she thought. *If this relationship develops I hope you learn to relax a bit; we've got to work together.* She veered away from the subject. "Right then, let's see what we've got." She riffled through the pages. "OK. Born Dorothea Finch; first arrest for soliciting at age twenty. Soliciting... soliciting... der, der, der, more of same... more of same. Ah. Here's where she went up in the world – keeping a disorderly house, then a gap, keeping a disorderly house again." Angela grinned across at Gary. "No wonder Stanway remembered her so well! And that seems to be that. Perhaps she met her rich husband after the last conviction."

"You've got another page there," said Gary.

"Mmm, I just want to check I've covered everything here. OK, that seems to be all the arrests and what-have-you. So what else has Leanne found out?" Angela ran her eyes over the writing on the final page. Then she flopped the sheets into her lap and breathed out loudly. "Oh! *Bin-go!*"

Gary opened his eyes wide and looked at her. "Have we hit the jackpot?"

"I think so. Listen to this. 'Ten years ago at the age of fifty-five, she married a local businessman, Jeremy Massingham.' *But.* Listen! 'In her mid-twenties she was briefly married to an electrician by the name of Leonard Summers.'"

"Summers? But that's –"

"Yes, it is. You're absolutely right. Nigel Summers is the business partner of Ian King. It can't simply be coincidence. It just can't."

"I think we're about to find out," said Gary. He nodded towards the house they'd been watching. Angela followed his gaze just in time to see a light switched on in the front room.

"She's in, then," he said. "I wonder if she's worried."

"If she's got any sense she will be, deeply worried," said Angela. "She was much less at ease with me the last time we spoke."

"We're not exactly going to be welcome callers, are we?"

"No, Gary, we're not," said, Angela closing her bag and opening the door. "Come on, let's get it over with."

Gary's prediction was correct. When Mrs Massingham came to the door a few moments later, her opening stance was one of exasperation.

"Yes? Er… Inspector? Really, this is becoming too much. What on earth do you want now?"

"I'm sorry to bother you again, and so soon after our last interview, but some more information has come to light and I need to ask you some more questions."

"Well, can't it wait until tomorrow? I'd prefer to come to the station."

I know you would and I wonder why, thought Angela. She allowed a firm edge to creep into her voice. "I'm sorry, but we need to act on these things as soon as we can. May we come in?"

Dorothea made a last-ditch attempt. "I'm not at all sure I want you in my house, Inspector." As she spoke, Angela could see her mind busily active, and wondered at the nature of the calculations going on inside.

"We can speak on the doorstep if you'd prefer," she offered, keeping her tone relaxed and her smile pleasant.

Dorothea knew when she was beaten, but she'd obviously also worked out her strategy. "Oh, very well, come through here," she answered in a tetchy voice. She was clearly indicating that they should precede her down the passage to a room further towards the back of the house.

In the few seconds available, Angela glanced at Gary and slewed her eyes very briefly towards the front room door, which remained closed. As he stepped across the threshold, Gary made for this door and opened it, every inch the keen, young, courteous police officer who couldn't possibly have seen where Mrs Massingham was pointing because he was behind Angela.

"Oh yes, thank you, Mrs Massingham, just in here, is it?" he asked, pushing the door open.

"No!" Dorothea Massingham couldn't hide a note of panic and fear in her voice.

"Oh, I'm so sorry," said Gary, pulling the door shut quickly. "I do beg your pardon."

Mrs Massingham regained her composure and gave a tight smile. "I'm sorry; it's just that it's such a mess in there. I'm in the middle of decorating. It's better if we go into the dining room."

"Decorating, eh?" said Angela. "I know what that's like… total chaos and you end up wishing you'd never started." Her voice was full of sympathy. Behind Dorothea's back she gave Gary the thumbs-up and they exchanged the briefest of smiles.

The glance she'd managed to get into the front room had been enough. There was no sign of any decorating, but on the wall opposite the door was a large photograph. It showed Dorothea and Nigel Summers, dressed in evening clothes and holding champagne flutes, smiling at the camera at what was clearly some upmarket social function.

In the dining room, Dorothea moved swiftly round the table. They took seats at one end of the highly polished mahogany, while Dorothea perched herself on a chair halfway along the side.

"Very well, Inspector – fire away." Dorothea was nearly in control. Her voice was only one degree off having a squeak in it and she had the good sense to keep her hands out of sight under the table.

"We're trying to trace a woman who was seen outside Kirsty's flat shortly before the murder last Sunday."

Dorothea relaxed visibly. This was evidently not the kind of question she had braced herself to field. Something akin to a smirk even appeared on her face. "And this has *what* to do with me, exactly?" she asked.

"We need to speak to all interested parties who fit the description." *I really sound very formal at times,* thought Angela.

"I'm not quite sure why I should be considered an interested party."

"If you remember, we found a page of Massingham's letterheaded notepaper among Kirsty's effects."

"Ah yes, I remember. I didn't have an explanation for it last week and I don't have one now. It strikes me this link is very tenuous, Inspector, and I don't think it qualifies me to be considered an 'interested party'."

She was almost beginning to enjoy herself. Angela had no problem with that.

"I can assure you, I was here all day that Sunday, Inspector."

"Is there anybody who can verify that?"

"Unfortunately not." Dorothea was completely at ease now. Angela had offered no description of this unknown woman and could tell Dorothea recognized the paucity of the information about her. "Right, let's leave that for the moment, although I presume you'd be willing to take part in an identity parade should we decide to go ahead with one."

"Of course."

"Thank you, that's very helpful."

Dorothea dipped her head in a gracious gesture and the atmosphere in the room warmed up a little.

OK, thought Angela, *so you feel on solid ground with this subject. Let's take you where it's a bit more wobbly.*

Angela flipped over a page in her notebook. "So when did you open this modelling agency?"

"We've been going for four years now."

"Have you built up a strong client base?"

"I'm pleased with the progress we've made. Four years isn't long but we've made some good contacts."

"Was it difficult to get started? I would think it's a hard industry to break into."

"I know when to be pushy," replied Dorothea. "And we have some very good models on our books."

"That would be essential, of course. Still, I expect you find that part easy. You're quite experienced at running girls, aren't you?"

Dorothea paled a little. "I'm not sure what you mean, Inspector."

"No matter," replied Angela, knowing the shaft had hit its mark.

"I run a completely respectable business. Just what are you implying?" Her voice was cold, even haughty.

"I just think you'd be wise not to use past experience to build present endeavours. It went wrong for you before and it will go wrong for you again."

"I think I'd like you to leave now. I wish to telephone my s – "

"Your son, Nigel Summers, co-owner of Ivano King, Mrs Massingham? Yes, you probably do."

Chapter Twenty-seven

Dorothea's face became haggard. All the care taken in preserving and maintaining her appearance suddenly went for nothing and she looked about ten years older.

But there was steel in Dorothea Massingham's character. She made no attempt to rush into hasty speech. She took a deep breath and pulled herself straighter on her chair.

"I was going to say 'my solicitor'," said Dorothea. She'd gone very pale except for two bright red spots high on each cheek.

"I haven't charged you with anything," replied Angela.

"I would prefer it if you didn't play games, Inspector."

Angela stood up. Gary did likewise. "I'm not, Mrs Massingham. I'm trying to solve a murder, and it doesn't help when people withhold information. You own a property in Richmond, in your late husband's name?"

Angela wouldn't have thought it possible for Dorothea to become any paler, but that was what happened. "You must know I do, otherwise you wouldn't be asking."

"You might not be aware that it was raided this morning. Four women and three men were taken away. We are certain that at least one of them was held in the house against her will. The three men are now in custody and will be questioned tomorrow." An involuntary gasp escaped Dorothea and her hand clutched at her throat. Angela nodded at Gary and they moved to the door. "We *will* be back," she said, as she headed along the passage.

They both sat in the car and breathed deeply.

"Wow!" said Gary, after a few moments.

"Yes, all that leaves a very nasty taste in the mouth."

"Why didn't you question her more about the house?"

"I want to know exactly what was found there first, and what the people living there say about the set-up."

"Oh, yeah, that makes sense. Where to now; back to the incident room?"

"Not immediately. This woman in a suit is still hanging round the case like a spare part. I want her sorted. I've got one more little idea we can try. Head for Putney."

"Ah!" said Gary, as he pulled the car away from the kerb and set off.

From where they were parked they had a clear view of Eleanor Chandler as she came home from work. Today she wore an elegant maroon trouser suit with an off-white blouse. She moved in a rapid, purposeful manner.

"She looks in a bit of a hurry," said Gary.

"She does indeed, Gaz. I wouldn't be at all surprised if she's expecting a visit from the boyfriend. But have you noticed what she's wearing?"

"Oh wow! Yes. Top marks, Angie."

"Hold on, I don't know if I'm right yet, but it was Madeleine describing her blouse as elegant that reminded me of Ronald Sanders using the same word. And every time I've seen Eleanor Chandler I've noted how well turned-out she's been." She looked across at him. "I admit it's all very thin and wouldn't stand up as evidence, but it got me thinking."

"You might be right. Shall we go, then?"

"Let her get the kettle on and her jacket off first."

Eleanor was just about to get up from her chair and go upstairs when the front door bell rang about ten minutes later. She quickly applied a little lipstick and ran a comb through her hair. Ian had called her while she was still on the bus, saying he would be round "later" – which could mean anytime. Not expecting him so soon, she hadn't even made the bed from his previous visit. She went to answer the door.

"Ah… er, Inspector – ?"

"Costello," supplied Angela. "And this is D.C. Gary Houseman, if you remember. I'm sorry to bother you again, but I've got a couple more questions. May we come in?"

Eleanor cast an involuntary look behind and up the stairs. "I was just about to go up and… er… I've got to prepare for someone. I'm expecting a visitor."

Angela could see she was distracted and wanted to take advantage of the fact. "We really won't take up much of your time," she said.

"Oh… er… er… All right, then. Just come in here, will you?"

Angela and Gary followed her into the smart living room they'd sat in on their previous visit.

"I wanted to get more details about this showdown that you had with Kirsty."

A sudden flash of alarm appeared in Eleanor's eyes and she quickly lowered them, noticing some speck on her trousers and brushing it off. *Ah, I'm on the right track,* thought Angela.

"Showdown, Inspector?" replied Eleanor, with only the slightest hint of breathlessness. "I've already told you everything about that."

"Yes, I know, and you were very frank. I believe you said the incident occurred at work?"

Pause.

"Yes." Eleanor kept her eyes averted from Angela's, her trousers taking up all her attention.

You're just not a natural liar, Eleanor, thought Angela. She let the silence lengthen for a few moments. "I don't think that's quite right, is it?" she said, gently.

Eleanor gasped and stopped what she was doing. "I didn't have anything to do with Kirsty's death!" she said, her face flushed, her eyes darting wildly, and her lips quivering.

"Shall I tell you what I think happened?" suggested Angela.

After a moment Eleanor nodded, her face a picture of misery.

"You were fed up with the way Kirsty went on. She was blatant about her certainty that she would get Ian back and she flaunted it all the time; but you've got far too much dignity to have a blazing row in the workplace, where it would become gossip fodder. And you've worked there a long time. You *knew* it would become the talk of the office. Am I right?"

Eleanor nodded, her colour returning to normal. Angela's tone and manner were having a calming effect on her.

"You could just imagine it, couldn't you?" continued Angela. "'Look at Eleanor, hasn't had a boyfriend in all these years, and now she's fighting with Kirsty over the same man – what a laugh.' That's what they would have said, isn't it?"

"I'm sure they all know how I feel about Ian; they must do. I'm pretty tough, but… it was the idea of being the butt of all the jokes. That's what I couldn't stand," nodded Eleanor.

"So you got yourself up in your best suit and no doubt took a lot of trouble over the make-up; it wouldn't do to put yourself at a disadvantage, and you went to visit Kirsty at her flat just after lunch last Sunday, didn't you?"

Eleanor nodded. She had completely recovered her composure by now. "When I was Kirsty's age, I would have been intimidated by an older woman in a circumstance like that but Kirsty wasn't, not a bit. I'm telling you, she was one dirty little fighter. I came home wrecked. I can assure you, she was alive and well and, to be honest, wallowing in victory, when I left her."

"Wallowing in victory?"

"Oh yes. My mother always brought me up to behave in a ladylike manner at all times. I didn't think she'd succeeded until that Sunday when I realized that Kirsty and I just didn't have a level playing field."

Angela nodded. "What time did you get home?"

Eleanor spread her arms. "As I've said before, I don't wear a watch at the weekends and apart from registering that it's morning, afternoon or evening I don't have much of a sense of time. I just know it was around lunchtime, maybe early afternoon."

Angela nodded, pleased that her guess had proved correct. Now that she was here it seemed a good opportunity to explore. Angela always liked to feel the sense of any place that mattered in an investigation, but she had a problem. The location she wanted to look at was upstairs in the main bedroom. Getting into this would prove a delicate business. She took her time writing in her notebook as she considered how to pursue the matter. After a moment she turned to Gary and looked meaningfully at him. "Can you go over the details of this visit last Sunday Gary, please? We want to make sure we've got them properly, then we won't have to bother Miss Chandler again."

Gary met her glance with a completely expressionless face. "Yes, of course." He turned to Eleanor with a grin. "It honestly won't take long, I'm a very quick writer."

"He's had to learn how to be, working for me, I'm afraid," smiled Angela.

Eleanor nodded, completely relaxed. "No problem," she said.

"While you two are doing that, do you mind if I use your bathroom?" asked Angela. "Sorry, hate to take liberties but needs must."

"Not at all, Inspector. It's just up the stairs and round to the right."

"Thanks." Angela left the room and went upstairs. The route took her past the open door of the main bedroom. She went into the bathroom and closed the door behind her as noisily as she could. She immediately opened it again without a sound. She could hear Eleanor dictating to Gary from downstairs as she tiptoed into the main bedroom. She noted the disarray that Eleanor was so keen to clear up, the bedlinen, the discarded champagne flutes and bottle. She cast a quick glance around the room.

And froze.

Well, well, well, that's very interesting, she thought, as she took her mobile phone out of her pocket and quickly took a picture before creeping silently back to the bathroom where she flushed the loo and emerged, closing the door as noisily as before.

She breezed back into the living room a few seconds later.

Gary glanced up as she entered. "Nearly done, Angie," he said.

"That's great." She looked at Eleanor. "There's just one thing I need to ask you and then we'll get completely out of your hair."

"What's that?" asked Eleanor, visibly at ease now the worst was over and she could see this ordeal coming to an end.

"As I passed the main bedroom, I couldn't help noticing something that would help us to eliminate you from the enquiry, if you'd let us take it."

Eleanor gave a wry grin. "I'm not normally a bad housekeeper but I just haven't got round to things this week, and there are probably a few things in that room that should have been tidied away days ago."

"Sorry," smiled Angela. "I didn't mean to criticize; no, it's just that, if we could take it we can test it for prints and it'll save us asking you to come in to the station and get them done at a later date."

"Oh goodness, be my guest, Inspector. Just show me what you want." She stood up.

Angela saw Gary looking up at her with raised eyebrows. She smiled. "Have you got an evidence bag on you?" she asked as she followed Eleanor out of the room.

"Yep," he answered, pulling one out of his pocket.

A few moments later they were settling themselves in the

car. "OK, Gaz," said Angela, as she belted herself in behind the driver's wheel. "I need your help."

"No probs," he replied, putting the evidence bag gently down on the floor between his legs.

"I took myself off upstairs while Eleanor was dictating her story to you to try and have a bit of a snoop, as you probably guessed."

"Yes, I got that."

"Couldn't do much in the time available, but I now think I've got an idea how this crime was committed. I might be wrong, but I'm going to run it past you anyway and you can try and knock it down in flames, all right?"

"Yep, fire away," he said, as the car pulled away from the kerb.

As soon as they got back to the office, Gary raced along to the forensic department and Angela sought out D.C.I. Stanway. She took him through the events of their visit to Putney.

Attentive as always, Stanway listened to Angela without interruption and remained silent and pensive, staring at the blotter on his desk for a few moments after she had finished.

"It hangs together," he said, finally; and then, "But it depends on what forensics come up with. Let me know when you've got the results."

"Yes, sir." As Angela got up and went towards the door, the phone on Stanway's desk rang. He picked up the receiver and gave his name. As Angela turned to close the door behind her, she glanced at him and saw a look of alarm spread across his face. He waved to stop her going any further. She quickly stepped back into the room again and closed the door.

"Yes? Yes… Tone-Up Gym… I heard that."

Angela sat down and leaned forward, straining to hear the other side of the conversation.

"Yes. Yes, she's here with me now. How many? When…?"

Stanway turned a grave expression towards her as he listened, making notes on a pad in front of him at the same time.

Angela's eyes widened as Stanway finished the call and put the phone down.

"Sir?"

"News is patchy at the moment, but there's some sort of violent disturbance going on at the Tone-Up Gym."

"Does it involve any of my suspects?"

"Nobody's got any names as yet. It seems someone has locked himself in there with a couple of other people and is threatening to beat one or both of them up; it's not clear." Stanway moved rapidly from behind his desk and grabbed his coat from the back of the door. "Apparently a hysterical woman phoned the message in, yelling for help and saying, 'He's gone berserk!'"

"Who is it that's gone berserk, sir?"

"Good question." He moved out into the corridor, Angela in pursuit. "We'll go in your car, Angie; text Gary to meet us there."

Chapter Twenty-eight

If Angela had been a gambling woman, she would have wagered the journey from the office to the gym couldn't be accomplished in less than five minutes, even with the siren blaring. She would have lost her money on this day.

Stanway groaned as he swung the car round the corner and saw the crowd of onlookers milling around outside the premises. "Oh no," he said. "Just as I feared. A party going on." They nosed carefully past the bystanders to a convenient space.

"Uniform are on the case already, I see," he said, as they got out of the car and surveyed the scene. Across the road in front of the gym, several officers were making valiant attempts to keep onlookers moving along. The fruits of their labours only produced more rubbernecks stopping to ask what was going on and staying to watch. The presence of another police car, blue lamps flashing, made it even more improbable that anybody would go about their business.

"They've managed to get a bit of order, sir," said Angela as she realized a cluster of gym patrons had been huddled into the area immediately in front of the door. They were easily identifiable from their clothes – a variety of warm-up suits or shorts and T-shirts. Some had towels draped round their necks and one man was wrapped in a bath sheet.

"He's going to think twice before taking a shower here for a long time to come," remarked Stanway, nodding towards the man.

"At least his modesty is protected in that great big thing, and it's a fairly warm night." Angela gazed across the road and recognized the latest arrival, a man holding a very professional-looking camera. "Uh-oh, the press are here."

"That's just what we need. It'll be the telly next."

"No, sir, it will be quicker to get a radio crew here," began Angela, but Stanway was already striding across the road towards the hubbub. He'd pushed his way through to the most senior-looking uniformed officer by the time Angela reached him, and stood listening to a recap of the events.

"… As far as we can tell, sir, the chap came in pulling another man along with him. He said he was going to kill him but wanted to make him suffer first. He made everyone get out and pulled the other man into… er… something called the waiting room."

"The weights room," corrected a nearby voice. They swivelled towards the sound and found themselves looking at a man in a purple warm-up suit, a towel flung carelessly across his shoulders.

"Did you see what happened?" Angela asked him.

"Yes, at close hand; and it was pretty scary, I can tell you," affirmed the man.

"Are you OK, sir? Can you tell us about it?"

"Oh yes, it was a bit of a shock at first, as you can imagine. I'm OK out here." He pushed an expensive-looking pair of spectacles further up his nose and ran a hand through his hair. It's as the officer said…" Out of the corner of her eye Angela saw the HAT car arrive. Gary and the rest of her team piled out and came across to join them. "I was in reception when the door burst open. Two men came staggering in – I took them for drunks at first. One of them was shouting, 'Leave me alone, you bastard! Leave me alone!' Then I saw his head was held in an armlock."

By now the speaker, Angela and Stanway were completely surrounded by their team. "What happened then?" she asked.

"Tony tried to calm him down. He even went towards him – my goodness, I was impressed! He said, 'Daz! Daz, calm down, mate.' But the bloke – Daz, I presume; huge man, officer, you'll need to be careful – just kept hold of the other man. Must have a grip like a wrench. Anyway this Daz said something like, 'No! He's gonna pay for what he did!' Then he dragged the man into the weights room and locked the door."

"Is there anybody else in there with them – people using the weights, that is?"

"I was in there, actually, with a couple of others, but we all came out into the reception area when the shouting started, so, no; nobody but those two now."

Angela thanked the man, who rejoined the other gym patrons. Stanway looked at her. "You've met him, Angie. What do you reckon?"

"Well, sir, you can't really ever tell with people. I put him down as a gentle giant, but if so, he's obviously flipped. From what we've just heard, it's at least safe to enter the reception and speak to Tony and Sandra. I imagine Sandra was our 'hysterical woman'."

"Angie, I…" Stanway's expression was worried, but he couldn't argue with the logic of her statement.

Angela pressed what she hoped was her advantage. "If we request back-up, we'll have to take the time to brief them. Tony and Sandra are bound to be frightened. They need to know we're here. Also, we need a fuller picture of what's going on in the weights room and we're not going to get it out here. If we go in now, we may be in time to prevent grievous bodily harm, or even a death."

Stanway gave her a searching look. "You seem very keen to get inside. I hope you're not hoping to be a hero, Angie."

"No, sir. If Darren's locked himself and his captive in the weights room, I don't think there's any danger in the reception area, and… and…" Angela looked into Stanway's concerned face and decided to drop all pretence. "Sir, the thing is, jungle drums being what they are, Patrick's likely to get wind of what's going on very soon, if it hasn't happened already, and then he'll be here and I'll find myself under pressure."

Stanway nodded. "A husband standing out here full of anxiety won't help you to do your job."

"May I proceed, sir?"

"Do you have either of their mobile numbers to hand?"

"Yes, sir."

"Call them."

Angela brought up the number for Tony Chambers on her mobile and pressed it. He answered after it had barely begun to ring. "Yes?" His voice was very low and shaky. Angela could tell that much even though the noise from the street meant she could hardly hear him.

"Tony, it's D.I. Costello here. We're outside the gym."

"Oh, thank God! We don't know what to do."

OK, one frightened man, she thought. *Three, maybe, if you count Darren and whoever he's dragged in there. And I don't suppose Sandra feels too chipper.* "It's OK, Tony," she said. "We're all here and we're going to get you out of this. We've been told that Darren has locked himself into the weights room with someone and is threatening them. Is that true?"

"Yes. From the sounds he was making, it seems like he's got the other bloke pinned under some weights, but I can't be sure. We were trying to talk to him through the door, but he didn't answer. In the last few minutes it's gone a bit quiet." Tony's voice had become steadier as he spoke.

"Do you know who the other man is?"

"Nope, never seen him before in my life."

"And who's with you?"

"It's just Sandra and me. I yelled at everyone else to clear out when it all kicked off."

"Yes, most of them seem to be out here in the street. OK,

Tony, hold on; I'll get back to you soon." Angela finished the called and turned to face Stanway.

"So?"

"Sir, it's as the witness said. Darren has locked himself in the weights room with another man. It seems he's got him pinned under some weights and appears to be threatening him. There's just Tony and Sandra in the reception area. They were trying to reason with Darren, but to no avail. I think, sir – " Angela took a deep breath, "I think I should go in."

From the look on Stanway's face, Angela knew he was about to become very formal. She set herself to match him.

"D.I. Cost – "

"Yes, D.C.I., sir; this is the case I'm working on at the moment. Some of my suspects are in there."

There was a brief silence.

"Very well, Angie, but no unnecessary risks and I want to be kept constantly informed."

"Of course, sir."

"And you're not going alone." Stanway looked across at Gary.

"I'll go with her, sir," he said.

"Good man."

Angela cast a brief glance at all those among the crowd then turned slowly back to the front door of the gym and was surprised to see Stanway waiting there with Gary. "Sir?"

"In case Patrick does turn up, I'll be safer in there with a crazed giant than out here with your husband, Angie," he said, in what was clearly an attempt at a joke. Angela smiled to acknowledge it. He looked steadily at her and Gary. "OK, troops, here we go."

Chapter Twenty-nine

Stanway went forward to the door marked "Reception" and pushed it gently. A sudden movement came from the other side and it was pulled fully open by Tony. His face white, he had his finger to his lips. The three police officers slipped silently into the room.

"Thank God you're here," whispered Tony. Across the room, Sandra, on the floor, pushed up against the door to the weights room, looked through the keyhole.

Angela didn't waste any time on preamble. "What's happening in there?"

Sandra turned her face away from the door. It struck Angela that looking through the keyhole must be a futile exercise. Sandra confirmed her impression with her next words. "I can't see anything, really," she said, "but I can't help looking."

"Better come away from there, babes," said Tony. Sandra looked at the new arrivals and scrambled away from the door. "Yeah," continued Tony. "This is a real turn-up. I would have just said he was the archetypal gentle giant."

"But he's definitely obsessive," said Sandra.

Tony looked at her. "I s'pose. Once he gets his teeth into something he doesn't let go easily."

"Yeah, obsessive," repeated Sandra.

"It's very quiet in there," said Angela.

"It wasn't at first," replied Tony. "That bloke he's dragged in there was screaming and yelling and going on about all the things he would do to Daz, and then we heard a slap – well, a slap… it was quite a whack, really. The other bloke cried out in pain."

"Is the other man still alive?" asked Stanway.

Tony looked at him. The little colour that had returned to his cheeks ebbed away again. "Yes, he must be. I think I heard Daz saying, 'Get over here, you bastard,' and there was some scuffling, a dragging sound."

"This was after the slap?"

"Yeah. Yeah, definitely after."

"And Daz has locked the door from the other side, right?"

"Yeah, but it's a latch lock, so it can still be opened from our side if you have the key."

"Which you have?"

"Yes," answered Tony. "But I wasn't going to use it without you here. Do you want me to open the door?" The look on his face showed all too clearly that Tony would prefer to simply hand the responsibility over to the police.

"No, no." Angela hastened to reassure him. "We'll handle things. Will you bring us the key, please?"

"Sure thing," replied Tony, with obvious relief in his voice. He hurried across the reception area and disappeared into the little room behind the coffee bar counter. He was back again within half a minute, holding out the key to Angela.

She took it and cast a glance at Stanway. "Shall I try talking to him, sir?"

"Yes, give it a go," answered Stanway.

Angela approached the weights room and leaned close to the door. Wondering what she was actually going to say, she opened her mouth to call out Darren's name, but only a strangled croak emerged. She coughed and tried again. "Darren! This is Inspector Costello."

Silence.

"Darren!"

This time there was an anguished moan from within. She assumed this to be from Darren's captive. She couldn't be sure but though she'd heard only an inarticulate groan, she somehow felt she recognized the voice. She tried again. "Darren, I need you to speak to me."

This was followed by more silence, and just when Angela was about to speak again, Darren spoke from the other side of the door.

"What about?" She could hear a mixture of rage, distress and tension that she wouldn't have thought possible to discern from just those two words.

What about? Angela gave herself a moment to take a breath. *What do you mean, "What about?" I'm not here to talk about the weather.* The thought made her smile and she felt a bit more relaxed. It also allowed her to take due note of Darren's tone, and it gave her a clue as to how to proceed.

"Darren, I know you're upset, but this isn't the way to sort out your problems."

"Yes it is," came the reply. "He killed my Kirsty. I'm going to make him pay."

Angela recognized belligerence behind all the other emotions. She took a brief look round the room. Tony and Sandra, both on the suspect list, were seated at a table. Stanway and Gary were a little way behind her. They were all staring intently in her direction. *OK,* she thought. *Not a good moment to tell him that he's sparked off a major incident and the only way he's getting out of here is in handcuffs.* She turned back. "Darren, will you open the door and let me talk to you?"

"Not till I've sorted him out."

There was another moan from Darren's captive, and this time Angela recognized who it was. Ian King.

It suddenly occurred to her that Darren, in his overwrought state, might have assumed that she was alone. *Time to slip into the first person plural,* she told herself. "Darren, we need to get medical aid to Ian King."

"He don't need no medical aid. He won't need nothing ever again after I've finished with him." This was followed by another, stronger groan from Ian, who sounded as though he must be coming round from the blow that Darren had given him.

Darren's tone had lost some of his distress and tension. Talking to Angela was helping to steady him, but she didn't want to strengthen his resolve to injure his captive. She turned to Stanway and whispered, "I think we need to get in there."

"It might send him over the edge. We can't put a member of the public at risk, Angie. And I definitely can't put you at risk."

"Yes, but sir, he wants Ian to suffer, so he's obviously planning to do him some damage before he kills him. He's calming down now. It seems to me, we need to get to him before he's completely in control of himself."

"You think if that happens he'll then start to think very clearly, decide time's not on his side, and just deal the death blow?"

"Something like that, sir; I think we're between a rock and a hard place."

Tony's face appeared over Stanway's shoulder. "I really don't think he'd do anything. I don't think he's got it in him," he whispered.

Stanway looked at him. "We're talking about a man who's dragged his victim into that room and has already thumped him."

"Yeah, but…" Tony's voice tailed off.

"The thing is, sir, having interviewed the man I can see where Tony's coming from. You would be surprised by all this if you'd met Darren as well."

"Whereas, not having had the pleasure…"

Angela stared into Stanway's clearly troubled face. She watched him wrestle with the doubts, the fear and the worry of what could happen and the repercussions thereafter. "With respect, sir – I'm not convinced Darren would actually kill Ian, but I do think he can threaten to do so and hold out in this situation for a long time."

Stanway knotted his brow and took up the internal debate again, no doubt factoring in overtime payments now, as well. "What is your suggestion?" he asked.

"I'd like to let him know that we're coming in, sir. I might be able to get an idea, from his voice, how he reacts to that. If I unlock the door and push it open from this side, I won't be in any danger. And we can keep it all very low key."

He looked at Angela. After what seemed to be a very long moment, he nodded. "OK. Let's give it a try."

Uttering a silent prayer, Angie positioned herself close to the wall and put the key in the lock. As the key went in she heard a scrambling from the other side.

'What are you doing? What are you up to? You can't come in here!' What little equilibrium Darren had gained had now clearly disappeared.

Angela leaned well back from the doorway. "Darren, we need to talk to you."

"I'll talk – I'll talk all right. You won't be able to shut me up once I've finished with him!"

Angela, remembering the unresponsive face opposite her in his tiny office, seriously doubted this. "Darren, come on; you're not stupid and you know this isn't going to get you anywhere. Why are you doing this?"

Ian's voice broke into the conversation. "Inspector…?" He sounded a little dazed.

"Mr King, the police are here."

"Oh, thank God for that. He's got me strapped into some sort of contraption. I can hardly move. You've got to get me out of here. He's gone loopy."

"Try to remain calm, we're dealing with the situation."

"He done her! He done my Kirsty and he's going to pay!" Darren's voice rose an octave.

"Don't be ridiculous," answered Ian, his irritation clearly detectable through his fear.

"What makes you think he killed Kirsty?" asked Angela.

Pause.

"I got my reasons." Mr Taciturn was back.

"Do you know something you haven't told us?" asked Angela. The notion of reminding him of the seriousness of withholding evidence came and was immediately dismissed. But she received a sudden illumination. "Was it the aftershave? Did you smell Ian King's aftershave in the lean-to last Sunday?"

"Just went in there to check something on my bike, didn't I? Didn't think anything about it then, but I realized later."

"You told me you hadn't been in the lean-to at all that afternoon."

"Weren't going to tell you, was I? I was gonna sort it out myself."

Angela thought back to the scene outside when she'd first arrived. Several well-heeled people were standing around outside the gym. She thought of the man they'd spoken to, designer warm-up suit, designer trainers, expensive streaks in his hair; she had no doubt that a lot of expensive aftershave was worn in this place. "Darren," she called, "that doesn't follow. Probably a lot of people wear that aftershave, especially here."

"Yes, that's right, you tell him. This whole thing's ridiculous." Ian was fully conscious now. There was an awkward quality to his voice, as if he'd been to the dentist and the anaesthetic hadn't worn off. Angela wondered if Darren had loosened or even knocked out a tooth or two when he slapped him.

"You shut up! You bastard!" roared Darren.

There was the sound of movement followed by a slap and a dull moan. Surmising that Darren's attention had been deflected, Angie glanced over her shoulder at Stanway and Gary. "Here we go!" she said, and dashed into the weights room without giving herself a chance to think twice.

It all happened very quickly.

Stanway and Gary reached the doorway just as Darren straightened up from hitting Ian across the face again. He stared angrily at Angela.

It was then she saw the gun.

Nobody had said anything about a gun. She had completely forgotten about Darren's other hobby.

It was pointing straight at her.

Stanway and Gary froze.

"Stay there! Don't move!" shouted Darren. He gazed wildly round at the three police officers. Even the most amateur of psychologists would have been able to see that every vestige of his self-control had evaporated. His panic showed only too clearly, and Angela had no doubt about the danger facing her. Amazingly, if she could have spoken at that moment she would have remarked with wonder on how astonishingly, vibrantly alive she felt.

"You shouldn't have done that!" he screamed. He blinked and took a breath. His hand, holding the gun, steadied.

Angela saw a change come over him. It was unmistakable. He was resolved. He was going to see this situation through to its end.

She forgot all about being a policewoman. She had no thought about whatever protocol might apply to this set of circumstances, if she ever knew. She was aware of only one thing; that she was facing death. She did the only thing she could.

She bowed her head to pray.

With a strangled cry, Darren pulled the trigger.

Chapter Thirty

The bullet whizzed across the top of her head, missing it by a matter of inches, and ricocheted off the side of the weights machine behind her. Angela had closed her eyes and was only aware of the horrendous bang followed by a calm, peaceful core at the very heart of her being.

Darren's brief moment as a hard man was over. He dropped the gun and collapsed sobbing on the floor.

Stanway and Gary raced into the room. Gary rushed over to Darren while Stanway came to help the still bowed Angela. She opened her eyes, and raised her head slowly. "Are you all right, Angie?" he asked.

"I'm not quite sure. Am I still alive?"

Stanway smiled, the relief evident in his voice. "Oh, you're alive all right. That was the most amazing sight I think I've ever seen. How did you know to bow your head just at that moment? It was like a miracle."

"Yes, sir."

On the other side of the room, Gary helped the still weeping Darren to his feet and handcuffed his obediently presented wrists. Stanway looked at Ian, still held down by the weights. He called to Tony, now standing in the doorway with Sandra. "Could you get this chap out of that contraption?"

Tony nodded and hurried over.

Angela stood upright and looked at Sandra. "My husband might be outside," she said.

"I'll go and check," said Sandra, hurrying off as she spoke. "Sir?"

Stanway shook his head. "It's not a problem, Angie. Patrick's been a D.I. in his time and he knows how to behave at a crime scene. In any case, he's a coroner's officer and his lot will have to be involved."

"Why, sir, nobody's dead?"

Stanway gave a short bark of laughter. "Of course not… how stupid…" He looked steadily at her. "You were marvellous, Angie. You did very well."

"Thank you, sir." Angela suddenly became aware of a dark shape rushing into the room and wrapping itself around her. Patrick buried his head in her shoulder and she could feel deep sobs shaking his body.

"Don't ever, ever, ever…" said his muffled voice.

"No, darling, I won't."

"She was an absolute hero," came Stanway's voice from nearby.

"Don't want a dead hero, want a live Angie," muttered Patrick, without raising his head. Angela snuggled into the crook of his neck and hugged him more tightly. *Why on earth did I want to get him into charcoal grey with royal blue coordinates?* she asked herself and smiled as she recognized the incongruity of the thought.

Suddenly Patrick pulled away from her so that he could look into her face. He glanced quickly at Stanway and then back to her. "Well done," he said, before burying his head in her shoulder again. "But don't ever do it again."

"No, Paddy, I won't," she assured him. She felt very, very tired, more than a little bit shaky and would like nothing more than to go home and lie down. But she was on duty and there was still work to be done.

"I wouldn't mind sitting down for a minute."

"How stupid of me," said Patrick. He drew her gently with him into the reception room and over to a table. "Here," he said, depositing her on a chair. He hunkered down in front of her, placed a hand on each of her knees and looked into her eyes. "A cup of hot, sweet tea, I think."

She smiled at him. "You might think that, but I'm thinking, a large brandy."

Patrick gave a laugh. "Good idea. There must be some, somewhere." He got up and turned to where Tony and Sandra were sitting at one of the other tables. Tony looked up at him. "Brandy, perchance?" asked Patrick.

Tony cocked his head in the direction of the coffee bar. "On a shelf under the counter," he said.

A couple of ambulance men, whom Angie hadn't seen arrive, were helping Ian King through the door from the weights room to a seat. As he sat down, Darren was led past them. Ian looked morosely at him and called to Angela. "Well, some good's come out of this." His voice was not quite a lisp, and a vivid bruise had appeared on the left side of his face. "You've got your man, at least."

"Have I?" said Angela.

Ian King wasn't able to move his facial muscles much but he managed to look puzzled anyway. "Well, of course. It stands to reason."

Patrick arrived at her side with a glass of brandy, but she realised it would have to wait. She shook her head gently. "Sorry, darling, I haven't quite finished the job I set out to do."

Patrick hesitated for a second before giving an understanding nod. He put the glass down. Angela stood up, aware that she felt clammy and decidedly odd.

As it happened, although they were at different tables Tony, Sandra and Ian were all sitting close to each other. Angela looked at each of them in turn.

"Of course it stands to reason," Ian reiterated. "It was either Darren on his own, or one of them." He tried to throw a glance in the direction of Tony and Sandra, winced and stopped. "My money's on Darren. It must have been him stalking me, waiting for an opportunity."

"It certainly looked like somebody from this gym was involved," agreed Angela.

"Well, there you are then."

"Tonight's events have shown me a scarf is not Darren's weapon of choice," said Angela. "And in any case, he was in love with Kirsty."

"Well… it was a crime of passion, or whatever," replied Ian. "But I'm sure you've got your man, Inspector."

Angela stood very still and let her gaze travel across all the suspects. Mentally she included Nigel Summers and Eleanor in the picture. "Yes, I'm sure I have," she said. She was now aware of feeling very queasy and recognized the effects of shock setting in. She wondered how much longer she could stand.

Angela glanced briefly at Stanway; he gave a small nod.

But it wasn't to be. She stumbled and would have fallen if Patrick hadn't caught her. She found herself leaning over his arms, staring at the floor, and as the contents of her stomach hurtled up past her throat she was vaguely aware of Stanway stepping in to take her place and arresting Ian King on suspicion of the murder of Kirsty Dawn Manners.

Patrick took Angela home, put her to bed and she slept for ten solid hours. The next morning she still hadn't fully processed the shock of facing death one moment and finding herself still alive the next, but she felt completely refreshed. By the time Gary came to pick her up, she had begun to wonder how Ian had slept, if at all.

His face had been cleaned up, and a bandage covered the cut Darren had made on his forehead, by the time Angela and Gary came into the interview room and she spoke the preliminary introduction into the tape machine.

Dark circles under Ian's eyes gave a partial answer to Angela's query, but his demeanour hovered somewhere between petulant and peevish. "Inspector, is this some kind of joke?" he asked, as Angela and Gary sat down.

"It's no joke, sir. You are under arrest – "

"I was with Eleanor Chandler from about two o'clock on Sunday afternoon, which I know she's already confirmed with you. Would you like to explain to me how I can be killing one woman at the same time as I'm in bed with another?"

"You couldn't, not if that were true but, in fact, you didn't arrive at Eleanor's until a little after three."

"I can assure you, Inspector – " His voice was loaded with confident assurance.

"You forgot to put the clock in Eleanor's house back to the right time before you left."

Ian looked abruptly down at his hands, but he wasn't quick enough and Angela saw a look of horrified remembrance on his face. When he raised his head again he'd regained control of his features. She wondered what his stomach felt like.

"I noticed it when I was at the house yesterday," she said. "I took a photograph so I could check it against the time on my mobile, just to be sure."

"I presume you mean the clock above the bed. I've no idea what time it says, or said on that Sunday, but I can assure you my watch showed a little after two. Would you like to check my watch?"

Yeah, right; like I'm going to believe that, thought Angela. "That won't be necessary, sir."

Ian had completely recovered himself now. "So would you like to take me through this revised scenario? I seem to have lost an hour from my week."

"You got to Eleanor's a little after three o'clock. You went up to the bedroom first and she followed a short while afterwards.

While you were alone up there, I believe you moved the hands on the clock above the bed backwards an hour. Apart from Eleanor's watch, that clock is the only functioning timepiece in the house."

"Amazing; I do hope you're not going to try building a case on this flimsy piece of evidence," he said. "And would you mind telling me why on earth I would want to kill Kirsty in the first place? A sweet child and obliging in the sack but, quite frankly, an airhead. What on earth was my motive?"

"Kirsty wasn't such an airhead though, was she? She had very big ambitions. She discovered the link between Ivano King and Massingham Models *and* just what they were supplying. She wanted a significant piece of the pie, didn't she? And you couldn't have that, because then you'd be stuck with her. But left out of the equation she could bring the whole little empire tumbling down. You really were impaled on the horns of a dilemma, weren't you?"

Ian couldn't avoid running a tongue around his lips to moisten them, but he managed to speak in a normal voice. "You've got a good imagination, Inspector, but I hope you're not building that case on Eleanor's clock *supposedly* being an hour out. You're going to look very silly when this business falls apart." His eyes suddenly brightened. "She has a mobile phone, for goodness sake. She would have looked at that. She'll be able to confirm that I arrived around two and not three."

Angela ignored him. "But the real clincher is your latest collection. You weren't worried about Kirsty having got at some of your designs. The reality is, she knew who you'd stolen them from and could prove it."

Ian went white. Angela wouldn't have thought it possible for someone to look so pale and still be alive. It lasted for only a moment before colour seeped back into his face and he sat up stiffly, to make sure she knew he would not allow any slur to be cast on his professional integrity. "I can assure you, Inspector, there is no question about the provenance of my latest collection. It is entirely my own work."

Angela opened up the folder she'd brought into the interview room with her and laid out two pieces of paper. The first contained one of the designs taken from Kirsty's computer, and the other his statement about the attack in the street outside his flat. She waited a few moments. He looked at them and raised his eyes to hers, an amused, questioning look on his face.

"Your point, Inspector?"

"This is one of the looks from your collection?"

"You know it is."

Angela placed one index finger on the statement's signature and the other on the single initial "K" below the design and watched carefully as Ian cast his eyes again at the pages. She saw his eyes widen and he gave a short, involuntary gasp.

"You'll see the letter 'K' in your signature on the statement is completely dissimilar from the one at the bottom of the design," she said. "And it's curious that there's no 'I'."

He had a stab at nonchalance with a not very convincing shrug. "I was probably stressed. My signature changes when I'm in a hurry; I miss things."

"I have a more workable theory," said Angela. Asia had now been interviewed and Angela had seen the transcript. "After the *Passionista* reception, Nigel told you of a promising young woman called Asia, from Poland, who had come here hoping to get an internship. You interviewed her and realized that she's very talented. You, having lost your edge and looking for something fresh to produce for this year's fashion week, came to the conclusion her collection offered just the thing to win back your reputation. You also knew the woman was being offered – er – 'lodgings' in the Richmond house, which she would accept because it sounded so good and she didn't know any better. Oh yes, we know all about that," she added as she saw his eyes widen. "So she'd be out of the way. You were free to put her looks into production."

"What utter rubbish."

"The trouble is," continued Angela as if he hadn't spoken, "you didn't trace the initial contact to its source. Nigel doesn't chat up wannabes at parties. He's not bothered about giving talented young foreign students a helping hand, especially not when he's come equipped with his own arm candy. You should have asked him how he knew about this keen designer."

"Oh, should I?" Ian's voice was heavy with sarcasm.

"It was Kirsty who met up with Asia. Kirsty was striking out on her own, finding out what she could. Asia, doing the same thing, eager to network and try to get a foot in the door, would grasp at even the faintest whiff of a promising contact. It was almost inevitable they'd meet. It was Kirsty, wanting to build her own stock, who told Nigel about her. It also goes without saying that Kirsty would ask to see some of Asia's designs, which she would have stored on her mobile. I expect Asia sent them to Kirsty's phone by Bluetooth at the same party. Then Kirsty uploaded them on to her laptop later."

Ian said nothing but his face had become drained of all colour again.

"I'm sure you're right about what you told me last week. I'm sure Kirsty had got at your computer. She would have seen you'd got hold of Asia's designs, and no doubt came to the conclusion you were going to use them yourself. The morality of this didn't bother her, she just wanted to help you; so she made an attempt to change the initials on the ones on her own computer." Angela tapped the bottom of the page. "She went for the simplest option and cropped off the first initial, leaving only the 'K'. Careless, really, given the different handwriting, but I don't suppose she thought it mattered at that stage. She uploaded the design as a photograph, inserted it into a Word document where, as I'm sure you're aware, it's very easy to recover the original format and see what's been cropped." Angela pulled out a similar page from her file and laid it on top of the others. It was the same design but, here, the initials "A" and "K" could both be clearly seen.

Ian ran a tongue around his lips as Angela continued. "Kirsty was very, very proactive on your behalf. Of course it would have been better if she'd just deleted the ones on her computer, but I expect she regarded them as her little treasure – maybe a future bargaining point, who knows? However, I've no doubt whatsoever that if we look at the designs you're working from, we'll find absolutely no trace of the original 'A' and 'K'. They will have been expertly obliterated."

Ian shrugged, completely in control of himself. "I have a few different signatures. As part of the case against me, this will never stand up in court."

"It will if the owner of the original 'AK' turns up to give evidence."

His eyes opened wide and immediately narrowed again. *Ah! That's got you,* she thought. "It's an interesting thing about Polish names," she continued, as if going off on a tangent. "Obviously the Poles have their own way of turning names into pet names and diminutives, just as we have."

Ian relaxed back in his seat, playing along with Angela. His smile was an attempt at insouciance but there was a tension about him. "Oh, really? Do tell."

"Take the name Johanna, for instance, the feminine version of John, of course." Angela pronounced it *Yo-hanna* as instructed by Leanne. "In England a Johanna or Joanna would probably get called 'Jo', but it's not the same in Poland. In Poland it gets familiarized first to 'Yo-asia' and that in turn gets shortened to 'Asia'. And, interestingly enough, both the English and the Polish for 'king' begins with a 'K'. 'Krol' in Poland, but I expect you know that already."

"Fascinating," said Ian. He hadn't moved and there was still a smile on his face. Angela could sense the tension in him, though. She thought back over the conversation she'd had with Eleanor.

"Anyway," she said, as one wanting to get back to the subject, "about this alibi of yours."

Ian picked up the cue. He leaned his head back and let out a slow breath. "OK, Inspector, I'll admit, albeit grudgingly, that you've done a good bit of legwork there. But you've hardly got enough to charge me. Anybody can make a mistake about time. And if I decide any of this warrants calling in a solicitor, that's exactly the argument we'll be putting forward." He looked completely relaxed now. "Even if I arrived later at Eleanor's than I originally said, that doesn't mean I was at Kirsty's place, killing her."

"We can place you at the scene of crime, sir."

Ian leaned forward as one intrigued and keen on learning more. "And how on earth can you do that? Bearing in mind I'm supposed to have killed her and got to Eleanor's by – er – what is it now, three o'clock?"

"It is quite tight for time, sir, but you're a cool customer. Though I bet you felt undignified on that bike."

"Bike? What bike?"

"Darren's. I think you took it from the lean-to beside the Tone-Up Gym, cycled round to Kirsty's, killed her, cycled to the gym again and put it back. Darren's bike was seen outside Kirsty's at the relevant time. The whole trip wouldn't have taken more than ten minutes. Then it would have been straight back into your own car, parked nearby, and off to Eleanor's for a little after three. It's completely do-able. And on a Sunday when there's not much traffic about… well…" Angela spread her hands.

Ian threw back his head and laughed out loud. "Oh, very good, Inspector; that's priceless! This is better than the cinema." He calmed down and looked at her. "And how on earth am I supposed to know where I could get hold of Darren's bike?"

Angela gave a gentle smile. "When we met before you claimed that you tuned out of a lot of what Kirsty said to you, didn't you? But I don't think that's the case at all. I think you took on board, in minute detail, exactly what you wanted to know. You knew all about Darren's standing at the gym and the routine with the bike in the lean-to. You even knew you could take the bike through the lean-to door and avoid being seen in the reception. And you knew all this because Kirsty had told you."

"Fascinating, Inspector, but it's only circumstantial."

"Are you saying you're not familiar with Darren's bike?"

"No – well, that is to say, I've seen him cycling to and from work now and again, but I haven't taken any notice."

"So you're claiming never to have had anything to do with his bike?"

"Of course I haven't. Don't be absurd."

Pause.

"Then how do you explain the presence of your thumb and fingerprints on it?"

Ian went deathly white again. He stared at Angela. He opened his mouth once or twice but was unable to utter any words. Finally he managed to speak.

"That… that can't be."

"Ah, but it can."

He thought for a moment and suddenly his objections gained a new lease of life. "You're trying to trick me, Inspector. My record is as clean as a whistle. I've never even had a parking ticket. There's no way you have my fingerprints on file."

"Mmm," said Angela with an almost regretful little smile. "I think, Ian, you're going to look back on this time and realize it was a mistake to take a bottle of champagne to Eleanor's that day."

The build-up in the media was enormous, and once they'd arrived Angela could see why. She and Leanne quickly recognized the more famous designers with whom they found themselves rubbing shoulders, and they accustomed themselves easily to the atmosphere, the lights and the celebrities mingling with the crowds. They were special guests at the show of a brand-new talent on the fashion scene. They'd taken full advantage of the free champagne on offer and clutched a goody bag left for them on their seats. Father Martin looked into his bag as they stood about, stretching their legs during a brief interval. "I think my sister will be very glad of this," he said.

Angela and Leanne exchanged looks and smiled at him. They'd already "ooh-ed" and "aah-ed" over the expensive cosmetics, the perfume, the silk scarves and the chocolates. "Be careful how you proceed," Angela warned him. "You might find your mum fighting her for it."

"Oh, do you think so?" Martin looked a little alarmed. "Perhaps I'd better just filter everything through to the Christmas bazaar."

"Come on, we'd better get back to our seats," said Patrick. "Our one's up soon."

Obediently they followed him and took their places along one side of the catwalk. Patrick leaned over to Angela. "What with everything else going on, you never did get around to telling me how you got from that raid on the house in Richmond to front row seats at London Fashion Week," he said.

"Ah, well, it was all quite simple really," she replied. "Ian King might have been arrested but his company hasn't."

"Yes, I see that."

"OK. One of the directors has been charged with murder but that doesn't have to affect the rest of the company – not until the Financial Services Unit has built its case anyway. So…"

"Business as usual."

"For the moment. Nigel Summers is a very pragmatic man. He trusts Ian's artistic sense, and has come to the conclusion that if this is the collection Ivano King are putting out this year, then so be it."

"I see, just a name addition."

"Yes, Asia Krol at Ivano King. People are beginning to talk about her already and she really has produced some stunning looks."

"Looks?"

"Trade jargon, darling."

"Oh, OK. So, then what?"

"Well, I should think Asia will build on whatever success she achieves here to go straight to another fashion house and try for a deal, which will be very wise because, from what Stanway was saying the other day, it won't be long before Fraud move in and pull the plug on Ivano King."

"Oh, fantastic. Uh-oh – shh, the lights are going down. Here we go."

Angela leaned forward and looked towards the curtained end of the catwalk. Having been involved in Asia's rescue, she felt a little as though she was her protégée.

She didn't want to miss a thing.

Acknowledgments

Although London Fashion Week is a real event that takes place in London every year, the House of Ivano King is a complete fiction. Equally, there is no Catholic parish of the Immaculate Conception in or around the Richmond area in Surrey.

Writing might be a solitary occupation but getting published is a group effort and I can't let this opportunity slip of acknowledging the debt I owe to various people who've helped in the process.

First of all, thanks to Tess for some great one-liners and, as ever, your huge encouragement. And thanks to Lynn who read the manuscript through for me.

I'm very grateful to Tony Collins, Jessica Tinker, and the team at Lion Hudson for all their help and advice, and to my copy-editor Sheila Jacobs for her timely advice.

Gordon Berry, Ann Murphy, and Dave Howard of the Brent and Harrow coroner's office were always ready with information and patiently answered my questions about police procedures, even when they were up to their necks in cases – thanks, guys.

Did you catch D.I. Costello's first case in *Game, Set and Murder*?

ISBN 978 1 78264 072 1 | UK £7.99, US $14.99

It's the first day of Wimbledon. And a dead body is lying on Court 19.

Newly-promoted detective inspector Angela Costello recognizes the dead man as Croatian champion-turned-coach, Petar Belic. A double grand-slam winner, Petar was famous, and much loved.

However, Petar had an ex-wife who wanted him back; a girlfriend who wouldn't let him go; a business partner with secrets. Then there was the temperamental leading Brit, Stewart Bickerstaff, whom Petar had been coaching.

"The aces keep coming chapter by chapter."
— *Tony Jasper*, author
"A witty and intriguing whodunnit."
— *Cindy Kent*, broadcaster